THE BALLAD OF BLACK POWDER

T0281767

THE BALLAD OF BLACK POWDER

MICHAEL NETHERCOTT

WHEELER PUBLISHING
A part of Gale, a Cengage Company

LIBRARY OF CONGRESS CIP DATA ON FILE.
CATALOGUING IN PUBLICATION FOR THIS BOOK
IS AVAILABLE FROM THE LIBRARY OF CONGRESS.

ISBN-13: 979-8-88578-257-9 (softcover alk. paper)

Published in 2023 by arrangement with Michael Nethercott

To Helen, Genna, and Rustin: my posse

ACKNOWLEDGMENTS

Many thanks to the first readers of this novel:

Helen Schepartz, Rustin Nethercott, and my old comrade in words, Peter Selgin. Much appreciation for the clear eye of my editor Alice Duncan and for the work of Tiffany Schofield and all the folks at Wheeler / Cengage.

CHAPTER ONE

The body of Ida Sawbridge lay upon a weathered pine door set firmly on six upright barrels. This makeshift bier stood in the front room of the family cabin and was at present surrounded by half a dozen mourners. A spray of yarrow rested in Ida's folded hands and, next to the pillow beneath her head, the family Bible lay opened to *The Book of Psalms.* Specifically, to the page containing Psalm 139, a favorite of Ida's. After losing a husband and three offspring, the notion that *the darkness and the light are both alike* had always somewhat comforted her.

At forty-six, gray had barely touched Ida's long brown hair, which was now loosened so that it spread over her shoulders, giving her the look of someone much younger, perhaps even a child. Although a death spasm had twisted the woman's features, her daughter Elizabeth had managed to smooth them out adequately. If Ida did not look exactly *at peace,* she did seem beyond suffering.

In appearance, the daughter was a younger version of the mother, half her age. A serious and conscientious young woman, Elizabeth had seen to all the funereal details. She wanted her mother's body to "lie in state," a term she had heard used to indicate momentous events, such as displaying the remains of assassinated presidents. First Abe Lincoln and then, only two years ago, James Garfield had lain in state, and Elizabeth wanted no less for her family matriarch.

She reasoned that the old door was a particularly suitable choice, since it had come from the original home her long-dead father, Ida's husband, had built for his new bride soon after they wed. Ida had brought it along when she moved to this cabin to remind her of those good early years. It was usually kept leaning against an outer wall, awaiting service as a spare table should neighbors come for supper. Now it served as Ida's funeral bed. The barrels had once held sugar and flour and other foodstuffs and so, like the door, seemed to Elizabeth appropriate choices. Her mother was never happier than when bustling about her stove, baking, frying, and conjuring up grand meals from the humblest scratchings. It was a wonder that, with all the food Ida pressed on them, her family members had remained lean and fit.

Now, though, that family consisted of only Elizabeth and her brother Tom. At least here in Wyoming Territory. Elizabeth did not count Cousin George in her tally. Her sisters had married and left the territory in pursuit of remote opportunities, and Elizabeth's own husband had died three winters back. After the diphtheria had taken him, Elizabeth moved back in with her mother to help with raising Tom and other chores. But Tom was fifteen now and parentless and would need to find his manhood sooner or later. Since their mother's death two days ago, he'd become notably sullen and had said little to Elizabeth or to anyone else.

Except for a neighbor woman whispering a prayer over the body, everyone in the room seemed pledged to silence. Ida Sawbridge had been well liked hereabouts, and no one took any pleasure in the occasion of her death. True, sometimes the passing of a less-appreciated soul might provide some welcome distraction, but such was not the case with Ida. Her absence would be lamented.

The front door creaked open, and two

men entered. They were both tall, wore thick mustaches, and each looked about fifty. The similarities continued with their attire: long duster coats and slouched hats. The one in front, though, was a white man. His companion, who lingered behind him, was black. The first man had a definite air of authority, and that, combined with the deep scowl on his face, caused the roomful of mourners to promptly leave the cabin, all but Elizabeth and her brother.

George Gault maintained his scowl as the neighbors filed out, then shifted his gaze to the dead woman. He cursed under his breath.

"We heard you were away," Elizabeth said coolly. "That you and Saturn were off horse-trading."

"That's right," Gault muttered, still studying the corpse.

"I sent word for you. One of your men was supposed to ride out and let you know. Did he find you?"

"He did." The scowl altered now, becoming something more pained. "He damned well did."

Elizabeth sighed. "Then you heard, Cousin George."

She would have preferred not to call him that, but addressing him as simply "George" would have implied an undesirable familiarity. And to call him "Mr. Gault," as the men who worked for him did, was intolerable. He was — or had been — Ida's first cousin, making him Elizabeth's first cousin once removed. In truth, she would rather have had him even farther removed than he was.

Gault finally tore his gaze away from the dead woman and settled it on Elizabeth. "Tell me," he demanded.

"Didn't your man explain what happened?"

"I want to hear it from you."

"There's not much to tell," Elizabeth said. "Mama went to bed two nights ago and seemed fit and fine. But, come yesterday morning, I heard her hacking something terrible, and, when I got to her, she just rolled over, and, minutes later, she died. No time to even summon the doctor."

"You're leaving out something, ain't you? I was told you found a bottle."

"I did. A bottle of elixir she'd bought. Partly empty on the table beside her bed."

Elixir. Gault spat out the word. "Would that be the same elixir those show folks were selling a few days ago? That so-called major and the Indian girl?"

"Yes. Mama bought a bottle from them."

"And why the hell would she do that?

13

Didn't she know those traveling people and their ilk are all frauds? Hucksters?"

"Mama was a trusting sort. You know that."

"Trusting's one word for it," Gault said. "Another's foolhardy. Damned foolhardy. Where's that bottle?"

From a nearby shelf, Elizabeth took down a half-empty blue bottle and handed it to Gault.

He read aloud the label. *" 'Major Pompay's Fabled Fortifying Elixir. Effective on a Multitude of Ailments, Aches, and Discomforts. It Will Do Wonders.' "* Gault grunted. "Yeah, sounds like the kind of hornswoggle Ida would fall for. How much she pay? A dime? A quarter?"

"Seventy-five cents."

"*What?* And you just let her fling her money away like that?"

Elizabeth stood her ground. "Mama had those ongoing knee problems, so she was hoping —"

"Damn it, girl! I figured you had more sense than Ida. You should have intervened."

"I saw you at the show, too. Why didn't *you* dissuade her?"

"I only stopped by there for a few minutes. Long enough to see what them pie powders were about. Nothing but two-bit players tossing out their wobbly tunes and a few hunks of Shakespeare. That puffed up Major Pompay — who I'd wager was never any major at all — and that heathen girl who was spouting verse. Them and the rest. Yeah, I noticed you there. You and Ida and Tom here — though I was surprised your mother let the boy go to such a fast show. But I left just as they commenced to selling their wares. I would've stayed if I knew Ida was going to buy into their trickery."

Gault shifted his gaze back to his deceased cousin.

The other man, who had remained silent till now, removed his hat and spoke quietly. "My condolences, Miss Elizabeth. And to you, Tom. Your ma was a fine lady."

"Thank you, Saturn," Elizabeth said.

"She was kindness itself," Saturn added.

"Ida only bought this two days ago, yeah?" Gault was not letting up. He raised the bottle and gave it a shake. "Only half filled. She sure took a fancy to it, looks like."

"It appears so," said Elizabeth.

Gault snorted. "Even allowing for that, something claiming to be 'effective on a multitude of ailments' ought not kill a body." He uncorked the bottle and sniffed it. "Cheap alcohol and spices, I'd venture. And God knows what else. Did you see her

15

drinking the stuff?"

"I did not," Elizabeth said. "I thought she was saving it for the next time her knees vexed her."

Gault turned to Tom. "How 'bout you, boy?"

Tom shook his head, looking like he wished to be anywhere but there.

"Well, drink it she did." Cousin George recorked the bottle and set it down on a nearby table, not gently. "And now she's dead."

"You're saying there's a connection?" asked Elizabeth.

"You must think so yourself, or you wouldn't have mentioned the elixir when you sent word to me."

"I just . . . I just thought it worth noting."

Gault sneered. "I bet you did, Elizabeth. Your ma was never really sick a day in her life, was she? Nothing more than aching knees. Went through birthing seven babies and weathered a dozen waves of smallpox and scarlet fever, and she never once took ill. You telling me that out of nowhere she ups and dies for no good reason? Listen, I've heard my share of troubling tales about folks sampling these potions. Concoctions that damned charlatans like Pompay sell off their show wagons. People get sick drinking

16

the swill, and more'n one have gone to their graves."

"You're talking in a general sense," Elizabeth said. "Not specifically about that Major Pompay's troupe. We don't know for certain if —"

"I *can* know for certain. I can track down those hucksters and make my inquiries."

Elizabeth looked hard at him. "Make inquiries . . . That's not what you really mean, is it? You mean to bring violence to those people, whether they deserve it or not. I know the sort of man you are. And so did Mama."

"Don't you tell me what Ida thought of me! I was always good to her. Didn't I let her come stay on my land here after her man died? Her and her children, you among them, girl. Remember, she was a Gault before she was a Sawbridge. Ida was kin, and I took care of her. She appreciated that."

"Of course, she was appreciative," Elizabeth said. "Gratitude was in her nature. But that doesn't mean she didn't see you for what you are. A rough man with bad ways and bad intents. She kept you in her prayers, but she also kept her distance. Or hadn't you noticed?"

Gault's eyes blazed. "High and mighty,

ain't you? You're the type who contents herself by looking down at a man like me. A man who gets things done, who builds up his ranch and makes a success of himself. A man who makes things right when others are afraid to."

"Oh, is that what you do?"

"You damn well know it. Just as you know what I'm fixing to do now. I'm going to take some hard men and ride out after Pompay and his crew. I'm going to do right by Ida. And don't pretend that ain't what you want me to do. You're more than content to abide my 'bad ways and bad intents' when it's in keeping with your own wishes. I've lived long enough to know that's how most people steer their lives. Don't try to deny it."

Elizabeth started to say something but stopped herself and looked away.

A thin smile played across Gault's lips. "No more smart words? What a big damned surprise." He reached into his coat pocket, pulled out a small cloth sack, and dropped it on the table where he'd put the bottle. The sack made a soft clink as it was set down. "That's to see to any expenses for Ida's burial. I won't be waiting around to see her stuffed in the earth."

Elizabeth shifted her gaze to the money

sack but said nothing.

Gault turned to leave, then paused and looked at Tom. "What about you, boy? Want to ride out with me and see justice done for your ma?"

"No!" Elizabeth moved to her brother's side. "He's too young for such things."

"Is he? How old are you, Tom?"

"I'm just on fifteen," Tom answered softly.

"I wasn't much older when I left home and made my own way. Now, was I sixteen or seventeen when I cut up that Dutchman in a knife fight? I don't rightly recall. Sure I can't entice you to join my little excursion, Tom?"

Elizabeth put an arm around Tom's shoulder. "Good-bye, Cousin George," she said firmly.

Gault took one last long look at Ida's body, then left the cabin.

Saturn replaced his hat and addressed Elizabeth. "Sorry again about your ma's departure. Like I say, she was the best of ladies. Do let me know if I can be of help in any way." Then he turned and followed Gault out the door.

Elizabeth walked over to the funeral bier and placed a hand on her mother's cold arm. She closed her eyes and stood there silently for some time.

Finally, Tom asked, "You praying, Lizbeth?"

Without opening her eyes, Elizabeth said, "I don't know if I'd call it praying, Tom. I honestly don't know."

Saturn found Gault standing by their horses, staring off across the open range. It was a mild afternoon in early autumn, clear skied and windless. Saturn thought he saw a slight misting in his boss's eyes.

Gault cleared his throat. Without looking at the other man, he said, "I was fond of Ida, Saturn. I truly was."

"Yes, I suspect you were."

"She brought something good to this sorry world." Gault smoothed his mustache. "We'll stop back at the ranch, get fresh mounts, and head out."

"Who you planning on taking along, boss?"

"Taking you. And I figure Billy and the Finn."

"Billy's pretty young for this kind of chore, ain't he? Not young like Tom, of course, but —"

"Billy's young, but he's steady. I need steady hands. When I stopped by to see that damned show, I noticed they had this rough-hewn fellow traveling with them.

Armed and looking like he knew a thing or two. I'm guessing he's a bodyguard of sorts for in case they run into bad situations. If that man's in the mix, I want steady hands by me."

"Instead of Billy, you could take Davis."

"No, I need Davis to run things while I'm gone. Dammit, Saturn, you fret over Billy like he was your own boy. Just 'cause you share the same shade of skin, don't mean you need to mother him so. Anyway, I've fixed my mind."

George Gault climbed onto his bay's back, and Saturn mounted his own blue dun. Gault drew a cheroot from his pocket and lit it. Staring dead ahead, he blew out a stream of smoke and spurred his horse forward. The two men rode out.

CHAPTER TWO

Alworth Nevins pondered how best to approach Mr. Gault about joining his impending vengeance ride. Knowing his request would be denied out of hand, Alworth had prepared several counter arguments.

He first planned to tout his own skills as an educated man and florid writer who could deftly chronicle the upcoming adventure. He immediately abandoned that proposal, guessing at the disdain with which it would be met. George Gault hardly tolerated the young man's university background and avid journal writing, never mind seeing it as an asset. Next, Alworth entertained the idea of offering his services as a useful conduit between Mr. Gault and this Pompay fellow who, like himself, seemed to be of a more genteel bearing than Gault and the other men. Again, disdain, if not outright hostility, was the anticipated response.

Alworth's final proposal — the last arrow

in his quiver — hinged on a bit of fabrication. A lie, actually. He would profess his heartfelt admiration for poor Ida Sawbridge, a woman among women whose death was injustice personified. The truth was that he had barely had any contact with Ida since he first signed on at the Gault ranch two months before. Once or twice, at a distance, he had ridden by her cabin and exchanged waves. She had smiled at him, and the smile was a warm one. So, yes, Alworth possessed a passing fondness for Mrs. Sawbridge, which he hoped he could expand into a claim of strong dedication. He would declare that he felt honor-bound to accompany his employer in pursuit of righteousness.

Of course, Alworth wouldn't share his real reason for wanting to join the pursuit. Two nights ago, he had been one of the many spectators at the local performance of Major Pompay's Nomadic Review of Entertainment & Edification. (Those words were painted on the troupe's gaudy touring wagon. Alworth had noted the idiosyncratic spelling of *Pompei.*) On the whole, the theatrics had been adequate at best, nothing like the polished shows that played in New Haven. More akin to the roaming bands of Connecticut amateurs he had seen back in Danbury. Still, one specific recitation had gripped him, mesmerized him . . .

Certainly it was not the first time he had heard the Juliet balcony speech, but Shakespeare never felt so compelling. To hear *Wherefore art thou, Romeo?* from the lips of that young Indian woman, clad in her buckskin dress with an owl feather dangling from her braided black hair, struck some deep, strange chord in him. Two Robes. That was what Major Pompay had called her, Two Robes. A Lakota Sioux, Pompay had said.

Alworth had tried to put his reflections on the girl down in his journal but wasn't sure he had captured the true depth of his feelings. What he knew for certain was that he desperately wished no harm to befall her, and he'd just overheard Saturn say that Gault was hell-bent on a revenge that might well include Two Robes. It was no secret that Gault bore no love for the red man — or woman — and his dark intentions regarding Pompay could well spill over to include the Sioux girl. Alworth was unsure if his own presence would have any effect should Gault overtake the traveling troupe, but he meant to find out.

As rickety as Alworth's claim of allegiance to Ida Sawbridge might be, it seemed his best bet, and he armed himself with it as he went to seek out Gault. He found him standing outside the ranch house in consultation with the cook. Gault was issuing brisk orders for supplies to be gathered for the impending ride. The cook left to fulfill his assignment, and Alworth stepped forward to make his case.

He drew in a fortifying breath. "Mr. Gault, I'd like to join you on this journey."

"I've already picked my crew." Gault started to walk away.

"I understand, sir," Alworth called after him, "but one more man would give you an advantage."

Gault stopped and looked back at him. "An advantage? And you reckon you're the man to give me that?"

"Well, sir, I . . . That is, your cousin Ida was a very good . . . an exemplary . . . What I mean . . ." Under George Gault's scrutiny, Alworth sputtered to a halt. Abandoning his prepared speech, he simply said, "I want to ride with you."

Gault narrowed his eyes. "How long since I hired you? Six weeks? Seven?"

"Eight."

"That long? And why the hell do you think I took you on?"

"I'm not sure, Mr. Gault."

"Truth be told, I ain't sure either. Just an

odd damned whim, I guess. Curiosity as to how a tender tyro from back east would fare here in the real world. It's a far cry from your days at Harvard, yeah?"

"It was Yale, sir."

Gault snickered. "Pardon my mistake."

"And, actually, I only completed one year. After that I —"

"Get ready. We leave in twenty minutes." Gault turned abruptly and strode away.

Alworth Nevins watched Gault's retreat. He took a moment to wonder at what had just transpired, then hurried off to fetch his gear.

Saturn Hayes and Billy Fowler waited together by the corral. Despite their differences in age and background, the fact that they were the only black men on the ranch bonded them. They mingled well enough with the other drovers but found in each other a camaraderie that bordered on kinship. Billy was not yet eighteen and had been working there for a year and a half now. Mr. Gault hadn't asked his age then, and Billy never bothered to offer it. Tall and sturdy, he looked older than his years. Clearly he knew his way around horses, and that was good enough to get hired on. Likewise, Saturn never offered his age, though not because he wished to hide it. Being born a slave, unlike Billy, he never knew the exact year of his birth, but figured it to be somewhere in the early thirties. That would put him at fifty and some, roughly three times Billy's age.

Having saddled their horses, they had left them within the corral as they waited for Gault. Billy had chosen one of the duns, while Saturn had gone with his own blue roan, Foggy. Even though Gault had ordered him to get a fresh mount, Saturn never felt right astride any steed but Foggy. The two men leaned with their backs against the corral rails speaking in low voices.

"I got a bad feeling about this, Billy." Saturn chewed on his mustache.

"How so?"

"I don't know if chasing down these folks is the right thing or not. Either way, I don't see no pleasing outcome to it all. Mr. Gault has his fire up, and that's never a good thing."

Billy shrugged. "He's calling the tune, so it's his dance, right? Man pays me, I go waltzing. That's just the way of the world, I figure."

"Way of the world . . ." Saturn repeated the words slowly as if dissecting them. "I've seen enough of the world to be wary of its

27

ways. I'll say that for a fact."

Billy grinned. "You're wary of damned near everything, old man. You spy a single steer limping along, you say a whole stampede's a comin'. You catch one lone cloud in the sky, you swear that heaven's 'bout to explode and drown us all. Never met a man so eager to be gloomy."

"You're lucky enough not to have known chains, you young rabbit. Me, I *have* known 'em. And, suchwise, I've known plenty of troubles and trials. Makes a man see things in a certain light."

"Yeah, makes him see midnight when everyone else is staring at blazing sunshine. No way to live, if you ask me."

"I don't recall asking you," said Saturn. "That'll be some amazing day when I need to hear what an overgrown child thinks about things."

Billy laughed. "I'd make you regret those words if I wasn't scared you'd shatter the minute I touched you."

It was their usual battle: in one corner, the elder who'd spent half his life in bondage; in the other, the youth born several years after Emancipation. Saturn might have taken more offense had he not believed that Billy, beyond his goading banter, respected what the older man had gone through in his life. Saturn had seen the look in Billy's eyes the first time he saw Saturn with his shirt off. The crisscross of old scars across the former slave's back made Billy catch his breath. Saturn had met the boy's eyes then, and something unspoken had passed between the two of them. Still, the banter continued to this day.

Fredrik Lampo, the one they called the Finn, now came walking toward them, accompanied by Alworth Nevins. Both were shouldering their saddles. The two men could not have been more different from each other. Alworth, considerably younger, was slender and smooth faced with a head full of black curls peeking out from beneath his overly pristine tan Boss of the Plains hat. Lampo, of indeterminate age, was barrel chested and red haired and wore his raggedy beard unusually long for a cowhand — it reached nearly down to his belt. His battered derby was anything but pristine.

Saturn turned his attention to Nevins. "Where you planning on going, Alworth?"

"With you all," Alworth said. "Mr. Gault says I'm to come along."

Saturn eyed him suspiciously, recalling Gault's stated desire to take only "steady hands" on this foray. "Is that so? Mr. Gault said you were joining us — him, Lampo,

29

Billy, and me?"

"He did."

Saturn looked at the Finn. "That so, Lampo?"

"Looks like it." Lampo's accent was thick, for he had only been in America a handful of years. None of the ranch hands knew a single thing about Finland, and Lampo seemed disinclined to educate them. In fact, he rarely spoke at all. A rumor had circulated that he'd been responsible for some particularly odious bloodshed back in his homeland, but, unsurprisingly, no one approached him on the subject. He carried a lengthy Bowie knife at all times, which further ensured his privacy.

Saturn sighed. "All right, saddle up and get ready. Mr. Gault will be along soon."

Smiling, Billy stepped over to Alworth. "You ready for some rough trails, greenhorn? You know, this ain't one of your fancy school outings we're going on."

"I know what we're in for." Alworth hoped he sounded confident.

Billy tipped back his hat and eyed Alworth as if making a careful study. "Hmm, let's see now. Does our Yankee friend here have the sand for this type of venture? I can't rightly say. Time will tell, though. Time will surely tell."

Alworth liked Billy, despite his cockiness. And he suspected that Billy liked him, too. They were the youngest hands in Gault's employ, which gave them something in common. Still, Alworth knew that, in terms of practical qualifications, his twenty-two years couldn't match Billy's eighteen. Alworth had grown up in a small Connecticut town, Billy on the prairie. Yet each had value for the other. The Eastern youth appreciated the other's horse knowledge, while Alworth's book learning interested Billy.

Unlike Saturn and many of the other drovers, Billy Fowler could read and write and owned a small satchel of reading material. True, most of that was nickel weeklies touting the exploits of Buffalo Bill and Jesse James, but he also kept a book of poetry that someone had once abandoned in the bunkhouse. Noting Billy's interest in the written word, Alworth had made him a gift of a dog-eared volume of Poe, the tales of which Billy gleefully declared were "god-awful terrifying."

Lampo and Nevins saddled up their horses, both gray mares, as Billy flung more good-natured taunts at Alworth.

Standing alone now, Saturn Hayes rolled a cigarette and muttered to himself, "Yessir, bad damned feeling."

31

■ ■ ■ ■

George Gault chose his weapons. Being the possessor of numerous firearms, his options were many. His Navy Revolver was an obvious choice; he always carried it with him, and, in its time, it had already drawn blood. Since Gault first purchased the Colt fifteen years back, its score included two men dead and two others wounded. It would do. For a rifle, he settled on the Trapdoor Springfield he'd recently acquired. Thus far, he'd only killed coyotes with it, but it was certainly capable of more varied service. For good measure, he chose another revolver, a Peacemaker, which he would keep in his saddlebag for luck. Along with Saturn's Winchester and whatever guns the others brought along, they'd be sufficiently armed.

Gault stuffed his saddlebags with the Peacemaker and a good supply of cartridges for all the guns. He draped the bags over his shoulder, took up the Springfield, and left his house. Stepping out into the early afternoon light, he did as he always did before leaving for a spell: he paused to look about him, to survey his particular kingdom. Yes, he had done well for himself. Damn well. From low beginnings, he had fought his way through a world that held no love for him. Fought and sacrificed and (when necessary) killed to arrive at his present situation. Several thousand acres of good grazing land, a thousand head of cattle, a thriving horse-trading business . . . something to be proud of, for sure.

He hoped soon to join the Wyoming Stock Growers Association, further solidifying his role as a man of property. As for wife or offspring, he never did acquire those, but he had come to the realization long ago that he was a man best left to his own designs. Of course, he had seen to his needs with numerous women over the years — most paid for, it's true — and that had been good enough. His requirements were basic and easily met.

As for his affections, they were few if any. He held no man as a true friend. On occasion, some fellow or other with whom he had business dealings might talk him into sharing a bottle of whiskey, but that did not count as friendship. Gault accepted those invitations out of commercial expediency, nothing more.

Regarding the men in his employment, none meant much to him, with the possible exception of Saturn. Hayes had been with him for eight years now, and Gault relied on his calm and dependability. If Gault had anything remotely like a confidant it would, oddly enough, be this former slave from Alabama. Saturn would listen to his boss's gruff musings, perhaps offering a brief reflection of his own, and that would suit Gault well enough.

If there was any soul for whom Gault felt deep fondness, it was Ida Sawbridge. Though three years his junior, she'd always shown an almost maternal affection for him, even when they were children. She had seen his pain close up as no one else ever had. Gault left home at sixteen, and, the few times when he did return, Cousin Ida was the one relation genuinely pleased to see him. First as a girl, then as a woman, she always had a smile and a gentle word for him. When her husband died, Gault offered her and her kids a place on his land, and she accepted. Damn Elizabeth for suggesting her mother mistrusted him, that she saw only the bad in him! No, Ida had cared for her cousin, George, even if no one else ever did. And now she was gone.

Gault made his way to the corral, where he found his chosen men all gathered. He saw that Saturn had saddled one of the mustangs for him. It was a good horse, and he approved. But he also noted that Foggy was saddled up.

"Saturn, I told you to switch out Foggy for another mount," Gault said. "He's too winded from the ride in."

Saturn tossed aside his cigarette. "Foggy and I are way too used to each other's company. You know that, boss. I'd be out of sorts if I had to take a different animal on the trail today. He'll do fine, I promise."

Gault was about to argue the point but thought better of it. "All right. Do as you like."

He took a moment to appraise the men he'd picked. Saturn, of course. And Billy Fowler. Though Billy was undeniably young and a bit too haughty for Gault's liking, he could be depended upon. Gault once saw him square off in a fistfight with another ranch hand, a broader, meaner fellow Billy dropped in two punches. Yes, he was worth having along.

Lampo the Finn, to be sure, was a dangerous man and would be useful. He'd been with Gault longer than anyone besides Saturn.

Then there was Alworth Nevins — who was standing there jotting in his blasted journal. Was it the lad's pluck that made Gault agree to let him come along? Maybe. Gault sometimes acted on impulse, and this was one of those times. That wandering college boy had left the safety of the East for the untamed West in pursuit of adventure. Well, by God, he was about to find some soon enough. Gault gave his mustache a tug and nodded to himself.

"All right, men, mount up," he commanded. "We've got some business to attend to."

CHAPTER THREE:
JOURNAL OF
ALWORTH B. NEVINS

EXCERPTS

I believe it was Tolstoy who said that boredom is the desire for desires. I think I understand all too well what the clever old Russian meant by that.

I left Connecticut over a year ago because the life I'd carved out for myself (or that had been thrust upon me) was painfully desireless. I had no real passion, no dash-fire, as I waded through my life as a scholar — nothing but a sense of obligation. My family had swelled with pride when I, a hatmaker's son, was accepted into Yale University. Of course, that had only come about because a distant relation, being childless but far from penniless, pulled a fistful of strings to arrange my placement. Perhaps I have some brains of the modest variety, but my pedigree is far from what one would expect of a Yale man. You might think that finding myself in that storied seat of learning would have satisfied and inspired me.

But you would be wrong.

Suffice it to say that when I chose not to return to Yale after my first year, anyone with whom I share an ounce of blood was horribly disappointed. Furthermore, when I explained my plan to journey west to live the life of a frontiersman, my sanity became a topic of heated debate. I pointed out that a well-known New York politico, Theodore Roosevelt, had done the exact same thing and how enthralled I'd been by *Hunting Trips of a Ranchman,* his colorful account of those travels. My father dismissed Roosevelt as a "stupendous chowderhead" and suggested I might be of the same breed.

Undaunted, I purchased a sturdy Stetson and a Remington single action revolver, both of which I understood would serve me well on the frontier. I spent the better part of a week learning to fire the weapon, gaining some real accuracy, I believe. So equipped, I left Connecticut, bound west. Father withheld his blessings.

Since I first found employment on Mr. Gault's ranch (and no one was as surprised as I when that occurred) I've generally declined my bunkmates' offers to visit town in search of "wild doings," in part because most of my cohorts are of a far rowdier

38

nature than I, but more because, after a long day of hard, unaccustomed work, I was in no shape to do anything but rest my bones. Upon hearing, though, that a group of traveling players had come to Willerton, I decided to go see their evening performance.

What can I say about Two Robes? Or, more exactly, my reaction to her? When I saw her standing there on the stage of the Wounded Wolf Saloon, dressed in the garments of her people with the verses of Shakespeare on her tongue, I was transfixed. She was staring straight ahead as if peering into another realm, one that the coarse men watching her could not begin to comprehend. It was as if two planets — those of the Plains Indian and of the white man — had converged in the form of this one being. I found her lovely in a quiet, unassuming way. Her long black braids framed a moon-shaped face, and her lips, when not speaking, were set in a thin resolved line. Diminutive and slender, I guessed her to be a few years younger than myself, perhaps eighteen or nineteen.

I had the feeling that, despite her poise upon the stage, she felt profoundly out of place in her surroundings, just as I often did in life — be it here in Wyoming Territory or at Yale or pretty much anywhere I've walked the earth. I think it was this sense of common unease that struck such a resonant chord in me.

Of course, it may be that my feelings of encountering a kindred spirit were nothing more than stupid romanticism. I've been accused of such in my time, and I'd be hard pressed to argue my way out of the charge. As I've mentioned, I found her compelling in face and form, so perhaps I worked up a fable of spiritual affinity to justify mere physical attraction. Perhaps. But, in my heart of hearts, I don't think so.

Hearing her give voice to the love words of fair Juliet greatly stirred me, and, when a drunk cowpoke next to me called out a crude remark, I damned near struck him. I refrained, and Two Robes ignored him, no doubt accustomed to such incivility. Without missing a beat, she continued her oration:

This bud of love, by summer's ripening breath,

May prove a beauteous flower when next we meet.

That verse hit me with particular poignancy. I knew full well that, following tonight's performance, the Lakota girl and her troupe would pack up and be on their way to parts unknown. There would be no *when next we meet* where Two Robes and I were concerned.

But I was wrong. It looks as if I will indeed set eyes upon the girl again, though not in circumstances I would want. By Mr. Gault's decree, we are to pursue and overtake Major Pompay's troupe, of which Two Robes is perhaps the most prominent member. In truth, it was she, along with Pompay, who, on the night I saw them, displayed for purchase those bottles of elixir — a potion that seems to have caused the death of Ida Sawbridge. George Gault is known hereabouts as a man who always gets what he wants, and what he wants at present is hot revenge. And Two Robes is one of those who will likely feel its heat.

CHAPTER FOUR

She stood beside the show wagon watching the mounted men — three Indians and one white — to see how things would play out. The men and horses were clustered together about forty yards ahead. A heated exchange was in progress.

Major Pompay, at the reins of the paused wagon, leaned down toward Two Robes. "What are they saying?"

The young woman kept her eyes on the men. "How would I know? I believe they're speaking Arapaho. I've told you before I speak only Lakota."

"It appears there's a bit of a disagreement going on." Pompay shifted his large bulk on the wagon seat, and the team of four horses, not one of them young, shifted as well. "Looks to me like that big brave in the coonskin cap has some manner of bee under his bonnet, and Nash is trying to settle him down."

"We'll see how *that* goes." Viola Hall had come up beside Two Robes and stood with folded arms. She was somewhere in her forties, blond and curvy, and had a good half foot in height on the Sioux girl. "I don't take Nash for no diplomat. Hopefully he won't get us all killed."

"I certainly hope not!" Pompay tilted back his Panama hat and wiped his brow. "I agree Nash may be a bit rough around the edges, but he does speak several of the local tongues, which is useful."

"Oh, he can utter some words all right," said Viola. "But that don't mean he can string them together in any worthwhile fashion. Sure, he can spit out a filthy joke with the best of 'em. Hell, *I* can do that. But I don't put much stock in his powers of persuasion."

Viola's argument seemed to be confirmed when the man in the coonskin cap shouted something and pointed a rifle at Nash. In response, Nash backed up his horse a few paces and placed his hand on his pistol butt.

"Oh lord," Pompay whispered.

Just as it seemed that violence might erupt, one of the other Arapahos said something firmly to his angry companion. This seemed to alter the situation. After a few more words, the man in the cap sneered, spun his horse around, and rode off in the same direction the wagon was bound. The other two Arapahos followed. Nash watched until the group had disappeared across the plains, then rode back to the wagon. He was a rangy man with a hawkish, half-shaven face. A crow feather jutted from the band of his hat.

Nash offered an unpleasant smile. "I saved us from some trouble there. Don't bother thanking me."

Viola snorted. "Are you joking, Nash? Looks like you came real close to getting some blood spilt. It was one of them who eased things down."

Nash glared at her but didn't argue the point.

"What was the trouble about anyway?" Pompay asked.

"Just a bit of red ugliness, Major," said Nash. "They're hunting for some saddle bum who shot one of their kin. White man who wears a fancy green sombrero. I explained to them we had nothing to do with it and that I wouldn't be caught dead wearing a green sombrero. I threw in that maybe *you* would wear one, but you were too damned rotund to manage a proper killing."

Pompay huffed. "Sir! You needn't be insulting."

"Anyway, two of them seemed to accept my word, but the bad-tempered one, who goes by Low Moon, wouldn't let things go."

The major sighed. "Well, they're gone now. We can continue our travels unmolested."

"Maybe," Viola said. "Maybe not. Seeing as Mister Low Moon and his pals rode off the same way we're going, we might cross paths again."

Nash smirked. "If we do, I'll handle it. You can bet on that."

Viola smirked back. "Oh, you're so brave and bold, you damn near make me swoon."

Nash cursed her, then jerked his horse around and rode on ahead.

"Viola, you shouldn't goad Nash like that," Pompay admonished. "You know we rely on him for safe passage through this risky country."

Viola laughed harshly. "I wouldn't rely on him not to piss in his own boots, never mind anything more important."

"Be that as it may, he's the card we've drawn. And he's a marked improvement over the last man we had, wouldn't you agree?"

"Sure, considering that the last man had more whiskey than blood rushing through his veins. At least Nash don't fall off his horse five times a day."

"As I say, a marked improvement. Let's continue our travels. Would you mind spelling me at the reins for a bit, Viola?"

"Spell your own self, Major. I'm hopping back in the wagon. Me and Two Robes need our beauty rest. Come on, girl."

The two women climbed back into the enclosed wagon, and Pompay, with a theatrical grumble, shook the reins and headed the two horses in the direction Nash had gone.

The interior of the show wagon was nothing like the vibrantly painted red, blue, and yellow exterior. The space was bleak and untidy, crammed with food supplies, pots and pans, bedrolls, portmanteaus of clothing, a few props, and crates of Fabled Fortifying Elixir. There was just enough space for the women to sit on the floorboards as they did now and, in the evenings, to stretch out to sleep. Pompay and Nash did their slumbering on the earth, an arrangement that the major never failed to moan about. Prior to Two Robes joining the troupe, Pompay had several times suggested that he and Viola share their repose together but was always solidly rebuffed. Since Two Robes had arrived the month before, those proposals had stopped.

As the wagon continued it bumpy progress, Viola waxed poetic on the failings of the man charged with their safety. "I know Nash is supposed to be a tough hombre and handy with his irons, but I don't trust him an inch. We'd be better off being protected by a mangy old hound, if you ask my opinion."

In truth, Viola Hall did not need to be asked her opinion on any subject under the sun. She was more than happy to offer it uninvited. As Viola moved on from the topic of Nash to that of the shortcomings of the male beast in general, Two Robes sat silently, occasionally nodding but barely listening. In their time together, the Lakota girl had learned that this was the easiest way to navigate conversations with the other woman. Eventually, Viola would pose some question or other to her, but that might be a while in coming.

Between nods, Two Robes smoothed out her blue calico dress and let her mind wander. She noticed there was a rip in the garment that would need mending. It was the only piece of clothing she had kept from her time at the Carlisle Indian School back in Pennsylvania. When she left that white man's school last year, she tried to put as much of the memory behind her as possible.

From age fourteen to eighteen, that had been her home, a place where her Lakota ways were firmly forced out of her. Sometimes with the tools of education, sometimes with the rod. She and all the other children — Cherokee, Ojibwa, Seneca, Apache, and the rest — had their traditions stripped away and replaced with new ones that never felt right. Some of the children had been forced into the school, while others were handed over by their parents. In Two Robes' case, she'd been orphaned at a young age and passed among various relations, the last of whom decided to wash their hands of her by shipping her east to Carlisle. She remembered little of her itinerant childhood, those memories being buried beneath the white teachings.

When she came of age, Two Robes decided to leave. Not only the school, but the east itself. She said farewell to the Indian girls who had been her friends at Carlisle and, with the help of an elderly Quaker woman who'd befriended her, purchased a ticket for the transcontinental railroad. By now, she had no real connection to South Dakota or her people.

She chose Wyoming Territory as her destination because her benefactor, Mrs. Lund, once told her that the famous Buffalo Bill came from there and, in addition, was himself a Quaker. Not that that meant anything really, but, lacking actual plans, Wyoming seemed as good an end point as any. Before she left Pennsylvania, Two Robes burnt the drab smocks she'd been forced to wear in the white man's school. The calico dress she now wore had been a gift from Mrs. Lund, so she kept it, her sole material connection to that life.

She only wore the buckskin dress, along with the owl feather, for the performances. That also had been a gift — of sorts — from Major Pompay. But his purpose in giving it had been less than charitable. He told her the buckskin added to the novelty of an Indian maiden spouting Shakespeare. Several weeks ago, Two Robes had seen one of the troupe's performances in Cheyenne. She listened to Viola's singing and the major's oratories and thought to herself, *Perhaps I could do that.* After all, she had learned large swaths of poetry while at Carlisle. Since her funds had almost run out, she summoned up the courage to approach the major and ask if he might consider taking on a new player. He agreed to her offer. Though the pay would be nearly nothing, she'd at least be guaranteed food in her belly and the shelter of the wagon.

"And, believe me, darlin', I know men. Get what I mean?"

Had Viola just asked her a question?

"Ah, yes, I think so," Two Robes said.

"Uh-uh. I know my way around. I've met a lot of folks in my time, and I've lived in a lot of places."

"I see."

"Yep, and I've had a lot of professions."

"Such as?"

"Oh, it don't matter. Let's just say that they all show up in the Bible. Some more favorably than others."

Two Robes went back to nodding.

"Anyway, my point is," Viola continued, "you don't live the life I've lived without learning how people's gears spin. 'Specially where men are concerned. Nash is a wastrel for sure. As for our dear major, he's just lucky no one's strung him up before now."

"Hang him?" Two Robes frowned. "Why would someone want to do that?"

"Let's just say that ol' Pompay don't always play on the honest side of the street. Why, I once saw him sell a man a stuffed monkey with a wig glued atop it, claiming it was the genuine missing link. The major told me he learned that trick from P. T. Barnum himself. Now, I don't know if that's true, but I do know we lit out of that town quick as lightning with that man and his four brothers a nipping at our heels."

"What about the things we've been selling?" Two Robes asked. "The lucky rabbits' feet and the —"

"Oh, they're rabbit feet all right. I can't say, though, if they've been certified as to their luckiness. I'd venture that they're not particularly *un*lucky. Except where the rabbits were concerned."

"What about the elixir?"

Viola was sitting next to one of the bottle-filled crates. She lifted out a blue bottle and thrust it forward. "Why, gal, can't you just see that it's filled to the brim with vim and vigor? Good for all that ails you? It's a damned miracle, yes indeedy!" She laughed loudly and replaced the bottle.

Two Robes asked no more questions about the business the major and Viola were engaged in — and that she was now party to. It struck her (not for the first time) how naïve she was regarding the ways of the world. The Carlisle School had not prepared her well for what lay beyond its walls.

"It's a living," Viola said philosophically. "And, Lord knows, I could ramble on about a ton of worst ways to make one. Don't get me started."

Two Robes had no intention of doing that.

She shifted her position, moving a little away from her companion and, in doing so, knocked over the bugle leaning next to her. It was the battered old instrument that the major played during the performances. He claimed it had seen service at Gettysburg, but, like most of what came from his lips, Two Robes suspected it wasn't true.

"Careful, hon," Viola said. "Don't go damaging that. You know how the major likes to blow his own horn!"

Since joining the troupe, Two Robes had heard Viola make the same joke a dozen times. And, each time, Viola burst with laughter as if the jest had just occurred to her. Two Robes no longer bothered to smile in response.

She now asked something she'd been wondering for some time. "Was the major really an officer in the war?"

Viola grinned. "Not too damned likely! Can you see him leading a battalion across some bloody battlefield? Hell, he can barely lead our sad little group. What's more, near as I can figure, his name ain't even Pompay. He just plucked that from some book on history to give himself flourish. Didn't even spell it right. But here in the West, anybody's got the right to make something new of themselves. Lord knows, that's what *I'm* doing. I partnered up with the major so I can travel about and sing for the masses. Ain't it glorious?" She laughed loudly again. "I'm no Jenny Lind, mind you, but I'm good enough for the drunks and drovers who stumble in to see us."

"You sing fine," Two Robes felt obliged to say.

"I thank you for that, hon. But *you're* the real deal in this troupe. When you toss out that poetry of yours, it's like the sound of doves flying high. Guess they taught you a thing or two in that school of yours back East."

Yes, they did, the Lakota girl thought to herself. *They taught me that I'm of two worlds but belong to neither.*

CHAPTER FIVE

George Gault and his men pulled into Willerton late in the afternoon. Gault dropped a couple of coins into Lampo the Finn's palm and told him to take Billy and Alworth over to the Wounded Wolf and get themselves a beer. But one beer only — Gault didn't want men swaying in their saddles.

While they were at the saloon, they should ask around if anyone knew anything about Major Pompay's travel route. Gault would do the same at the sheriff's office, not that he expected much there. He took Saturn with him, and they found Sheriff Rawley at his desk, hunched over a dime novel with the intensity of a man studying calculus.

Rawley looked up. "Gault. Nice to see you." His tone and expression suggested this was not the case. "Can I help you with something?"

"I strongly doubt it." Gault stared down at the gaunt lawman. "But I'll try my luck anyway. Wondering what you know about that Major Pompay and his people."

"Just that they put on a show here a couple nights back. I caught a bit of it. Not too bad I thought. 'Course, we don't get much entertainment in town, so I can't really —"

"I wasn't looking for your opinion on the show, Rawley. I expect you heard about my cousin Ida."

"Yes, of course. I'm so sorry. Ida was such a very nice —"

"Like I say, I don't need your opinion on things. You heard about her drinking that elixir Pompay was hawking, yeah? And how she died right after?"

"Maybe I did hear something along those lines."

"I don't suppose that, representing the law as you do, you took any action."

"Action? What action would you expect me to take? Those folks were long gone by the time I heard about Ida."

"I dunno, a woman in your jurisdiction gets poisoned, maybe you try to track down the ones responsible." Gault leaned forward and placed his hands on the desk, putting him inches from Rawley's face. "Maybe you wire some of your brother lawmen to let them know this Pompay is on the prowl.

Maybe you do something that shows you've got a thimbleful of guts, and that the badge on your shirt is more than a goddamn decoration."

The sheriff tried to look offended. "Now, see here, Gault. You can't —"

"Stow it. Did you get wind of where those show people were heading? What their route is? Do your ears work at least, even if your brains and balls don't?"

"I heard nothing!" Rawley tried to puff up his narrow chest in an unconvincing show of fortitude. "Now get the hell out of my office. I'm done with you."

Gault's right hand shot forward and caught the sheriff's shirtfront. With his left, he backhanded the man's face. Rawley let out a high-pitched cry.

Saturn took a step forward. "Mr. Gault! You don't want to do that."

"I think I do." said Gault and drew his hand back, poised for another strike.

The scene was interrupted by a large figure that suddenly filled the doorway. Gault dropped his hand and turned, as did Saturn, to take in the newcomer.

"Thank God you're here, Oakes!" the sheriff called out. "Gault here was trying to kill me!"

"Hardly," said Gault. "A few slaps

shouldn't kill a man. Leastwise not a real man. No need for you to get involved, Oakes."

Oakes was that rare example of a man whose name fit him just right. Certainly physically. He was tall and solid as an oak, even if he lacked the silent dignity of that tree. Gault knew him well enough, since Oakes had worked for him the previous year. He'd been fired for talking back to his employer one too many times. Meaning *one* time — that's all it took to fall from George Gault's graces. Since then, Oakes had somehow wormed his way into a new job: town deputy.

"Well now, just what do you think you're doing, Gault?" Oakes had a little smile on his lips that suggested something other than warmth.

"I'm done what I was doing. Step aside, and I'll be off."

"What's the hurry, *Mister* Gault?" Oakes belabored the title, and his smile widened. "No time for an old pal?"

Oakes' hand now moved to the pistol on his hip. In response, Gault rested his palm on his own holstered revolver.

Seeing what was playing out, Rawley jumped to his feet. "Are you men crazy? You're going to start trading bullets in this small space?"

"You're right, Sheriff," said Gault. "That would be damned foolish. Here, hold my gun while I work things out with Oakes here."

Gault gingerly withdrew his revolver and, clasping the barrel, held it out to Rawley. Just as the sheriff was reaching for it, Gault swung back around toward Oakes and struck the deputy hard in the temple with the grip. Oakes dropped heavily to the floor.

"Changed my mind," Gault said. "I think I'll keep my gun."

He slipped the revolver back in its holster, then drew back his foot and gave the fallen man a sharp kick in the ribs. Oakes cried out.

"You . . . you villain!" Rawley blustered. "Kicking a man when he's down!"

"Ain't hardly started," said Gault. Drawing back his leg, he landed another fierce kick. "No one threatens me, you hear, Oakes? No one!"

Gault delivered yet another kick before Saturn grabbed him by the arm and pulled him away.

"That's it, boss! That's it! You don't want to kill him, do you?"

Gault had a look in his eyes that suggested maybe he did. "All right, Saturn, let's go."

As the two men exited the room, Rawley called after them. "You've stepped over the line, Gault! You can't get away with this kind of savagery! No, you can't!"

George Gault was breathing hard as he headed down the street. Saturn caught up and stepped in front of him.

"Hold on now, boss." Saturn raised his hands to halt the other's progress. "You know you can't go on like this, burning things up this way. I understand you feel mighty bad about your cousin's death and all, but raising Cain like this just makes things worse. You can bet Oakes and the sheriff ain't gonna let this drop. Next time we're back in town here, there's sure to be hell to pay."

"I can handle that," Gault said.

"Folks might not feel too kindly toward you when they hear about things. You might find you've got few friends left hereabouts."

"What, you think I've got friends *now*? I'm accustomed to carving out my own path. Always have been."

"I'm just wondering if this here particular path is the best one to be taking. I mean the one that has us chasing down those show people. After all, we don't know for certain if —"

"Do I need to cut you loose, Saturn?"

Gault snapped. "If you don't have the stomach for this, you can head back to the ranch right now. I'll keep on with the men I've got."

Saturn pulled on his mustache and slowly shook his head. "No, no, I'm not saying that. I'm just raising up my concerns."

"All right, I've noted them. Now let's go fetch the others."

They had just started back down the street when Billy and Lampo came toward them. Beer suds clung to the Finn's long beard.

"Learn anything?" Gault asked.

"A little," Billy said. "The barkeep says the fat major mentioned they were heading north past Horse Creek. Town called Black Powder. Doing more of their shows and all."

Gault nodded. "I know Black Powder. 'Bout a day and a half's ride. We'll put in a few hours now and camp the night. We'll pull in before nightfall tomorrow. Now where's Nevins?"

"He should be along," said Billy. "Alworth took a notion to go buy himself a Holy Bible."

"A Bible? Right this minute? What for?"

Billy shrugged. "Couldn't tell you, Mr. Gault. That boy's got some peculiar ways."

Alworth Nevins left the mercantile with his

purchase in hand, though not the one he'd intended. Yes, there were a couple of Bibles for sale, but they were thick, heavy tomes that would have barely fit in his saddlebags. Had he thought it through, he'd have known that would be the case. But he had acted on impulse. As they were riding into Willerton, the idea had struck him that a Bible might act as something of a talisman. Not that he expected to read it. His purpose in obtaining the book was one of self protection, of defense against undesired outcomes. In accompanying Mr. Gault on his quest for vengeance, Alworth was surely placing himself in peril. Though he couldn't anticipate the exact nature of that peril, he could feel it in his gut.

Instead of his first choice, he had settled on the only other religious book available at the store: *Sketches of Eminent Methodist Ministers.* It had only a third of the pages of the Bible and, thus, was manageable. He hoped it would be sufficient for his purpose.

Alworth was fully aware of the illogic of his thinking. If his chums back at Yale had been privy to it, they'd no doubt have accused him of being superstitious and showered him with jolly abuse. And, the thing was, he wasn't even a particularly religious person. His time in the pews was sporadic at best. No, something else was moving him. Was it a sense of his own mortality? Surely, he was too young a man to dwell on the reaper's scythe. But, when following the dictates of someone as reckless as George Gault, that scythe was more than a fanciful symbol. It was a very possible reality that might take the form of a rifle bullet or a renegade's arrow.

In his time, Alworth had witnessed only one death, but it was a jarring one. This was just a few months back somewhere outside of Lincoln, Nebraska. At a country fair he attended, one drunk farmer plunged a pitchfork into the chest of another drunk farmer, mortally wounding him. It was a mad, ludicrous act, and the man responsible looked shocked by his own actions. The dying took several minutes and was a terrible thing to behold.

The man who perished was not much older than Alworth, which caused him to ponder, *I could cease to exist. Just a moment's bloody work and all I am could vanish into nothingness. My story would end forever.* Now, as he made his way up the street, that memory returned and weighed on his heart. Yes, as a bullet, arrow, or pitchfork, the scythe could appear out of thin air and, in an instant, deliver you to oblivion.

He found himself at the sheriff's office. Thinking that Gault might still be there, he peered through the front window. Inside he saw a skinny man whom he recognized as the sheriff bandaging a tall bruiser with a bloodied forehead. Not seeing Gault, Alworth decided against entering. He stepped back and noticed several sheets of paper tacked to the outer wall. Wanted posters. He took a moment to look them over. They offered brief descriptions of dangerous men, individuals who had killed for either passion or profit. Bold emissaries of the reaper.

Alworth clutched his eminent ministers tighter and continued down the street.

CHAPTER SIX

WANTED
FOR MURDER, BANK ROBBERY, AND
CATTLE RUSTLING
$3,000 REWARD
FRANK BAKER

32 years old; 5 feet 9 inches in height; weight 180 pounds; thick neck and stocky build. Dark hair and beard. Dark eyes. Missing a front tooth resulting in a noticeable gap. Surly in temperament, inclined toward drink. Baker has a history of involvement with several outlaw crews, including most recently the McNulty Gang.

WANTED
FOR BANK ROBBERY
$750 REWARD
T. C. HECKETT

About 24 years old; 5 feet 7 or so tall,

slight build. Dirty-blond hair, worn some-what long. Blue eyes. Pleasant face, clean-shaven. Comes off as friendly; inclined to smile when not involved in criminal activities. No known killings but seems confident with a pistol. Rides with John McNulty.

WANTED
FOR MURDER AND BANK ROBBERY
$5,000 REWARD
"BLOODLESS" JOHN MCNULTY

Nearing sixty years old, but carries himself with a younger man's bearing. Slender and sound of limb. Perhaps 5 foot 10 in height. Gray haired, he wears a neatly trimmed beard of the Van Dyke style. Irish born with a notable accent. Well-spoken and calm in deportment. Leads the McNulty Gang, which is responsible for a number of bank robberies, one reputed train robbery, and at least four deaths, including a U.S. Marshal. The sobriquet "Bloodless" comes from his reputation for having never been touched by a bullet, despite many violent encounters.

CHAPTER SEVEN

John McNulty was not a man you could easily rile. Despite the potential violence of his profession, his temper almost always remained in check. Back in County Kerry, there had been a time or two when he'd given in to unflattering rage, but those instances had been rare and could be attributed to youth. Even in 'forty-eight, in the midst of the Famine, when he joined the Young Irelander Rebellion up in Tipperary, he had remained cool. While his comrades, provoked by the enemy, screamed profanities and shot wildly, McNulty had calmly loaded his rifle and seen to the task at hand.

Now, over thirty years on, that same demeanor marked his life here in America. While his days as a political rebel were behind him, he considered his present work, in a way, an extension of righteous rebellion. Though no longer rising up against an unjust crown, was he not fighting a different brand of tyranny? It was a tyranny that kept good men poor while bankers and robber barons gobbled up wealth with soulless abandon.

Not that he dwelt too deeply on the philosophy of being a brigand. McNulty had chosen his course and would follow it to its logical end. He could well guess what that end might be, but one never knew: he might live decades more and pass into eternity while dozing in some tranquil garden. Never bet on the day of one's departure. McNulty would press on and, as in times gone by, simply see to the task at hand.

At the moment, the outlaw leader's usual calm was being tested. As was common these days, it was Frank Baker doing the testing. When the band's number was greater, Baker's venom had been diluted by the presence of several leveler heads. Now that death, capture, and departure had depleted their ranks, only McNulty and T.C. remained to deal with their companion's vehemence. Of course, T. C. Heckett couldn't be depended upon to offer any real counterbalance to Baker. The young man, though certainly a more affable type, possessed his own style of unpredictability. The barroom, poker table, and cathouse were constant sources of distraction for T.C. and so rendered him less than reliable in many situations. But bank robbing wasn't one of them. In the midst of a robbery, the youth was rock steady, wielding his pistol and casting a steely gaze as if he were the deadliest of desperados. It was a fine bit of acting.

They were standing now on the outskirts of a town whose name they never learned, grazing their horses in an open field. In reality, it was not a proper town at all, more like a scattering of shacks and shanties, but it had been enough of a place for Baker to find trouble there. McNulty had intended on letting Baker's actions pass with a strong reprimand, but the other wasn't content to leave it at that.

"You know what I think?" Baker, thickset and burly, faced off against the older man. "I think I'm getting real damned weary of you always harping on me all the time. Just 'cause I've thrown in with you don't mean I need your advice on my leanings."

McNulty smoothed his beard and fixed his gaze on the other man. "I wasn't offering advice, Baker. I was issuing a warning."

"You was, was you?"

"Your grammar is appalling, but yes, as I've stated, it was a warning." John Patrick McNulty's accent was deep and flowing, like the River Ferta on whose banks he'd been raised. His years away from his home nation had little changed it.

Baker scowled. "And don't think I don't recognize when I'm getting insulted."

"I'm sure you've had enough experience to do so. My point, Baker, is that should you ever again display such thuggery as you did back there, you're done for."

Baker narrowed his eyes. "And just how do you intend to see me done for?"

"One option, of course, is that I could shoot you dead. That would be the most decisive play. Barring that, I could expunge you from our merry band here."

"What the hell's 'expunge'?"

"It means to eradicate. To purge. Or, in terms you can grasp, I could toss you out of my gang."

"I don't belong to no gang of yours. I just happen to be riding with you for a spell. I figured throwing in with Bloodless John McNulty would be an obliging thing. I'm beginning to think otherwise. Besides, it ain't much of a gang any more, is it? Just you and goddamned T.C."

The subject of that blasphemy offered a grin. "My, oh my, now who's flinging insults?"

"Shut up, boy," growled Baker. "This is

69

between McNulty and me."

"Then get on with it," T.C. said. "I wouldn't want to intrude on a lovers' spat."

Baker turned his attention back to the Irishman. "Like I was saying, there's just you and him. 'Less you want to count that *creature* over there."

Baker thrust a thumb toward the fourth person in the field, sitting on the ground a little away from the others. It was a young female — though, by her look and garments, she might have passed for a boy. She was skinny and pale with cropped light-brown hair, and her eyes looked enormous in her narrow face. Her outfit consisted of a faded shirt and trousers. She probably hadn't reached her eighteenth year, maybe not even her seventeenth.

McNulty addressed Baker firmly. "No need to belittle Quinny. If you have more poison to spout, aim it at me and me alone. All right, enough of this parrying. I'll say it one last time: I won't tolerate any more of your brutish behavior."

"I was only hunting a little fun." Baker offered a leering grin, revealing his missing front tooth. "That cherry back in town had a quick look to her, and I just thought I'd try my hand. Can't blame me for that."

The blood rose in McNulty's face. "I

surely *can* blame you! You accosted that lass in the street and tried to drag her into an alley. If T.C. hadn't intervened, who knows what —"

"If you're worried that some kin of hers mighta caught wind of things, hell, we'd have been long gone before any trouble showed."

McNulty's usual reserve was gone. "Damn you, Baker! That's not how we conduct ourselves."

"Don't get high and mighty with me, McNulty! You and T.C. have squandered plenty of cash on whores and jezebels. Ain't like you're courting fine ladies with flowers and sweets. Hell, maybe you're just jealous 'cause you wanted a turn with that filly I caught."

Cursing, McNulty moved toward Baker with clenched fists. In response Baker balled his own fists and braced himself. Before contact could be made, T.C. stepped between the two men and pushed them apart.

"Whoa now!" T.C. said. "Don't we have troubles enough without stirring up our own? Last batch of wanted posters I saw, there were some real choice bounties on our heads. Maybe we shouldn't hang around squabbling like this, making targets of ourselves."

71

McNulty took a moment to steady his breathing. "Of course. Let's be on our way."

Baker exhaled deeply himself and mounted his horse. The rest followed suit, including the girl called Quinny, who rode a pinto pony. Baker headed out first in the planned direction, and the other three followed.

As McNulty drew his blood bay alongside T.C., he said with a slight smile, "Fancy the day when young Master Heckett is the one acting the voice of reason."

T.C. laughed. "Yeah, I surprised my own damn self!"

The outlaws spent the night on the banks of Horse Creek. They kept the fire low, the blaze just high enough to heat their coffee and supper. As always, McNulty acted as cook. In the months since she'd joined them, Quinny had offered more than once to take over those duties, but the Irishman insisted he enjoyed the task. He said it settled him down after whatever commotion the day brought his way. T.C. occasionally referred to him as "old Mother McNulty" for the way he took care of his brood. McNulty never seemed to take offense.

After they'd eaten, Baker and T.C. pressed

for details of their next robbery.

McNulty, lazily poking the fire with a stick, took some time to respond. "I haven't yet figured out our next bit of work. For the present, I think staying on the move is in our best interest. Maybe head west toward Fort Sanders."

"I thought we were gonna make a strike up Bordeaux way?" Baker asked.

"We may yet," McNulty said. "For now though, we'll lie low. As T.C. pointed out, the bounties for our capture have gotten quite high."

T.C. smiled. "For our capture . . . or demise."

"Or demise," McNulty repeated quietly.

"To judge by those wanted posters," said T.C., "you boys' skins are a helluva lot more valuable than my own. They're offering a few thousand for each of you. Me, I only rate seven hundred and fifty dollars. Couldn't they have pushed it to an even eight hundred? Makes a body feel unloved."

"You're worth less 'cause you ain't gunned down nobody," Baker said. "Me and McNulty are proven man killers. You got to stuff coffins to get respected."

"It's nothing to brag about." McNulty tossed the stick in the fire and watched as the flames devoured it. "Taking a life is no mild thing."

"But you done it all the same," Baker said. "That 'bloodless' they slapped on your name is a touch confounding, yeah? Sure, maybe you ain't gotten your own blood spilt, but you sure as hell spilt other fellas'. They say you made quick work of that marshal back in Buford. I got to admit I admire such gumption."

"I'd rather you didn't, Baker."

"Are you afeared of their ghosts?" Quinny spoke now, addressing McNulty. She was seated across the fire from him, firelight and shadows playing over her bony frame. "Those folks you killed, I mean. Are you afeared their ghosts might come visit you in the night?"

Baker let out a loud laugh. "Jesus! Sometimes I think this one is tetched for sure. You believe in that bunkum, girl? You think a passel of spooks is hovering about waiting to pounce on you?"

"I think I do believe in them," Quinny said softly. "I may have seen one in the woods once. A little girl with a streak of white in her hair. I told Ma, and she said it must be her sister who died of the croup." She shifted her gaze to the dying fire. "Now I guess Ma might be a ghost herself."

Baker laughed again. "Tetched for sure!"

"Leave her be," T.C. said.

"Yes, Baker," McNulty added. "She doesn't need your ridicule."

"I'm used to folks poking fun at me," said Quinny. "Ever since I was little."

McNulty studied the girl across the burning embers. Since the day he'd first come across her just north of Cheyenne, she had been an enigma. Living rough, stealing to eat, she seemed more dust than flesh. They'd found her sleeping in a buffalo wallow, wrapped in a blanket she'd pilfered from an army wagon. She reminded McNulty of the famine orphans he'd encountered back in Ireland.

Moved by pity, he'd swung her up behind him on his horse and brought her to the nearest town. There he paid for her to obtain a warm bath and a hearty meal. He even bought her a dress, but this she refused to wear, preferring the trousers and shirt she'd been found in. When Baker and some of the others joked about their leader's intentions with the girl, McNulty shut down such talk firmly.

Her name was Quinny, or so she told McNulty. She accepted the man's kindnesses with few words, leaving him unsure as to what she thought of him. But when he attempted to ride off without her, she planted herself before his horse and refused to move. After a brief debate, McNulty gave in and purchased her a pony. She'd ridden along with them ever since, waiting on the outskirts of targeted towns while the men did their illicit work.

"In answer to your question," McNulty now said to her, "I fear no ghost. Why should I? After all, I come from a land rife with phantoms and fairies. Besides, aren't we all ghosts waiting to be born? Someday I'll wander the Elysian Fields with the shades of the men I sent there." He added under his breath, "And perhaps with that of the man who sends *me* there."

Quinny nodded solemnly.

T.C. chuckled. "If they gave out medals for cogitating, by God, John McNulty, you'd have a chest full of them!"

McNulty smiled gently. "That may be so. All right, I'm ready to get some slumber. I suggest you all do the same."

He burrowed into his bedroll and, in what seemed like seconds, was snoring deeply. Baker pulled out a whiskey flask and gave it his full attention. Quinny continued staring into the embers, her eyes looking even wider than normal.

"Hey, Quinny," T.C. called quietly. Receiving no answer, he raised his voice.

"Quinny . . ."

Seeming not to hear him, Quinny stood, walked over to her tethered pinto, and began untying her bedroll. In the light of the nearly full moon, T.C. could see her clearly. He rose and joined her.

"You know, I've been thinking to give you something," he said with some hesitation. "Sort of a gift, I suppose."

"A gift?" She didn't meet his eyes. "Why?"

"I just figure you don't have much to call your own." T.C. reached into his coat pocket and withdrew something. "Here you go."

Nestled in his hand lay a small, short-barreled pistol. Quinny studied it for a moment, then looked at him quizzically.

"It's a genuine Philadelphia Derringer," T.C. explained. "Like the one Booth used to dispatch Lincoln."

"Why would I want such a thing?"

T.C. shrugged. "You're a wisp of a gal, and this world's a mean place sometimes. If that meanness gets too close, it might be useful having something handy to fend it off." He pressed the derringer into Quinny's hand. "I won it in a poker game a while back. Three sturdy kings! Been carrying it around ever since. I've got some shots for it in my saddlebag I can get for you come morning."

Without another word, Quinny pocketed the derringer, pulled free her bedroll, and found a piece of ground to lie down. As usual, she chose a spot somewhat away from the three men. T.C. returned to the fading fire and dropped down beside Baker.

"Don't tell me you've taken a shine to that little scarecrow," Baker said.

"That's not how it is."

"Never seen such a strange girl." Baker passed T.C. the flask. "Dresses like a boy and huddles like a mouse."

"I guess that's her right." T.C. took a pull of the whiskey.

"What was you giving her there?"

"Just a pretty little bauble I found."

"Hah! Pretty things are wasted on that one, don't you figure?"

"Probably so." T.C. handed back the liquor.

Baker capped the flask, then rolled over in his bedroll.

T.C. sat up for some time, watching the embers turn from red to black to gray. At one point, he heard McNulty, deep in slumber, call out something. Though he couldn't make out the words, T.C. thought he detected a note of longing there.

CHAPTER EIGHT:
MCNULTY'S DREAM

He was walking down a narrow, tree-lined lane, such as he had known back in Ireland. These trees, however, were ponderosa pines, common to Wyoming Territory, but certainly not to his home country. A thick bluish mist swirled about him and, strangely, seemed to be infused with sound. A humming, almost a chanting. He had the sense that he was bound for somewhere particular, though where exactly he could not say. He only knew that he must reach his destination soon or things would not be right.

The blue mist grew heavier and, with it, the intensity of the sound. He hastened his pace, eventually breaking into a run. He found that his limbs were as strong and supple as they had been in his younger days. He ran so fast that his feet nearly left the ground. But that fleetness was short lived, for suddenly his legs froze in place, as if rooted to the earth. At the same moment, the fog thickened to an even greater degree, becoming nearly solid and weighing him down. The sound was now a bellow. For several seconds or an eternity, he struggled to move forward. Panic filled him. He opened his mouth to cry out for help — from whom he had no idea — but no words would come. The fog became something else now: the embodiment of despair.

Then a break appeared some yards ahead. The oppressive mists parted, and a face could be seen. A feminine face, a face he knew. A realization hit him with the power of a strong blow: *this was his beloved.* She was his destination, his outcome, the one he had always desired. This surprised him. Had he thought about it, he would have called her an unlikely choice to fill such a role in his heart. He would perhaps have named the O'Donnell lass who'd lived across from his family and for whom he had always pined. Or Bridey Mahoney, with whom he had first shared his passion. But it was neither of these. It was *her.*

The mists closed in again, and the face vanished. With new resolve, he freed himself from his inertia and pressed forward. Despite the unnatural weight of the fog and the deafening roar in his ears, he resumed running. As he pierced the mists, he found his voice and cried out to her, *I'm coming! I'm coming to you!*

CHAPTER NINE

Alworth woke to a firm kick to his rump, delivered by a growling George Gault.

"Get the hell up, Nevins," Gault commanded. "How many times do I need to say it?"

Alworth scrambled to his feet. "Sorry, Mr. Gault, sorry. Guess I was deep in my sleep."

He received a grunt in reply. They had camped for the night in a rock-bordered pass somewhere east of Pole Creek. Dawn had just broken. Gault hadn't allowed a breakfast fire, so cold biscuits and dry prunes, hastily consumed, were the morning's fare. Within minutes, the five men were saddled up and back on the trail.

Saturn sided up to Gault. "We should roll into Black Powder by day's end. What's the plan then, boss?"

"You know the plan. We rout out Major Pompay and his people."

"Then what?"

"Then they get what's due them."

"And what exactly do you figure that to be?"

"What are you getting at, Saturn?"

"I'm just speculating as to what we're doing here. If you got a grievance with this Pompay fella, maybe the law can —"

"The law? I believe you were there yesterday when I visited Rawley. You think that weak son of a bitch is gonna set things right?"

"Maybe not him, but could be the law up in Black Powder can do something."

"I *am* the law right now, Saturn. Just 'cause you don't see a badge on me, don't mean it ain't so. Until I set things right by Ida, I'm the goddamn law."

Gault fished out a cheroot and lit it, then spurred his mustang forward, leaving Saturn in his wake. Billy Fowler came up alongside his friend, and they rode side by side.

"You had a good palaver with the boss man just now?" Billy asked. "Hey, you think he'll give us a bonus for making this ride with him?"

"Maybe he'll pay for our funerals. Is that enough of a bonus for you?"

Billy grinned. "You never miss a chance to have a sour thought, do you, Saturn?"

"I just try to see things as they truly be.

83

Not like some I could name who wouldn't know the truth of things if it came up and bit off their particulars."

Billy winced. "Now that's harsh, old man. I expect it's *my* particulars you're referring to."

Saturn couldn't suppress a smile. "I didn't name no names, did I?"

"Careful now. You keep needling me like this, I may forget you're a hundred years old and give you a thrashing."

"You just try it, you damned sapling. We'll see then who's king of the roost."

" 'Less I'm mistaken, that would be Mr. Gault, wouldn't it?"

Saturn took a moment to answer. "That's right, Billy. I'm just hoping he ain't one of those kings who leads his army straight off a cliff."

"Now, where'd you come up with that? I'd guess it was from some storybook, only I know that you and the written word don't get along."

"Hell, you think you can hurt my feelings with that?" Saturn leaned down and spat in the dust. "I don't need no books to understand life. I've learned more in my years than a dozen other men could do. When you hit my age, you come find me, and we'll see if you learned half as much."

Billy laughed. "The truth is, when I'm your age, you probably *will* still be kicking around. You're too damned ornery to die."

A half hour later, Saturn cursed softly and pulled up his horse.

Billy pulled up his own. "What's troubling you now, old man? Too much excitement?"

"It's Foggy." Saturn dismounted, knelt down, and began examining the blue roan's front hooves. "I've been noticing for a while now he seems to be hobbling a bit. Yeah, he's gone and cut his hoof on something. I'll need to see to it."

The other three men had now turned around and joined Saturn and Billy. Saturn explained the situation. Gault ordered his men to climb down and give the horses a few minutes rest while Foggy was tended to.

Alworth had gone a little ways off to relieve himself and didn't notice as Billy sneaked up behind him.

"Rattlesnake!" Billy shouted.

Alworth jumped and barely managed not to soil himself. "What? Jesus! Where?"

Billy was bent over with laughter. "Oh my! Oh my! You're sure a brave man, Alworth. Nothing scares you, no indeed!"

Alworth was looking all around. "I don't see any snake."

Billy straightened up, still laughing. "My mistake! Guess it was a trick of the light."

Alworth buttoned up his trousers and cursed. "You're a regular jester, aren't you, Billy Fowler?"

"Some folks say as much." Billy slapped Alworth on the back. "Don't worry now, you'll toughen up — in ten or twenty years maybe."

Alworth headed back toward where the others were standing. He was paces away when the air thundered with several loud blasts.

It all seemed to happen at once. Saturn cried out and fell to the ground. Foggy reared, staggered, and landed beside his master. Gault yanked his Springfield free of his saddle and yelled *"Down!"* Everyone dropped to the earth. Guns were quickly drawn. Another shot flew over Gault's head, narrowly missing its mark.

Gault called over to the fallen Saturn. "You hit bad?"

"Shoulder," the other man groaned.

"Lay low. Anybody else shot?"

No one was. Billy, sprawled out a distance away from the others, started to crawl toward Saturn.

"Billy!" Gault called out. "What the hell you doing?"

"Going to check on Saturn there."

"He'll keep. You stay where you are. I don't need another man with a bullet in him. Anybody see where it came from?"

Alworth pointed up toward a rocky outcropping to his right. "I just saw a glint up over there. Maybe a rifle barrel."

"I see it, too," Gault called out. "Okay then, when I say so, Billy and Lampo, you all start firing that way. You, too, Saturn, if you can."

"I can," Saturn said through gritted teeth.

"Here, Lampo." Gault slid the Springfield over to the Finn. "It's loaded. You're the only one sharp-eyed enough to hit something from this far, so do your damndest. Alworth, you're closest to me, so you get the call." Gault pulled out his Navy Revolver. "When I make a run, stick to me close as the devil. We're aiming for that cluster of rocks up over there. The rest of you, stagger your shots, but don't let up. Keep whoever that bastard is occupied. All right, we're going for it."

Gault made a scrambling run for the rocks. Alworth sucked in his breath, tightened his grip on his own pistol, and followed close on Gault's heels. Bullets kicked up the dust around them. Lampo and the others returned fire. The running men reached the shelter of the rocks and dropped down behind a large boulder.

"Okay, Nevins, here's the play," said Gault. "I figure if we head up along this cut here, that bushwhacker can't see us. At least till we get fairly near him. Once we make it over that ridge up there, we should get a glimpse of the son of a bitch. I'll give the word then, and you start firing in his direction. You won't likely hit nothing, but you'll distract him. Meanwhile, I'll peel off to the left and loop around."

"So you can get the drop on him?" Alworth had read that line somewhere, and it felt apt for the current situation.

"That's right. Come on, let's move."

As the gunfire between the men below and the bushwhacker continued, Gault and Alworth began their ascent. As Gault had conjectured, they seemed to be in a blind spot, for no shots came their way. A five-minute climb brought them to where they could see their quarry just above them. He was kneeling and firing down at Lampo and the rest and hadn't noticed the two men twenty yards away. The intervening rocks blocked their view of him, so that they could just make out the man's hat and shoulders, but not his face. Gault caught Alworth's eye and gestured with his revolver to indicate that the younger man should start firing. Gault then moved off to the left and vanished among the rocks.

Alworth extended his right arm, resting it on a small boulder, and took aim at the man above him. It occurred to him that this was the first time he had ever pointed a gun at anyone, never mind with the intention of drawing blood. Or, perhaps, taking a life. His finger was curved around the trigger, but his hand was far from steady. He wrapped his left hand around his right wrist in an effort to stabilize it. He needed to fire now, had been ordered to do so, but found that his trigger finger resisted. Damn it! Gault was depending on him. Billy and the others were depending on him. Alworth suddenly wished that his *Eminent Methodist Ministers* wasn't below in his saddlebag. Having it at hand might have provided some measure of fortitude. Casting off that notion, he sucked in his breath, screwed his eyes shut, and fired.

When he opened his eyes, he saw that his shot must have gone astray, for the bushwhacker was still kneeling there. Clearly, though, the man knew he was under attack, as he looked desperately about, seeking the source of the shot. His face was still obscured. Alworth fired again, and, as before, the shot went wild. Now his location had been revealed, and the man shifted his rifle toward him and fired. The bullet whistled inches past Alworth's right cheek, and he flung himself to the ground. A moment later, another shot rang out, but of a different timbre. A pistol as opposed to a rifle.

Alworth looked over his boulder and saw the scene unfolding above him. The man was no longer kneeling but standing now, though unsteadily. At last fully visible, his hat had fallen from his head and his shirtfront was stained red. He still held his rifle. Not far away stood Gault, smoking revolver in hand. Gault fired again at the man. The bullet struck home, but not before the bushwhacker had gotten off his own shot.

Gault swore and clutched his right side. The other man did a jerky little spin, dropped the rifle, and collapsed facedown. He twitched once or twice, then ceased to move. Still holding his side, Gault stepped forward. Slipping a boot under the dead man, he flipped him over so that the glassy eyes aimed skyward. Gault holstered his pistol. Alworth holstered his own and scuttled up to stand beside Gault.

He stared down at the lifeless form. "He looks familiar. I think I saw him yesterday in the sheriff's office."

"Name's Oakes," Gault hissed. "Deputy goddam Oakes. I gave him a little thumping yesterday, and I guess he held a grudge." He let out a low moan and drew his hand from his side. It was bloody.

"Jesus, Mr. Gault," Alworth said. "You're wounded."

"Not much. I can make my way down just fine."

"Do you want me to gather up his weapons?"

"No, I don't want his damn guns. Let them rust out here with his corpse."

"We're not going to bury him?"

Gault let out a hoarse laugh. "Sure we are. Why don't you go pick some flowers and round up a preacher?"

Alworth was on the verge of replying but held his tongue.

Gault pointed off to the left. "I saw he has his sorrel tethered just over yonder. Go get it and lead it down. I'll meet you below."

Gault bent over, tore the tin star off Oakes' shirt, and pocketed it. He turned and moved away. Alworth took a moment to study Oakes' face, staring into the strange dead eyes as if searching for some answers there. Then, with a slight shudder, he headed off to find the horse.

When he returned with the sorrel, Alworth found Gault, his shirt unbuttoned, being tended to by Lampo. Saturn, fully shirtless, his left shoulder bandaged with torn cloth, sat close by Foggy, unsaddled now, who lay on his side groaning softly.

Saturn was stroking the dun's head and cooing, "You be easy now, boy. You just be easy."

"How's everyone doing," Alworth asked.

Billy tried to sound chipper as he helped Saturn pull his shirt on. "Good, real good. Mr. Gault's bullet went clear through. And ol' Saturn's wasn't deep at all."

"Deep enough," Lampo muttered.

"The Finn dug it out with his Bowie knife," Billy said. "He should study up to become a surgeon. Ain't that right, Lampo?"

The Finn grunted.

"The thing is," Billy continued, "an old relic like Saturn here is too simple to know how to get shot properly."

Without looking away from his horse, Saturn said. "I'll mend, but Foggy here . . . Poor ol' Foggy."

Gault buttoned his shirt over his bandaged ribs. "You know what we got to do, Saturn."

"Foggy's been with me a long time," said Saturn quietly. "A long damned time."

"You know what we got to do," Gault repeated, sliding out his Colt. "Now you go walk away a little, Saturn. I'll see to this. Billy, help him up."

Saturn shook his head. "No, no sir . . ."

"Now, listen, Saturn. You see how Foggy is. He's got to be —"

"I'm the one to do it," said Saturn firmly. "I won't let no one else. Not another soul in this whole damned world but me. Help me up, Billy."

Gault nodded and holstered his gun.

Leaning on Billy, Saturn got to his feet. "You all leave me and Foggy alone for a minute."

Billy, Gault, and the others walked a short distance away. They turned their backs but could make out Saturn speaking softly. Low, pained words. After a minute, they heard the gunshot. They waited a little, then rejoined Saturn. He stood stiffly, his Winchester cradled in his arms.

Alworth looked down at the dead horse, then whispered to Billy, "Will we bury him?"

"Too much work burying a horse," Billy answered. "Let the earth take him."

George Gault looked around at his men. "Here's the way of things. We're going to

93

keep on toward Black Powder. I've been winged, but nothing I can't tolerate. I'm fit to ride. Saturn, your wound is worrying. You're gonna take Oakes' horse and head back home."

Saturn didn't argue. "If you say so."

"I'll ride back with him," Billy said. "To make sure he gets there all right."

Gault shook his head. "No, I need you with me, Billy. Saturn can ride alone."

"But, Mr. Gault, even though the bullet's out, it's still a bad wound. You said so yourself. It'd be better if I was with him."

"I said he goes back alone. This ain't something we're gonna debate over."

"But Saturn's my pard. I don't like the idea of him —"

"That's it, boy!" Gault's eyes narrowed. "Don't go challenging me."

Billy Fowler drew himself up to his full six feet. "He's my pard," he said again, a new note of defiance in his tone.

"Billy!" Saturn called out. "Quit it now."

"Listen to him," Gault said, low and menacing. "Listen to your pard."

Saturn came close to Billy. "Don't be fretting about me, young blood. I don't hurt much, and it ain't so long a ride."

After a moment, Billy shifted his gaze from Gault to Saturn. "I guess you know your own mind, old man."

"Guess I do," said Saturn.

"Mount up, Billy. Lampo. Nevins." Gault issued the command, then took the sorrel's reins from Alworth and passed them to Saturn. "I know he ain't Foggy, but he should be good enough to get you back to the ranch." Gault waited till the others had moved away, then said quietly to Saturn, "I'm sorry you took that bullet. It's clear enough Oakes meant to put it in *my* hide, not yours."

"Things may not be too hospitable back in Willerton," Saturn said. "Once word gets out about Oakes. 'Specially if he came after you in an official type way."

"I doubt Rawley sent Oakes to come gunning for me. The big idiot probably did it of his own accord. Hey, Saturn, look here . . ." Gault pulled out the tin star. "Finally got my own badge." He smiled thinly. "Everything's proper now."

Saturn looked away. "I'd best be heading back now."

Gault pocketed the star, then took a minute to replace the sorrel's saddle with Saturn's own. When he was done, he handed Saturn a fresh cheroot. "Here's for the ride."

Gault turned and walked off toward his own horse.

Billy rode up and nodded down at his friend. "I'll see you back home."

Saturn nodded back. "Yes, home."

Billy rode off with the others. Saturn watched the four riders disappear into the distance, then placed the cigar between his lips, took one last look at Foggy, and hoisted himself onto the sorrel. Soon nothing was left in that place but the lifeless body of the blue dun and, up in the high rocks, that of the man Gault had killed.

CHAPTER TEN

Ida Sawbridge's burial was well attended. Elizabeth was pleased. All the neighbors came out that morning and a fair number of townsfolk, plus three or four of Cousin George's men who were still about. (She would have expected Saturn Hayes to pay his respects, but she figured Gault had taken him on his quest for retribution.) Representing the family, of course, were only the two of them, Elizabeth and Tom. She had written letters to her far-flung sisters, but who knew when they would receive them.

The reverend did a fine job and, at Elizabeth's request, read aloud the 139th Psalm. One line stood out for her: *If I ascend up into heaven, thou art there: if I make my bed in hell, behold, thou art there.* Standing over the open grave, she thought to herself that, yes, if indeed there was a heaven to be ascended to, the Lord would certainly greet her good-hearted mother with open arms.

As for making one's bed in hell, Elizabeth found herself thinking of Cousin George. Undoubtedly, he was the breed of man for whom that line was written. And wherever he might be at this very minute, was he, in fact, making his stay in hell more of a done deal? All in the name of Ida Sawbridge . . .

Elizabeth drove all thoughts of George Gault from her mind. She'd be damned if she would let him intrude on Mama's burial day. After the psalm reading and eulogy, two men began filling in the grave. Elizabeth closed her eyes, but she could hear each shovelful of earth as it struck the coffin lid, and the fierce permanence of death clutched at her heart. During the day's preparations, she had kept tears at bay, but now they overwhelmed her, and tremors shook her body. Some neighbor woman drew her close and whispered comforts to her. Elizabeth nodded and stammered her gratitude. She fought the urge to cover her ears to block out the hideous sound of dirt striking boards.

When it was all over, Elizabeth looked around for Tom. Her brother had accompanied her to the burial site but, once there, had stood far off to the side, betraying little emotion. Since the hour of Ida's death, Tom had become quiet and distant. Elizabeth had tried to draw him out, to gauge his feelings, but he had resisted such attempts. Mourning the loss of his mother had apparently taken a great toll on the boy. More than Elizabeth could have predicted.

Tom was usually a good-natured, if perhaps naive, fifteen-year-old lad. He'd often confide in his sister the small trials and tribulations of his young life. Now, when she tried to reach out to him, he cut her off abruptly, even harshly. She had a feeling that something besides sorrow was gnawing at him.

Tom was nowhere to be seen. Elizabeth hoped he had walked back to their cabin, which was less than a mile away. A gathering was to be held there shortly, food provided by the neighbors. She now declined several offers to be accompanied home, saying she'd like to spend a few moments alone with her mother. When everyone else had headed off, she stood at the foot of the grave and offered such prayers as she could muster.

In her grief, she found it hard to remember the exact words, so she tried making up her own prayer. That felt awkward, so she resorted to speaking directly to her mother, telling her of the numerous vittles that the neighbor ladies were expected to bring today. This seemed better than any religious entreaty, for wouldn't Mama have delighted in hearing of the savory dishes that would be gracing her table?

Elizabeth had just offered an account of Mrs. Clay's vinegar pie when she heard footfalls behind her. Turning, she found herself facing a short, gaunt man with a grim look on his face.

"Sheriff Rawley . . ." This was hardly someone she expected to be visiting her mother's graveside.

Rawley touched his hat brim. "Ma'am. Sorry to intrude. Just wanted a word with you. In my capacity as a lawman, you understand."

Elizabeth eyed him warily. In her few interactions with the man, she had never been impressed by his abilities nor convinced of his character. "You see that I've just buried my mother, don't you?"

"An unhappy occasion, to be sure. Everyone hereabouts knows what an upright person she was. Alas, the same can't be said of your cousin George Gault."

"Why come here bothering me about *him*?"

"That's the thing, ma'am. George Gault has intruded on my peace of my mind, which is why I have to intrude on yours.

Yesterday, he stopped in at my office and created real mayhem. He beat me, threatened my life, and bludgeoned my deputy. Now maybe that's all hard for you to believe . . ."

"It isn't," said Elizabeth flatly.

Rawley smiled coldly. "Then maybe you'll be inclined to do the right thing here. My deputy set out alone last evening to track down your cousin and bring him to justice. For what he did to authorized agents of the law, you understand. Actually, Deputy Oakes went against my better judgment, since I suggested he wait till Gault returned here when we could do the job safely."

"Get to the point. What is the 'right thing' you want me to do?"

"Only this. If the deputy isn't able to apprehend Gault, and you learn your cousin has returned to the area, send word to me immediately. Then I can round up the men needed to confront him without incident."

Elizabeth tried to imagine Cousin George allowing himself to be arrested without incident. She couldn't.

"All right, I'll send word," she said. "Now please leave me to my mourning."

Rawley touched his hat again, pivoted, and strode away.

Alone again, Elizabeth tried to return to

her one-sided dialogue with her mother but had lost focus. After a few more silent moments, she left the gravesite and started for home.

Less than a quarter mile from the cabin, she came upon Tom by the side of the road, sitting against the base of a cottonwood. She approached him, and he looked up at her, his eyes red from recent crying.

She dropped down beside him and placed a hand on his arm. "Oh Tom . . ." Her voice broke a little. "It's such a sad day for us. Such a terribly sad day."

This time her brother didn't move away, or even look away. He kept his reddened eyes firmly fixed on hers. His lips were quivering; words began to form on them, then sputtered off.

Elizabeth saw that he was trying to give voice to something. Something hard. "Yes, Tom?"

The boy gave a little moan, then pushed out the words: "I've got a thing to tell you, Lizbeth. A pretty bad thing."

CHAPTER ELEVEN

The morning after the encounter with Low Moon, Two Robes had climbed out of the wagon and been greeted by the sight of a large, wide-winged eagle circling high above. This had touched her heart, for it made her think of Eagle Singing, her closest friend from her early days at the Carlisle School. Eagle Singing had been an Apache girl whom the whites labeled Alice, but who never stopped referring to herself by her original name. Eagle Singing had been bold in a way that Two Robes always admired. Beyond the eyes of the whites, the Apache girl would sometimes enact the ceremonies of her people. Once, when Two Robes was suffering from a fierce headache, Eagle Singing stole some barrel hoops and performed her version of the hoop dance to heal her. Two Robes felt much better afterward.

But no one had been there to perform a

hoop dance for Eagle Singing herself when she was taken to the infirmary with severe dysentery. The white man's food, so different from the diet she was raised on, had never sat well with her. She died the next day, just sixteen years old. Two Robes had prayed for her spirit then, but not with the white man's words.

The great bird above her soared beautifully. To the Lakota people, the eagle was seen as a messenger who delivered their prayers up to the Creator. As she had done on the day of her friend's death, Two Robes offered prayerful words for Eagle Singing in the next world. And too, she offered a plea for safe passage for her own self and her companions. The appearance of the eagle, circling above them in wide, perfect loops, was surely a good sign, wasn't it? Then why did she have this feeling of apprehension? *O Winged Sister, rider of the sky, let no harm befall us.* The eagle circled a few times more, then angled off and disappeared in the distance.

It was late morning now, and they'd stopped in a narrow gulch to tighten a loose wheel on the show wagon. Major Pompay assisted Nash with the task, afterwards complaining at the effort needed to lift his large bulk from the earth. In regaining his footing, Pompay's Panama hat tumbled to the ground, where Nash accidently stepped on it, crushing the top.

"Damn it all, Nash! I was fond of that hat!"

"Then keep on being fond of it,"Nash said. "It'll still fit on your skull, won't it?"

Pompay set the hat on his head and groaned. "It's utterly smashed. The crown's caved in."

"Don't be such a big baby. It looks fine. Here, I'll spruce it up for you." Nash pulled the crow's feather from his own hat and shoved it into the band of the Panama. "There now! Don't you look the sport."

Pompay yanked out the feather and thrust it back at Nash. "I've no use for your mockery."

Nash laughed nastily and stuck the feather back in his hatband. "Suit yourself. It won't rub *me* none if you don't wish to take on a bit of style."

"Look who's talking style." Viola Hall came up beside the two men. "I'll tell you plain, Nash. I've seen more stylish fellas than you sprawled in horse shit after a night's carousing."

Nash turned on her. "Why are you always jabbing at me, woman? I'm not being paid to take your bad-mouthing."

"I figure you're being paid to take whatever we dish out at you."

"Then you figure wrong. Push me any more, and I'll quit being so sweet tempered."

Viola's laugh boomed like a cannon. "Sweet tempered? Funniest thing I've heard in a year! Got any more hilarities, Nash? You seem to be chock-full of 'em."

"All right, all right." Major Pompay raised a pacifying hand. "We've all vented some steam. Now let's resume our travels."

"Not till we get one thing straight," said Nash. "I'm done taking guff from this soiled dove here. Starting now, she keeps her big mouth shut around me or I'll leave you all in the dust. Let angry renegades and whoever else take the pickings."

Seeing that Viola had a reply ready to fly, Pompay stepped forward intending to intervene. He was too late. "Gee whillikens, Nash." Viola cocked her head. "Remind me. Wasn't it just yesterday you got us on the bad side of those Arapaho warriors? And the week before, didn't you insult them three *vaqueros*? Pure luck we haven't wound up as vulture food by now. I don't see how we could end up much worse if we parted company. Likely we'd prosper. Jesus, what a waste of flesh we're saddled with."

Nash's face darkened, and his eyes blazed. "Why you evil, whorish —"

Pompay flung his busted hat to the ground. "Damn it to Hades! Can't everybody just simmer down? We need to pull together here. Like the fingers of a hand. Like . . . Like —"

"Like stiffs in a graveyard." Viola turned and headed to the back of the wagon, calling over her shoulder, "Rouse me when we reach Black Powder."

Two Robes, who'd been watching it all unfold, closed her eyes and shook her head. Perhaps the morning eagle hadn't been a good omen after all. Perhaps it was a sign of discord and danger. In truth, wasn't the eagle at its heart a bird of prey? When she opened her eyes, she saw that Nash had climbed back on his horse and was lighting a cigarette. It was hard for her to guess his mood. He stared ahead, seeming to look at nothing at all.

The major retrieved his Panama hat and examined it ruefully. "Don't know when I'll again find such a worthy *chapeau* as this one. Good-bye, faithful friend." He hurled the hat away, ran a hand over his bald scalp, then looked up at Nash. "Don't pay Miss Viola much mind. She has a fiery disposition, as do many artistes."

"As do many goddamn strumpets," said Nash.

"You may be right there, sir. But do know I value your knowledge and protection on our trek here."

Nash grunted and spurred his horse forward.

Pompay now turned to Two Robes. "It takes great skill to keep such a disparate group as ours intact. I'm pleased to say that you, at least, give me no cause for heartache. Much appreciated, my comely Sioux maiden."

He pulled himself up onto the wagon seat and took the reins. Two Robes climbed into the enclosed back.

As they resumed their bumpy travel, Viola, seated on the floor, greeted the Lakota girl with a wan smile. "Maybe I do run my mouth off a touch. It's my curse and my gift. But I'll tell you true, I've got no use for that damned Nash."

"Why do you hate him so?" Two Robes asked.

"Is it that obvious?" Viola giggled. "Maybe 'cause he reminds me of a husband I once had. Long, lanky piece of dung, always boasting and courting trouble. Matter of fact, Nash reminds me of *two* husbands I had, the first the same as the second. Can I give you a little advice, hon?"

Two Robes knew she'd be receiving that advice, whether requested or not. "I suppose so."

"When you choose yourself a man — and a fine-looking filly like you should have your pick of 'em — don't settle for the first one who flings some pretty words at you. There's plenty of yahoos out there who know how to bait their hook with sweet prattlings."

"You think Nash is someone who flings pretty words?"

"Hell no! But I'm talking about menfolk as a group. What I'm getting at is, don't waste your life hoarding fool's gold. Lord knows I've done that a heap in my time." Something like sadness showed in Viola's eyes. "Yeah, Lord knows . . ." She went quiet and seemed in no hurry to speak again.

Two Robes was not used to a silent, sorrowful Viola. She attempted to draw her back. "You must have met some good men at one time or other."

The merry Viola returned. "Ha! Why, sure I have. A few here and there. Trouble is, they usually blow through like tumbleweeds. Can't get hold of them nohow. There's one fella in particular . . ." Again, she went quiet, but this time the look in her eyes was one of fondness. After a moment, she fluffed her blond curls and grinned. "Who knows? I've still got my looks and my spunk. I may yet land some half-decent drover or a shopkeeper. Hell, maybe I'll even get me a dentist like that Doc Holliday way over in Tombstone. A man who can shoot *and* pull teeth . . . now there's a catch!"

It was late in the afternoon when they accepted the fact that Nash was not returning. While on the trail, he'd never before left the wagon for more than a half hour, and then only to scout ahead a bit. He'd been gone now for nearly three hours. They had stopped to talk it over and were standing together in the curve of a swooping steppe, amid sagebrush and shadow.

"No doubt your jibes drove him away, Viola," Pompay said. "A man can only bear so much taunting."

Viola looked defensive. "I had to bear my share of taunts from *him,* didn't I?"

"I'd say that, more often than not, you threw the first stone. Or, at the very least, threw it with more gusto."

Viola shrugged. "You could be right there. But maybe it wasn't me at all, did you think of that? Maybe it was your own cawing and complaining about that fool hat of yours.

Sure, that could've put him over the edge."

"I had every right to lament the loss of my hat! It gave me dignity and panache."

"I've no idea what 'panache' is, Major, but you and dignity ain't exactly two things I think of lined up together."

"See? See? That's the very type of insult I was referring to!"

"It's the type I shine at, so don't expect me to hide it under a bushel. That's in the gospels. You can look it up."

"I assure you I know my Good Book."

"Then you're acquainted with the commandments, including the one about not bearing false witness. Ain't that what you've been doing by accusing me of running Nash off?"

"And you accused my hat of running him off! You ridiculous female!"

"Don't get snappy with me, Pompay! I can take you in a fight, fair or foul!"

"No more!" Two Robes, who'd kept her peace up until now, had had enough. "Nash is gone! Does it matter why he left? He's just gone."

Pompay exhaled. "Yes, quite right. We must live with the fact that the man has abandoned us."

"Or maybe that Low Moon character got him," Viola offered. "Could be he was waiting up ahead and settled yesterday's squabble with a blade or bullet."

Pompay gave a little shudder. "I hope that's not the case. If it is, the Arapaho could still be waiting beyond to extend his bloody wrath to us three."

"We're in agreement there," said Viola. "I'm all for avoiding bloody wrath." She laughed. "Never had much stomach for it. All right, I'm gonna fetch the shotgun in the back, and I'll come ride alongside you, Major. It'll help settle your fragile nerves."

With a huff, Pompay again took his place at the reins. Viola went to get the gun.

Two Robes cast her gaze around the great expanse of muted-green sagebrush. A man could lie low in it, crouching, watching, and not be detected. Or a body could be stretched out here undiscovered for a long time, perhaps forever, the flesh steadily forsaking the bones. Her gaze was drawn upward. A great bird in flight. For a moment, she thought it was her eagle, returned to comfort her.

But no. This was a vulture — never a harbinger of comfort.

CHAPTER TWELVE

"Look at our leader there," Billy said in a low voice. "Yesterday he told us he didn't want no man swaying in the saddle. Today, that's just what he's doing."

Alworth, riding beside Billy, followed the other's gaze. Up ahead, George Gault was clearly making an effort to stay firmly astride his horse. Not infrequently, he would slide to one side or the other, then abruptly right himself. Since parting ways with Saturn, he had already stopped three times to rest.

"Seems like his wound's catching up with him," said Alworth.

"It surely does," Billy agreed. "Guess Mr. Gault's just made of skin, bones, and blood like the rest of us. He should own up to that."

They watched as their boss teetered to the left. Lampo the Finn, riding next to him, reached out a steadying hand, but Gault waved him off.

Billy shook his head. "The man's stubborn as a rock."

"I can't argue that."

"Say, Alworth, what are you doing here anyway?"

"You mean out West?"

"That's a mighty huge question right there. But, no, I mean on this here expedition of ours. Not to give offense, but you don't seem like someone Gault would be eager to include on a rough run like this."

"If you must know, I asked to come along."

"Now why the hell would you do that? Looking for something perky to write in that journal of yours?"

For a moment, Alworth thought of sharing the truth with Billy, who was as close to being a friend to him as any man within two thousand miles. But that truth, half formed in his own mind, would no doubt seem ludicrous to Billy. *I've come along so that I can act as protector to a Shakespeare-quoting Indian girl I saw only once and have never spoken to.* That wouldn't sound insane at all, would it?

Instead, he said, "Sure, that's it, Billy. Just looking to spice up my journal entries."

Eventually, they came to a tight cluster of small, weathered buildings, little more than shacks. There was one horse tethered outside, which they tied theirs next to. They all entered the largest building, one with a crudely painted sign above the door that read SUTLER. Inside, they found what passed for a shop: a warped deal counter and two or three tables covered with a chaos of tins, jars, and wrapped packages. Atop a pile of barely folded garments sat a scrawny, unkempt cat missing an ear. The presumed sutler, seated on a barrel and drinking from a clay jug, looked to be a human version of the cat, though possessing both ears.

"Customers." The old man spat out the word as if identifying violators rather than valued patrons.

Gault, unsteady on his feet, leaned on one of the tables. "We're looking for some show people." His voice struggled to stay above a whisper.

"Shows?" The sutler stood, set the jug aside, and dragged a stained shirtsleeve over his lips. "No shows out here, that's for damned sure."

Gault expanded on his request.

The old man listened, a look of disdain fixed on his face.

"No! No! No!" The sutler waved his hands wildly, as if swatting flies. "No show people, no fancy people, hardly no living people at all here. I tell ya, I made good money back in Arkansas during the War of Northern Aggression. I followed Bobby Lee's army selling 'em whiskey, tobacky, and whatnot. Yessir, that was a living. But now, it's all run to shit. They were s'posed to aim the railroad out this way, so I set up here. Never happened! Now nary a soul wanders by. And no damned show people!"

"But someone's here," said Gault. "His horse is outside. 'Less it's yours."

The sutler scrunched up his face. "Ain't mine. All I got's a mule out back, a swayback ol' piece of crap that I ought to make hash out of. No, that horse belongs to a fella who rode in earlier. He's over in my saloon now drinking whiskey. You all can buy some, too, 'less you want to purchase some genuine Paris ladies' undergarments first. For your wives and sweethearts."

"We'll talk to that man," Gault said. "See if he knows anything. Bring us to him." Seeming to draw on some hidden reserve of strength, he stood erect and took the sutler by the arm.

"Don't be manhandling me!" the old man bleated.

They all crossed over to another of the buildings, the "saloon," which was half the size of the store. Entering, they found one occupant — a lanky, hawk-faced man seated at one of the two tables, a glass in his hand and a bottle before him. His hat lay on the table next to the bottle, a long crow's feather protruding from the band. The man looked up at them, his eyes narrowing in anticipation of trouble.

Gault studied him for a long moment before speaking. "I recognize you. Damned if I don't."

Though weakened by his wound, Gault displayed a quick hand. Before the seated man could react, Gault had the Colt aimed at him.

The man extended his palms. "Whoa, look now, mister . . ."

"I recognize you," Gault said again. "I saw you back in Willerton three nights ago. You travel with Major Pompay and his band."

"*Used* to. I used to travel with them, but we parted ways earlier today. I swear to God. My name's Nash, mister. We've got no quarrel, you and me. I've got no love for Pompay and his flock. That's why I'm not with 'em now." Cautiously, he lowered his

117

hands. "I'm guessing you've got no love for him either."

Gault kept his pistol leveled. "What's your grievance with them?"

"Pompay's a fool, and the woman what travels with him, an ex-harlot goes by Viola, has a sharper tongue on her than Beelzebub himself. I've had my fill of the lot of 'em."

"There's an Indian girl, too, right?"

"Yeah, but she don't give much trouble."

"Indians are always trouble."

"Mind lowering your iron, mister? It's hard to have a pleasant discourse when staring down a barrel like this."

"Keep your hands on the table, and maybe I will."

"They're right here for all to see. Like I say, we've got no quarrel."

"Pompay's bound for Black Powder, up toward Chug Water, yeah?"

"Last I knew."

After a moment, Gault slid the Colt back in its holster. "All right, Nash, I've got a proposition for you."

Nash let out a sigh of relief. "Always open to hearing what another fella's got to offer."

"I aim to track down those show people," Gault explained. "As of this morning, I'm down a man. Seeing as you're acquainted with Pompay and know his ways, I figure

118

you could be useful to me. It'll put some greenbacks in your pocket."

"If you don't mind me inquiring, what's *your* grievance with the major?"

"He killed someone I cared about. That's more than you need to know."

"Fair enough. I wouldn't have thought Pompay able to pull off a killing, but if you say he did, I believe you. You pay well?"

"Damned well."

Nash lifted his glass. "Should we have a drink to seal the bargain?"

"No. We ride now."

"As you like." Nash downed the whiskey and grimaced. "What is this swill anyway, old man? Rat poison?"

The sutler snarled. "It's my secret blend, damn you! It was a favorite of Stonewall Jackson. Now, anybody else want to buy something before you go?"

When no one else replied, the Finn asked gruffly, "Got any peppermint sticks?"

Gault's reserve of strength only lasted the length of another three miles' ride. That's when he listed to the side and fell to earth. The others dismounted and gathered around, Lampo kneeling beside him.

"How is he?" Alworth asked.

The Finn examined Gault, who lay still,

softly moaning. "He needs a rest."

Nash stared down at the sprawled man. "I'm starting to have my doubts here. How's he gonna lead us on if he can't keep in the saddle. What happened to him anyway?"

"Man shot him," Billy said.

Nash smiled grimly. "Yeah, that'll halt up a fella, for sure. Will he die?"

"Hope not," said Lampo.

"Hmm . . ." Nash scratched his bristled cheek. "Seeing as I just got employed by him, I'd prefer he not expire before my pay's due."

Lampo glared up at him. "If he lives, you'll get paid."

Nash pursed his lips and turned away.

It was already past midday, and Black Powder was still a fair ride away. They'd found themselves in the shade of a pine grove, which seemed as good a place as any to pause and give Gault a chance to rest. Lampo instructed the others to water the horses at the creek that they heard just below them. He remained with Gault.

At the water's edge, Nash muttered to himself (though well within hearing of the others), "I should take a better measure of the company I choose."

After Nash had watered his horse, he

headed immediately back for the grove. Alworth and Billy, seeing to their own horses and those of the other two, lingered at the creek.

"I don't know that I feel too fondly toward Nash there," Alworth said.

"Can't say I do myself." Billy dipped his hat in the running water and drank from it. "He's sure no fit replacement for Saturn."

"And with Gault down, it looks as if Lampo is taking charge."

"Well, he's the senior man among us."

"I know, but he makes me uneasy. He's strangely quiet. Too much so for my taste."

"The Finn don't say much, but if that big ol' knife of his could talk, I bet it'd have some frightful tales to tell. Scarier than Mr. Poe's. Sure, Lampo's a rough man. But then, so is Gault, least when he's not been shot through."

"All rough men," Alworth said quietly. "I wish Saturn was still with us. Somehow he seemed to balance things out."

"Now, don't ever breathe a word of this to Saturn," said Billy, "but I'd say the reason I've stayed working for George Gault as long as I have is because of him. If that old fool wasn't around to set me right now and again, I'd probably have vamoosed long ago. Hell, I sure hope he makes it home all right." He drew two of the horses from the water. "Okay, I've got mine and Lampo's. You bring Gault's up with you when you're done."

Billy led his two horses away from the creek.

Alworth remained there a while longer, his eyes lost in the swiftly moving current. A fragment of verse came to him from his year at the university. It was Longfellow, he believed, lines composed as the poet stood on a bridge observing the rushing waters below him.

For my heart was hot and restless,
And my life was full of care,
And the burden laid upon me
Seemed greater than I could bear.

Indeed, Alworth's heart beat hot and restless in his chest, and the burden before him, when he pondered it, felt unbearable. True, if Gault was unable to continue his hunt, then the burden would be lifted. But if he recovered enough to ride — and Gault was a tough, indomitable man — then Alworth had decisions to make. And actions to commit himself to.

CHAPTER THIRTEEN

Saturn was passing through a stretch of woods, trying to concentrate on the ride itself — and not on the memory of the bullet that had torn into his shoulder. Nor the one he had put into Foggy. The sorrel was doing just fine and seemed a reliable-enough creature, but he was no Foggy. What horse could ever be? Despite a persistent pain where the bullet had entered, Saturn was feeling stronger than he'd have expected to feel. Lampo had done good work with that blade of his. Saturn should have no trouble making it back to the ranch before nightfall.

Getting shot might well have been a blessing, seeing as it spared him from whatever was in store for the others. He'd have wanted to remain with them all just to watch over Billy, but the boy would have to look after himself now. Which was fitting, of course. A young fella needs to learn. So

Saturn would return to the ranch as Gault and fate would have it. Funny how you never knew what trail would lead you where.

Saturn found himself thinking now on a thing that happened back in Alabama when he wasn't much more than a child. One night three slave men from his plantation, three brothers, made the getaway together, creating a real commotion the next day. Though they all started out side by side, the destinies of the three went in wildly different directions: one was recaptured, another made it to freedom, and the third drowned in a swamp.

Young as he'd been, Saturn had learned something important then: the world will do with you what it wants, no matter your intentions. Of course, being born a slave had pretty much drummed that in already, but something about the tale of the brothers made the lesson especially memorable. Like some dark and weighty parable from the Holy Book.

He'd just emerged from the tree line when Saturn spied two riders approaching from some distance away. As the gap between them closed, he saw that it was a man and woman. No, not a man — an almost-man, not much more than a boy. Then they were near enough so that he knew exactly who it was.

"Lord almighty. Elizabeth . . ." He spurred the sorrel forward.

They converged and pulled up their horses.

"My God! Saturn! We actually found you." Elizabeth had traded her dress for trousers, shirt, and a wide-brimmed hat. "Where's my cousin?"

"He's a ways back," Saturn said. "Pushing on toward Black Powder. But what in heaven's name are you two doing out here on your own? No telling what might befall you. Weren't you burying your ma today?"

"We saw to that this morning," Elizabeth said. "We didn't wait for the gathering afterward, just took to the trail."

"What's so important that you lit out like this?" Saturn asked.

"We need to talk to Cousin George." Elizabeth nodded toward her brother. "Tom does."

Tom Sawbridge looked away and fiddled with his reins.

Elizabeth held her brother in her gaze. "Right, Tom?"

CHAPTER FOURTEEN

It was late in the day when John McNulty and his crew pulled into Lowfield, a modest-sized town with only one bank but three cathouses. The bank was not their objective. As McNulty had already made clear, they'd hold back on any robberies, letting things cool down for a spell. Though Baker and T.C. were eager to make another haul, they were content with the present substitution of garters for greenbacks. When they'd woken that morning, McNulty had announced his intention of journeying there. It struck the others as odd that, after insisting they lie low, he wanted to mix with civilization. But the prospect of brothels and saloons kept them from debating the issue.

"All right, McNulty, aim us at the wagtails," Baker said as they walked down the main thoroughfare. "Wait, never mind. Judging by the sign over that doorway there, I figure that's where we're bound."

The sign read Gentlemen Welcome.

T.C. laughed. "It's almost like they knew we were coming and put that up just for us. I feel downright honored. Come, gentlemen, let's go announce ourselves in a lordly manner."

McNulty caught T.C.'s arm. "You don't want that place, believe me. I've been there, and it's well worth avoiding. No, the establishment you want is that one down on the right, just past the billiard hall. The rates and the ladies are superior. Go enjoy yourselves. I'll be by shortly."

"We bow to the wisdom of age," T.C. said. "Come on, Baker."

McNulty watched the two men head down the street. Once they were out of sight, he turned and entered the building he'd just deterred them from. He stepped into the parlor, a gaudy display of crimson splashed with gold, where several girls and patrons were milling about. Even if McNulty were recognized, he wasn't likely to find trouble here. One sinner more or less in this place wouldn't much matter.

It had been close to three years since he'd last been here, and the madam was a woman he didn't know. He approached her. "Good day. I'm wondering if a lady named Viola is still employed here."

"Sure is," said the madam. "But these days she generally goes by Deucey."

"Deucey?"

"Yeah. Just head up the stairs, third door on your left. You can settle up with her."

McNulty climbed the stairs and found the room. He knocked, and a voice within told him to enter. He put his hand on the doorknob but surprised himself at his hesitation. He felt nervous in a way he had not for a long time.

"Like a schoolboy . . ." he muttered to himself.

He drew in a breath and entered.

On the edge of the bed sat a dark-haired young woman dressed in undergarments. She stood and smiled. It was not a warm smile, nor a particularly welcoming one. It was, perhaps, a smile of calm obligation, with a suggestion of reluctance. The circumstances that led women to these places were not always pleasant ones.

"Beg your pardon," McNulty said. "I must have the wrong room."

The smile went away. "I don't suit you?"

"It's not that. I was seeking a particular lady. One by the name of Viola."

"I *am* Viola. Though I mostly go by Deucey."

"It's Miss Viola Hall I'm looking for. She's

older than you, by a bit I'd say. And blond."

"Oh, I know that Viola!" The smile returned, now with some warmth. "When I first came here two summers back, she was real nice to me. I was sorry to see her go."

"When did she leave?"

"Just over a year ago, I'd guess. She went off with a traveling show, of all things. I was hoping maybe she'd stop by again sometime, but, once a girl takes off from here, she usually don't come back. Anyway, Viola could sing real pretty, and she joined up with that show to become a songstress."

McNulty nodded. "Yes, as I recall, she had a pleasing voice."

"She'd make up her own songs. Nice ones, too. Want to hear something real funny? Like strange funny? A young Mexican drover stopped in for a quick one this afternoon. Pretty chatty fella. He mentioned running into some theater people on their way to do a show up north somewhere. I wonder if that could be Viola's people."

"When did he see them?"

"Just this afternoon."

"And heading north you say? Did he mention any town in particular?"

"He didn't."

"Is that man still about."

"Nah. He wasn't dallying none. Did his

business with me and rode right out. Sorry Viola isn't here to see to your needs, mister. But if you fancy a throw, I'd be obliging. I can give you a kind price."

"Thank you, but no. That wasn't my purpose in seeking her out."

"No?"

"No, not that at all. You see, I had a dream last night . . ."

Later, upon reflection, McNulty would wonder what led him to tell the girl everything: the country lane, the blue fog, the loud humming, and Viola's face appearing in the midst of it all. Viola's face, the face of his beloved. And how that unexpected revelation had burrowed into his soul and motivated him to ride the length of the day to find her.

Deucey listened wide eyed, then said, "That's the loveliest thing I ever heard. And the amazingest! First you dream about Viola, then you show up here asking about her, and I tell you a fella may have just seen her. Don't that all strike you as mysterious?"

"Yes, mysterious." McNulty placed some coins in the girl's hand. "Thank you, miss."

"But I didn't do anything for you."

"You've aimed me. That's worth much." McNulty tipped his hat and left.

■ ■ ■ ■

T.C. was homing in on a pretty flush, ace high. One more heart would do the trick. He'd surprised Baker (and, in truth, himself) by deciding to skip the cathouse and seek out a poker game. He'd felt the tingling in his scalp that always let him know that luck was with him. He'd experienced that tingling several times in the past and, on each occasion, had won big at cards. His mother once told him he'd been born with a caul — a mask of flesh, easily removed but startling to behold — and that those born with it were naturally lucky. Whenever he felt the tingling, T.C. figured it was the ghost of his caul informing him that he should hasten to a poker table. So, this evening, he'd left the strumpets to Baker and devoted himself to flushes and full houses.

He'd found a draw game in progress and had been winning steadily but modestly. The pot was large for this hand, and a flush could kick things up to a new level for him. He called for one card and peeked at it. Queen of hearts! He bet large, knocking out three of the other players. One remained, a particularly foul-tempered blacksmith.

When the cards were revealed, T.C.'s flush vanquished the smithy's straight.

T.C. raked in his winnings. "That's what I like! I'd been planning on some other female company tonight, but I'll take that flirty little queen for sure. She was the last card dealt me, a nail in your straight's coffin, friend."

"Ain't your friend." The smithy shoved his cards toward the next dealer. "Don't be so goddamn chipper when you're taking a man's money."

"I guess I'm just inclined to sunniness," said T.C. "Can't blame a fellow for that."

"I can blame you with my hammering hand. Right in your jaw I can."

"Easy now," one of the other players said. "No cause for getting riled."

"I don't like when a man's too chipper in winning. It ain't seemly." The smithy tossed down his glass of whiskey. "Deal the cards."

The blacksmith's mood was sweetened slightly when he won the next hand. That mood was short lived. T.C. won the hand after that, celebrating the display of his full house with a loud bellow.

"None of that!" the smithy barked.

T.C. shrugged. "Just feeling my pleasure, friend."

"I already said, we ain't friends. I'd never

have a pissant like you for a friend."

"Now you're just being hurtful. A better man wouldn't begrudge me enjoying my good fortune."

"You think you talk so smart, don't you?"

"I like to think I can turn a phrase."

"So goddamned smart." Having refilled his glass, the blacksmith again emptied it. "So chipper and smart. Who's dealing?"

"I believe you are," T.C. said.

The smithy cursed and dealt.

"Don't mean to disparage your dealing skills," said T.C., "but you gave the fella to your left an extra card."

"Did not," the smithy grunted.

"He's correct," the other player said. "I've got six cards."

"Misdeal." T.C. smiled. "It happens to the best of us."

The blacksmith flung the remainder of the deck on the table. "I'm done with your sass. Your sass and your shit."

T.C.'s smile remained fixed. "My sass *and* my shit?"

"Don't rile him, stranger," one of the others cautioned. "He's got a temper."

"I see that."

"You'll see it all right." The smithy jumped to his feet, his chair crashing to the floor. He was a big man. "How 'bout we see to it

133

right now?"

T.C. let the smile slip. "I'm going to pass on that. Obviously, in a fistfight you'd destroy me. No question about it. And I sure don't want to resort to guns. I've always found pistols and poker to be a bad mix. So, please, sir, be seated and deal a new hand."

The blacksmith stared down at him, clearly unsure how to proceed. Finally, he scooped up what was left of his money and stomped out of the saloon.

T.C. laughed. "I sure hope I didn't offend him. Seemed like a lovely fella."

As dusk settled in, McNulty sat on a bench outside the Lowfield Mercantile watching two small girls play a game of graces. Each brandished her pair of dowels cleverly as they flung the wooden hoop through the twilight air. It was a serene thing to watch. The girls danced nimbly about, intent on their play, seemingly ignoring the coming darkness. If they noticed him observing their game, they gave no indication. They could have been frolicking alone in a flower-filled meadow at the world's edge, and not here in the dirt street avoiding the dung and spittle at their feet.

McNulty watched the game and pondered

his next move. *North.* North was a big place. Were the performers heading due north toward Bordeaux? Or northwest toward Albany County? Or northeast toward Black Powder or even, beyond that, into Nebraska? There were many possibilities. And, of course, there was the very real possibility that these traveling performers were not the ones Viola was aligned with. What made him even consider they might be? He smiled to himself. *His dream.*

Yes, truth be told, he was being dragged forward by a dream, a mad vision whose meaning he could only guess at. Viola had been central to that dream. Of course, on one level she was only a sporting woman whose company he'd paid for several times in the past. But there had always been something more, hadn't there? They had talked together and laughed together, and, once, she had cried into his shoulder at the memory of a baby she had born who died in the birthing bed. In their time together, fleeting as it might have been, there had always been something beyond the exchange of coin.

So he would let himself be dragged along by a nocturnal fantasy. After all, as he'd told Quinny last night, he hailed from a land steeped in dreams and fairy lore. Tomorrow morning they would head north. But, again, which north? He closed his eyes for a moment. Let the mad dream be his guide. It came to him: northeast. He would try his hand at Black Powder and see what happened. He rose, took a last glance at the playing children, and went to find his men. He came upon Baker as he was leaving his brothel.

"Where's T.C.?" McNulty asked. "We're heading out."

Baker scowled. "Whatta ya mean? We just got here. I haven't even had myself a drink."

"We're leaving. We'll join Quinny outside town and camp there for the night. We ride out first thing in the morning. Now, where's T.C.?"

Baker led the way to the saloon, where they found their companion watching his two pair lose to three of a kind.

"Settle up," McNulty said. "We're riding out."

T.C. looked up at him. "But my luck just took a bit of a dip these last few hands. I know I'm due for a favorable streak."

"Not tonight. Come on."

They left the saloon and headed back to where their horses were waiting. Night was nearly upon them. Riding out of Lowfield, they passed the spot where the girls had been playing. They were both gone, and McNulty saw that they'd left behind their grace hoop. It had somehow broken in half and now lay abandoned in the dust, barely visible in the descending darkness.

CHAPTER FIFTEEN

The town of Black Powder owed its existence to war and death. Its founder, having sold gunpowder to both the Union and the Confederacy, had made a tidy fortune from that two-faced commerce. After Appomattox, he invested a good sum in building the town, only to succumb to a burst lung a year into the project. Still, the place thrived after a fashion and was a preferred stop for travelers and drovers seeking repose, supplies, or an evening's distraction.

Major Pompay and his companions pulled into town late in the day and made hasty arrangements with one of the saloons to perform there. Despite being abandoned by Nash, their ride in had been fairly uneventful. They'd encountered a small band of Cheyenne who seemed uninterested in them and some vaqueros with whom they briefly conversed. Pompay even talked one of the young Mexicans into buying a bottle of elixir.

Now, with little time to spare, they made hurried preparations. As usual, Viola took to the streets, handing out playbills and bellowing the time and location of tonight's show. Pompay, with Two Robes' help, unloaded the props and set up the backdrop — a painted screen made to tolerably resemble theater curtains. The saloon had no stage per se, just a slightly elevated platform that would have to suffice. Abhorring the idea of performing bareheaded, the bald major made a quick visit to a nearby shop and was delighted to find a new Panama hat to replace the one Nash had trampled. Two Robes and Viola switched into their costumes: for the Lakota girl the buckskin dress, for Viola a red gown, vaguely Elizabethan and noticeably faded.

Soon the saloon filled with patrons, some male, some female, some sober, many not. Viola conducted the initial passing of the hat (there would be another at the end), and the show began.

As was customary, Pompay started things off by blowing some violent notes on his bugle and declaring, "Greetings! I and my company are pleased — nay, honored. Profoundly honored — to meet the illustrious citizens of . . ." Here he paused, forgetting for a moment which town they were in that night. "Black Powder! We shall henceforth endeavor to provide you with the most cultivated and enlightening entertainments the noble stage can offer. You will be forgiven if, in the course of our program, you mistakenly imagine yourself in the galleries of Stratford-upon-Avon or the fabled Globe Theatre."

"Or in the shit end of a pigsty!" some wag offered.

The resulting laughter was raucous and punctuated with vulgarities.

Pompay grinned widely, as if savoring the joke. "Ah! I see that the wit of the Black Powder citizenry has not been exaggerated. I'm even more convinced that your appreciation of our efforts tonight will be great indeed. Let us commence! Afterward, you'll all be the recipients of a unique chance to purchase the most life-enhancing elixir known to man. But now, prepare to welcome that world-renowned, golden-voiced *chanteuse,* Miss Viola Hall!"

To a weak smattering of applause, Viola came forth and commenced a warbly rendition of "Silver Threads Among the Gold," which earned a leaden response. The follow-up of "In the Gloaming" was equally ill-met. Only when Viola launched into "You

Naughty, Naughty Men," replete with winks and wiggles, did the audience show their recognition of high culture.

Next on the bill was Two Robes, whose recitation of Shakespearean speeches and sonnets seemed to leave the observers more perplexed than entertained. Thankfully, she received no lascivious suggestions or racial taunts, reactions not unheard of during their shows. The evening continued with more songs from Viola, some acted-out scenes from antiquity, and Pompay's bombastic patter between acts.

After the last of the entertainments, it was time to hawk the elixir. Since Two Robes had joined the troupe weeks before, she'd been assigned the task of displaying the bottles, one in each hand, while Pompay did the talking and Viola handled the money collecting.

Pompay always saved his peak verbosity for the pitch. "Dearest friends," he began, "your reception this eve has been exceedingly heart warming. It would be no embroidery of the truth to state that I feel like I'm among brethren here. And as I would with my very own brothers and sisters, I'd do everything within my power to ensure your health and well-being. Which brings me to the bottles now displayed by our lovely Lakota lass here. 'Fabled Fortifying Elixir' is what the label reads, and, by God, that's what you'll find in each and every bottle. Are you troubled by palpitations? Distemper? Headaches? Joint pains? This potion will alleviate all those troubles. And, if I may be so indelicate, women's difficulties are also addressed. Yes, even the curse of Eve will be mitigated by this elixir. Am I right, Sister Viola?"

"Damned right!" Viola called out.

Pompay continued. "This concoction is composed of too many healthful ingredients to list, including some developed by Two Robes' own mystical race. Suffice it to say that no reasonable person would miss the chance to obtain a bottle — or several — of this amazingly beneficial panacea."

Apparently, there were a large number of unreasonable people in the audience, for only three bottles of elixir were sold. The night's yield was hardly inspiring: the hatful of coins plus the profits from the fabled fortifier.

They made camp in a field behind the churchyard, an arrangement Viola found unnerving.

"I don't like sharing a patch of ground with the dead," she complained. "Soon enough, we'll get our own chance to burrow under the dirt. Don't need to rush it."

"We've over here, and they're over *there,*" Pompay said. "It's not like we're stretching out between the tombstones."

Viola shuddered. "I don't even like being in eyeshot of graves when I'm trying to sleep. It makes me wonder if I'll wake in the morning or slip right into my eternal repose. How 'bout you, gal? What's your opinion on slumbering with corpses?"

"It doesn't bother me," said Two Robes. "As the major says, we're over here, and they're over there."

Though she echoed Pompay's words, her meaning was not so much one of physical proximity but of a spiritual one. The dead were with the dead — be it in the heaven of the whites or on the sky-road of the Lakota — and the living were here in the world, breathing, struggling, smiling, weeping. The dead were beyond those things. Her mother, her father, Eagle Singing, the other lost Carlisle children, the fallen of the war, Lincoln, Crazy Horse, William Shakespeare . . . all, all gone beyond the things of the world.

No, she did not fear the dead. If anything, she envied the clarity of their position. The dead no longer needed to wonder where

143

they fit in the scheme of things. Not one occupant of that churchyard over there was troubled now by who they were or should have been or could never be. All those lives beneath the soil were completed, finalized, forever inscribed on the scroll of history.

Viola and Pompay were still bickering.

"If I cozy up alongside those carcasses," Viola was saying, "I doubt I'll sleep a drop! Not a blasted drop!"

Two Robes walked a distance away from the others and stared up into the star-filled night. The sky-road — called the Milky Way in the white man's astronomy — was up there somewhere, though not visible in the spring. The soul of every person, the *nag-iwho,* was destined to travel there at its allotted time.

Two Robes sighed. It was beautiful, the eternal blackness above. Terrifying in a way, but beautiful.

CHAPTER SIXTEEN: JOURNAL OF ALWORTH B. NEVINS

The stars are particularly compelling to-night. Like a million vivid eyes gazing down upon the affairs of men. Or, perhaps, like a multitude of white flames. Or a vast fortune of bright silver coins.

Or maybe they're bullet holes streaming light through a black wall. Yes, that would be more in keeping with the nature of this day. Earlier, I shot at a man for the first time. Though I missed him, my intent was, I suppose, to kill him. That's what my life has come to. I'm a world away from the halls of Yale and the lectures on transcendentalism and Socrates. Now I ride with tough, lethal men like Lampo, Nash, and my employer, Mr. George Gault. I'm with them, though not *of* them.

As I'd feared, Mr. Gault's grit and sheer force of will have asserted themselves. Resting these last several hours seems to have given him back his strength. While not fully recovered, he's been able to stand on his own and move about our campsite. He informed us that, come morning, he'll be ready to lead us on to Black Powder, where Two Robes and her companions are expected to be.

Tonight, the reality of that approaching encounter has fully hit me. And, too, my complete lack of a plan. In petitioning to join this pursuit, what did I think would happen when we finally came face to face with Major Pompay's group? Did I imagine I'd wedge myself between them and Gault and, using persuasive discourse, talk him out of wreaking vengeance upon those people? Did I expect Lampo, Nash, and Gault himself to nod thoughtfully at my skillful words and agree to let bygones be bygones? Was I that much of a fool?

When the others had all gone to sleep, I sat with young Billy Fowler around the fading campfire.

After sitting quietly for a bit, I spoke to him in a low voice. "You said before that you've thought of leaving the ranch, of leaving Mr. Gault, and might have if it wasn't for Saturn. What about now?"

"You mean cut out in the middle of our expedition?"

"You seemed ready to this morning when

you wanted to head back with Saturn."

"But I didn't, did I?" Billy looked me in the eyes. "I signed on to work for Gault. Even if he ain't my favorite of God's creatures. I always figured if you signed on for a thing, you're obliged to see it through."

"Even if that thing's immoral?"

"You're saying what we're doing here ain't moral? That man Pompay, he's responsible for killing poor Ida Sawbridge, right? Sold her the poison. Mrs. Sawbridge was a pleasant lady, and it's a damn pity she's gone."

"Do we know for certain her death was Pompay's doing?"

"Saturn was there in her house, heard Gault and Miss Elizabeth talk it all over. So, yes, it seems to be."

"But the folks with Pompay . . . Maybe they really had nothing to do with her death. Maybe they didn't know what Pompay was selling."

"Where you going with all this, Alworth? Where's your mind wandering to?"

I went silent. For a time, the only sound was the crackling of the fire.

After a while, Billy said, "Trouble with you, greenhorn, is that all that fine Eastern education has left you in a whirl. Like some sailor in a storm, you try to keep your boots firm on the deck, but the sea keeps tossing you back and forth."

"And what does the sea represent in your little parable?"

"You're conscience maybe? Or maybe your fear of not being the man you think you ought to be?" Billy laughed. "How the hell should I know what it means? You're the one who went to college."

I laughed, too, softly.

Then Billy said, in a near-whisper, "You do what you need to do, Alworth."

He left me there at the fire and went off to bed down.

Now here I am, alone with the white stars and the red coals. Alone with my thoughts on this page, my spiraling, storm-battered thoughts. Before dawn breaks on the land — and before my companions rise, intent on their merciless task — I need to decide where I stand. To use Billy's words, I need to finally push aside my fear and be the man I ought to be.

CHAPTER SEVENTEEN: McNULTY'S DREAM

It was the same setting as the other dream: a country lane bordered by tall trees. This time, though, the trees were not ponderosas, nor any tree that he had ever known. They were strange imposing things with black trunks and dark-red limbs. The thick trunks, instead of simply growing straight, were coiled like lengths of rope. They reminded him of the rigging on the ship that had brought him to America years back. Had he heard somewhere that that ship had eventually sunk — or was that just something his dreaming mind had made up? Either way, the ship had been called *The Bold Roamer,* and the trees were like thick coils of black rope. He did not like the look of the trees.

The heavy, humming mist of the other dream had not come to this one. He was thankful for that. But in its stead, a thousand shadows filled the path before him. He could not be sure if the shadows were cast by unseen objects or if they existed unto themselves. There was something indefinably perilous about the shadows, something that made him unsure of his footing. He had the sense that he should avoid treading on them. Perhaps it would have been better to contend with the blue mist.

He could not see Viola's face this time, but he knew she was out there. He thought perhaps he could hear her voice raised in song, but it may have been a wind in the treetops. Forward; he must hurry forward. She would be there somewhere, of that he was certain. But he must not tread on the shadows. Wings. Wings would be useful. But he had only his limbs, which he now pushed forward. Boldness: that was the clarion call. He must be a bold roamer.

CHAPTER EIGHTEEN: GAULT'S DREAM

He was standing atop a mesa with Ida. Her long brown hair whipped about in the wind. Smiling, she held out a wedge of cornbread to him. *I baked it for you, George. Just for you.* He started to reach for it but then withdrew his hand. *I can't eat it yet. Don't you realize they killed you?* Ida kept smiling, still extending the cornbread. *But I baked it for you.* He became angry with her. Must she always be so kindly . . . even when she'd been killed like that? He wanted to knock the cornbread from her hand but, instead, turned abruptly away. He stared down at the prairie spreading out far below.

The landscape was on fire — high, vicious flames climbing up the sides of the mesa. They would soon reach the top.

CHAPTER NINETEEN

"Damn it! Damn it to hell!"

Gault's shouting woke the others. They scrambled to their feet, Lampo with his knife in hand.

Gault stood at the edge of the pine grove, staring down the trail they'd rode in on. "That weak-kneed son of a bitch!"

Billy swayed on his feet, hardly awake. "What son of a bitch?"

"Nevins!" Gault turned to them and spat on the ground. "He's gone. Musta taken off sometime in the night or before dawn. He's abandoned us."

Billy looked over to where the horses were tied. Alworth's gray was gone.

"Maybe he just rode off to scout," Billy offered without conviction.

"Like hell!" Gault said. "I know when a man's run out on me."

Nash yawned and stretched. "No great loss, is it? By the looks of him, that fella was nothing but a mail-order cowpoke. Who cares if he mizzled off?"

"*I* care," said Gault. "No one runs out on me."

"So what do you figure to do?" Nash asked. "Track him down and shoot him?"

Gault took a few moments to answer, during which he kicked at the pine needles underfoot. Finally, he said, "No, the hell with Nevins. I doubt we'll see him again. We're continuing on to Black Powder."

"You fit to ride?" the Finn asked.

"Yeah, you looked pretty wobbly yesterday," said Nash.

"I'm fit," Gault insisted. "Now saddle up. We've lost too much time as it is."

He grabbed up his bedroll and moved toward the horses. Lampo followed.

Nash sidled up to Billy. "Gault's a real tough bastard, huh?" He lit a cigarette and blew out a ribbon of smoke. "What's it take to lay out a man like that, I wonder."

"More than *you* got." Billy walked away.

Nash shook his head and muttered, "Right unfriendly fellas. Makes me almost miss Pompay's bunch."

Gault, now in the saddle, was breathing hard. He grimaced, flinched once, then drew back his shoulders in a posture of

153

fortitude. "I'm fit as hell," he said to no one in particular. "Fit as all hell."

CHAPTER TWENTY:
JOURNAL OF
ALWORTH B. NEVINS

When I rode away from our campsite, the sky was still black, and my innards were twisted into tight knots. If Mr. Gault should hear my horse's hoof-falls and wake, his response might be violent. Perhaps fatal. He was not a man who'd likely abide desertion. But my mount, responding to my *hushes,* was quiet as a prayer, and we made our escape undetected. I had never learned the gray mare's name, if she had one, but, on the basis of her reliability, I now decided to call her Steadfast. It occurred to me that, depending on how things played out, I might not be able to return her to Gault. If he had no tolerance for deserters, then horse thieves would definitely rate a black mark in his book.

I left the pine grove and rode on in the direction Gault had been leading us. The anxiety of being discovered immediately gave way to the concern of getting lost.

Working in my favor was the fact that I'd made this journey in reverse about two months prior, so I was passingly familiar with the route. But back then I'd been a passenger in a stagecoach, seated across from a traveling watchmaker who kept expounding on the virtues of balance springs and harmonic oscillators.

In contrast to that guided journey filled with another man's endless chatter, I was now alone in the silent pre-dawn darkness on a mission I had barely thought out. That first hour's ride brought me the most profound feeling of solitude I'd ever experienced. I might have been the last man in the world . . . or the first. A primitive loneliness filled me, almost weighty enough to make me stop in my tracks and give in to despair. But I pushed down the emotion and pressed on. Steadfast, living up to her newly bestowed name, did her part by bearing me onward without hesitation.

To maintain my focus, I conjured up an image of Two Robes, as best I could recall her. True, I had only been in her presence for less than two hours and, during that time, always had three or four besotted cowhands standing between us. Still, the impression she made was a powerful one, and it sustained me now as I traveled alone through the bleak land. I fixed my thoughts upon her eyes, so black and piercing, as they had stared beyond that foul barroom into some distant, unknowable universe. And I saw again her lips, moving so calmly and cleverly as they gave life to antique poetry. The sound of her remembered voice rose ghostlike, lifting through the deep silence around me.

Eventually, the sun crested the horizon, and the darkness melted away. A high sea of clouds, saturated with red, now revealed themselves and seemed to stretch on forever. The brightening landscape, though cheering in a way, brought with it a new loss of faith. As I looked around me, I began to doubt that I was on the right path toward the town of Black Powder. I was still riding northeast, I believed, but had lost any feeling of certainty. I knew I should be passing some buttes on my left and, indeed, I now saw some, but they lay much farther away than I thought they should.

I adjusted my direction several times, but with each shift, my confidence flagged all the more. My unease intensified when I came upon a pile of bleached bones someone had arranged in a sort of pyramid. I tried to convince myself they were those of a steer, but the length of them seemed wrong. I wondered where the skull was.

An unpleasant story from the past came to me unbidden, something my father had once told me. When he was six or seven, a beloved playmate of his had wandered off into the twilight woods in search of a runaway dog. My father called after the boy, warning him not to venture too far, but his cries went unheeded. The dog eventually returned; the boy did not. A year later, a hunter found the bones at the bottom of a ravine miles away. The child had wandered far and wide seeking his dog but, in the end, had found only mortality. When telling the tale, my father's voice always got low as he said the child's name: Thaddeus. Now, riding with uncertain aim, in a potentially futile search for the Lakota girl, that name began to spin around my head like a haunting whirlwind. Thaddeus. Thaddeus. Thaddeus. What fatal cliff — physical or figurative — might be waiting for me up ahead?

I must have added more than an hour to my ride, and my desperation continued to rise. Nearing the end of my rope, I finally ran into a piece of luck. This came through the appearance of a wandering saddle-preacher. He gave me detailed directions to Black Powder, a place, he lamented, where his preachings had fallen on deaf ears. But such were all these scattered towns, the preacher claimed, all islands in the dust rife with gambling, drinking, and whoremongering. Transplanted Sodoms and Gomorrahs, that's what they were.

Promising that I had no plans to partake in any of those colorful sins, I thanked him for his guidance, both spiritually and geographically, and, to show my gratitude, presented him with a gift. As we rode off in our separate directions, it occurred to me that I no longer had my protective talisman. But I didn't regret the loss. In accepting *Sketches of Eminent Methodist Ministers,* tears of pleasure had actually come to the preacher's eyes. I was glad to have brought a dram of joy to the prairie apostle.

And perhaps I was no longer deserving of protection. After all, I had broken faith with my companions, hadn't I? Some might even call my actions betrayal.

I rode on for another hour or so before my next encounter with humanity. This one was unquestionably more disturbing than the last. I had just emerged from a rocky gully when I came upon a sight that made me tighten the reins and bring Steadfast to an abrupt halt.

About forty yards ahead, in the shadow of

a tall cottonwood, I beheld two figures, one stretched out on the ground, the other crouching beside the first. Two horses were tethered a short distance away. Hesitantly, I continued forward. The stretched-out figure was a man, his wrists tied together with a rope that had been fastened to the tree, his feet likewise bound and staked to the earth. The crouching figure was a woman with long black hair. For a fleeting moment, I thought she might be Two Robes.

When she turned to calmly appraise me, I saw at once that she was not Indian, but Chinese. She looked to be about thirty. The restrained man was also Chinese and probably of the same age.

I came abreast of them and drew up. In contrast to the woman's calm, the man was gripped by what I can only describe as something demonic. His eyes were wide, yet unfocused, and profuse sweat painted his brow. His mouth was smeared with a thick white froth. Spasms wracked his body as he struggled futilely against his restraints. A moaning sob trembled on his lips, a terrible thing to hear. The man's traditional hair queue, lying across his left shoulder, had become undone. The woman was carefully braiding it as she looked up at me.

"What . . ." In my appalled shock, I could

hardly get a word out.

"The rabies. He was bitten by a wolf days ago, and he now has the rabies." Though the woman's accent was notable, her command of English suggested she'd lived in America for some time. "He is my husband, and he will die."

"Dear God! I'm . . . I'm sorry."

The man, seemingly unaware of my presence, now let out a loud, high-pitched cry. I shuddered. On impulse, I reached for my canteen and extended it down to the woman. "Does he need a drink?"

She released the queue and firmly held up one hand. "No! No water! He cannot stand water."

The realization struck me like a blow: the other name for rabies was *hydrophobia*. A fear of water. I quickly withdrew the canteen.

The man cried out again, and the woman rested her hand on his chest. Looking into his frenzied eyes, she said something soothingly to him in Chinese.

"What's your name?" It was an odd thing for me to ask at that moment, but it's what came out.

The woman looked back up at me. "Junying. And this is Cheng. He has been my husband for more than ten years."

"I'm sorry," I said again. "Why is he tied down like this?"

"When we knew he had the rabies, we decided together that this is what we must do. We did not want him running off to die alone. I am his wife."

"Can't we help him?" I asked.

Junying shook her head. "There is no help for him. He will die soon, and I will keep him company until then. Cheng was always a powerful man. He worked in the mines. His back was strong, and his arms were strong. But even a strong man cannot fight this thing."

"I suppose not," I said weakly.

"Last year, President Arthur decided no more Chinese workers could come to America. Soon you will no longer see men like my Cheng working the mines and the railroads."

I'd read about the Exclusion Act. Perhaps she was right, and Cheng was one of the last of his kind.

"He was always strong, and now I will be strong for *him.*" Junying looked back at her husband and began speaking again in their native language. The words now seemed to have the rhythm of a recitation.

"What are you saying?" I asked when she paused. I was aware that I was imposing on a private moment, but something compelled me to ask.

Junying didn't seem offended by my question. "A poem, a very old one by a poet named Li Bo. The name is *Farewell to a Friend.*"

She then recited the words in English. This is what I remember:

> You must depart and go away.
> I shall think of you as the drifting clouds.
> In the sunset, traveler, think of me.
> You wave good-bye as you leave this
>   place.

After finishing the poem, Junying closed her eyes for perhaps a minute. When she reopened them, she said quietly, "Legend tells us that Li Bo drowned when he tried to hug the moon's reflection in the Yangtze River. That would be a better way to die than this. I wish Cheng could have died back home hugging the moon."

After that, Junying had no more words for me. She returned to braiding her husband's queue. Seeing as there was nothing to be done, I rode away. Once or twice, I heard the dying man's pitiful cries in the distance, then no more.

■ ■ ■ ■

When I finally arrived in Black Powder, the town had just begun to stir with its morning activities. At first glance, I couldn't confirm the preacher's assessment of the place. Neither Sodom nor Gomorrah leapt to mind, but, after all, I was seeing it in the vivid light of day. No doubt, the tentacles of sin waited till dark to fully extend themselves. As I rode down the main road, I took in the buildings on either side: general store, hardware, livery, small hotel, accompanying restaurant, and, of course, saloons . . . all the enterprises one would expect in a Western town. Discounting a languid hound dog, the first beings I encountered were three gray-haired women clustered together on the side of the thoroughfare, deep in conversation.

I dismounted, tipped my hat, and greeted them. "Good morning, ladies. Perhaps you can help me."

The trio appraised me, clearly weighing my worth — if, in my present bedraggled state, I had any to weigh. Perhaps the gun on my hip gave them the impression I was a more fearsome character than I really was.

After a moment, one of the three parceled

out a response. "We don't know if we can help until we've heard your request."

"Fair enough," I said. "I understand a troupe of players led by a Major Pompay was scheduled to make an appearance here. Would you know anything about that?"

"Theater people!" The second of the elderly women sniffed the air as if smelling something rancid.

"That's right," I said. "Theater people."

"I hold no truck with that sort," declared the sniffer.

"Nor I," said the first woman.

"So you don't know if they arrived in Black Powder?" I asked.

"Oh, they arrived here all right," said the sniffer. "Put on their tawdry little show last night at one of the saloons. Of course, I didn't attend."

"Nor I," said the first woman.

"As for myself, I *did* attend." The third of the elders now spoke up. She was a tiny person, rail-thin and less than five feet tall, whose large spectacles took up a third of her face. Her dress and bonnet were pure black.

The sniffer could huff as well as sniff. "I must say I'm not surprised, Miss Peppers."

"Nor I," said the first woman, predictably. "You often make unorthodox choices."

165

Little Miss Peppers shrugged. "I do enjoy an occasional entertainment. There's no sin in that."

The other two women exchanged a glance. They clearly had a shared opinion on sin and Miss Peppers' relationship to it.

"I thought it wasn't such a bad show," the small spinster continued. "A little bit of song and Shakespeare does the heart good."

"Well, make your own choices, Miss Peppers," said the sniffer. "I just know that I'd never step foot into any of these whiskey hovels to watch actresses doing who knows what in their tight, unbecoming costumes."

Before the first woman could throw in her *nor I,* I asked, "Do you know where those folks are now?"

"They camped behind the churchyard last night," Miss Peppers said.

"And where's that?"

"I can show you, young man. I know it quite well."

I tipped my hat again to the other two women. A look of disapproval remained on their faces, meant to encompass, I imagine, myself, Miss Peppers, all tightly garbed theater people, and the world in general.

As I followed my guide down the street, I was suddenly aware of how exhausted I was from my sleepless hours. I lumbered more than walked.

Miss Peppers seemed to notice my condition. "A youthful gentleman like you should take care of his health. Proper rest and nourishment lead to a long life."

I ignored her sage advice, instead asking, "At the show last evening, was one of the performers an Indian girl?"

"Oh, yes. A lovely young lady and very pleasant to listen to. She's the one with the Shakespeare. Have you seen her perform?"

"I have," I said simply, leaving it at that.

We turned down a path leading to a small church, then walked around the side to an iron-fenced graveyard. There was no sign of Major Pompay's lavishly painted wagon.

Miss Peppers clicked her tongue. "Sorry. I suppose they left early this morning."

I'm sure I would have felt my disappointment much more keenly were I not so utterly fatigued.

The little woman looked up at me. "Maybe they're heading toward Bordeaux. That's the next sizable town above us. If you're still wanting to catch up with them, that might be your best bet."

"Yes, thank you." I started to leave but noticed that Miss Peppers still stood in place and was staring into the graveyard.

"Since I'm here, I think I'll stay a bit to

167

visit with Papa." She gestured toward one of the nearest headstones, on which the name Winfield Peppers was chiseled. "I like to check in on him and my clients."

Too tired to ask who her clients might be, I gave a little nod and headed off.

I write this now in a cramped, musty room of the Regal Rest Hotel, as falsely named an establishment as ever there was. To be true to my plan, I should mount up immediately, leave Black Powder, and hasten north. But my exhaustion and lack of sleep have left me barely capable of staying on my feet, never mind riding over unknown terrain in focused pursuit. And so, I've decided to log an hour or two of slumber before resuming my quest, hopefully with my wits nominally restored. But before I close my eyes, I felt the need to chronicle these last few hours before they fade into some strange, disjointed memory.

I think I've gained enough of a head start on Gault to be quit of Black Powder before he arrives here. I can only imagine his mood when he awoke to find me gone. Satan himself could not muster enough fire and ferocity to match George Gault when he fancies himself betrayed. Yet *have* I betrayed him? I reflect on what Billy said last night: *if you signed on for a thing you're obliged to see it through.* But which thing have I truly signed on for: Gault's vengeance or Two Robes' protection? Can my classroom readings in philosophy offer an answer to that conundrum? I doubt it. I've certainly flung myself into the maelstrom, haven't I? Maybe Father was right, and I don't belong out here — far west of the Mississippi and a world away from my beginnings . . .

But, damn it all, I've made my choice! Whether I'm on a knight's quest or a fool's errand, I must see it through. Come what may.

CHAPTER TWENTY-ONE

The night before, John McNulty hadn't shared much about his plans. With the arrival of dawn, he at least named their destination.

"Black Powder," the outlaw said as he saddled his horse. "That's where we're bound. Our Mecca, so to speak."

Frank Baker looked confused. "I've heard of Black Powder, but no town what's called Mecca. Is that in the territory?"

McNulty laughed softly. "Just outside it."

"So which we heading to, Black Powder or Mecca?"

T.C. came up and put a hand on the burly man's shoulder. "Don't worry over it, Baker. You wouldn't want to overburden that poor brain of yours."

Baker shook off T.C. "So which is it, McNulty?"

The outlaw leader sighed. "We're heading for Black Powder."

"They got a nice bank there?"

"As I told you before, Baker, we're laying off the work till things settle down a touch."

"Then what the hell we going there for?"

McNulty finished tying off the saddle. "Let's just say I have an inclination."

"Damn it, you Irish gump! What's happened to you? Once on a time, you were big bad John McNulty. You used to be reliable, leastways so far as puzzling out a job. Now you act like you're allergic to bank vaults."

"That's a lively turn of phrase, Baker, I must admit. You're not usually so piquant."

"You think hurling them ten-buck words at me will shut me up, but it won't. If you got such an inclination to go to Black Powder, why don't you just go your own damn self? What do you need me and T.C. for?"

"Because I feel better having you lads where I can keep track of you. But enough banter. Prepare to ride."

Baker puffed up his chest. "I could just light out on my own. Right here and now, I could light out."

"You could indeed," said McNulty. "The thing is, you've made similar threats nearly every day since you joined up. Yet you've never acted upon a single one."

"I still might. You never know. Don't you

be surprised if I do." Baker strode off and flung his saddle roughly onto his horse's back.

T.C. turned to McNulty and said under his breath, "All bluster and no balls, that's our chum there."

McNulty spoke quietly himself. "Perhaps Baker *has* overstayed his welcome. He's a shaky ally to be sure, and we may well profit by his departure. I could call his bluff right now and cut him loose."

"Do you think it's smart to go dwindling our ranks more than they already are? I know Baker's no darling, but we're down to a pinch and a peck here. We get any leaner, we'll have to strap a musket on Quinny there and send her into the fray. Though, come to think of it, I bet she'd fare handsomely."

T.C. looked over at the girl, who stood off to herself stroking her pony's head. She had turned upon hearing her name.

T.C. gave her a wink and called out, "Just singing your praises, gal!"

Quinny stared at him without emotion.

"Perhaps you're right, T.C.," McNulty said. "This may not be the time to decrease our numbers."

McNulty mounted his horse and rode over to Baker, who was just starting down the trail. The two men continued on side by side. Quinny hoisted herself onto the pony and gripped the reins. T.C. smiled up at her.

"Another day, another chance for glory, eh, Quinny?"

It took a long moment for Quinny to respond. "When I was little, we had a rooster we called Glory."

"Oh?"

"He was irritable and strutty, but I was passing fond of him." With that, she gave the reins a shake and trotted off after the others.

T.C. stood shaking his head and smiling to himself. "Peculiar little snipper . . ."

They came within range of Black Powder three hours later, midmorning. As usual, Quinny chose to remain on the outskirts of town, a couple of miles away, while the men went to do their business. In the past, sometimes that business would be robbing banks; other times it was not business at all, Quinny knew, but might involve a poker table or a sporting lady's bed. She had become accustomed to any and all of those possibilities. This morning, though, it wasn't clear what McNulty's intent might be. Quinny did not speculate one way or the other on the matter. As always, she accepted her benefactor's choices without scrutiny.

She sat on an outcropping of rock watching the men ride off. Her pony grazed close by. It was a fine clear day with just a touch of wind. She could hear the tumbling waters of a nearby stream, which sounded to her like a little song. A song about everything and nothing. A song about the countless things of the known world and, too, the emptiness between all things, the blank spaces where her thoughts and dreams resided. As it had ever been, life moved around her like some bodiless spirit — she might sense it, glimpse it, but never fully be part of it. Not that she was blind to it all; she could see the beauty of the rolling land, the ugliness of certain men (Baker being one), the kindness of others (McNulty and T.C.), the mottled splendor of her pinto, the lonely dignity of a mesa . . .

Certainly, she had eyes to see, but her vision was not like other people's. She had realized this truth from childhood on. If asked, she would have said she didn't wish to be like others, but, of course, no one ever asked. There was a certain safety in not being understood, a protective skin of sorts.

If anyone came close to understanding her, it might be McNulty. The old Irishman would look at her sometimes as if seeing one of the fairy folk from the land of his birth. He once even expressed as much to her. She liked that notion. From what she understood of fairies, with their flitting, unknowable ways, she might indeed be kin to them. It would not surprise her at all.

She leaned back on the rock and looked up at the sky. Her eyes fixed on a particular cloud, white as a bride's linen against the stark, bright blue of the heavens. The clouds were her faithful companions. Except during night or storm, they kept a constant watch on her, no matter her troubles or torments. The cloud she now focused on had the shape of a turtle. There for all to see was the oval shell and the head and the stubby little limbs (though the back left one was missing). There was even a little wisp that could be the tail. Yes, a puffy white turtle, maybe a snapper, riding the air looking for birds to eat.

A noise made her forget the turtle and sit up. Though her ears were usually keen, she had somehow not heard the approaching horse. About seventy feet away, below and beyond the outcropping, a lone rider sat paused on his mount, staring up at her. He was an Indian man, probably Arapaho or Cheyenne as were common hereabouts, with long braids dangling beneath a raccoon-skin hat. He was tall and stern, and his gaze bore into her. In his right hand he balanced a rifle, presently pointed upward but ready to drop into firing position.

The girl and the man appraised each other silently for a full minute. Quinny wondered at the other's intentions. She thought of the derringer T.C. had given her, but the weapon was tucked away in her saddlebag. Probably not the best place for it at such moments as this.

Because she could think of nothing else to do or say, she called down to the rider, "I was just watching the clouds."

The look of sternness on the Indian man's face shifted to one of bewilderment. Quinny couldn't be sure whether or not he understood her words, but his perplexed expression was one she often received from her fellow humans. After studying her a bit more, the man gave a slight nod and rode off in the direction that McNulty had gone earlier. Quinny watched until he vanished in the distance.

She returned her gaze to the sky, only to discover that her turtle had somehow changed into a buffalo. A great fat buffalo.

After the men left their horses at the Black Powder livery, McNulty started to give instructions but was cut off by Baker.

"Hold on now," Baker said. "I've already staked out a plan. I'm going to go drum me up a chippy. Figure there must be a whorehouse in the vicinity."

T.C. shook his head in disbelief. "Lord almighty! It ain't but ten or so in the morning. Let those poor girls rest a bit before they start their working day. Besides, didn't you get your fill last night?"

Baker smirked. "I got a big appetite."

"Which you will stifle," McNulty said resolutely. "I want you and T.C. to wander the town and see if you come across any sign of a troupe of theater performers."

"Theater performers!" Baker spat out the words. "Now why the hell would we want to do *that*?"

"Because those are my orders."

"Well, your orders and my desires don't line up," said Baker. "Like I say, I'm gonna go find a cathouse and start the day off proper."

"Perhaps you didn't hear me," McNulty said.

"Perhaps I don't give a good goddamn," Baker snapped. "That ever occur to you? Maybe I got my own notion of how to lead my life and don't need your opinion on such things."

McNulty smoothed his beard and sighed. "This really gets tiring, you know. Must our every exchange turn into a debate?"

"Baker does bring up a good question, though," T.C. said. "Why are we on the prowl for thespians? Seems a strange sort of task to give us."

"I have my reasons," McNulty said. "Now split up and see what you can discover. We'll meet back here in half an hour."

Baker hooked his thumbs in his gun belt. "I doubt I'll be ready by then. Maybe after I'm done pirooting, I'll go visit the local bank and get a little work in. Just 'cause you've gotten shy about tending to business don't mean *I* have."

McNulty's eyes narrowed. "You *will* stay well clear of any banks, Baker. I've explained this to you. For the time being, we're —"

"Each man to his own view," said Baker. "That's democracy, ain't it?"

"This is not a democracy."

"From here on out it is. Riding in just now, I got to pondering the situation. Simmering on it. I figure it's high time I stopped handing my reins over to you, McNulty. Consider our partnership done with."

McNulty's face darkened. "Maybe later. But, for now, when we're all together here in this town, our fates are linked. If one man acts recklessly, we all suffer. Thus you'll abide by my decisions."

"And if I don't? You ready to throw down here in the street, McNulty?" Baker stepped a couple of paces backward and rested a hand on the grip of his Smith & Wesson. " 'Cause I am. It'd be a goddamn pleasure."

"Are you off your head, Baker?" T.C. asked. "Look around you. There's folks in the vicinity. You want to make a spectacle of us?"

By way of illustration, a woman and child passed by within a stone's throw, and, across the street, a shopkeeper stood on his porch casually sweeping.

Baker tried out a look of bravado. "Maybe I *would* crave an audience. How 'bout you, McNulty? You're so eager for some theater. We could put on a fine little show, you and me."

The Irishman looked steadily at his challenger. "Tell me, Baker, have you ever actually shot a man face to face? I know you've planted bullets in men's backs. That's your specialty, so to speak. But locking eyes with an opponent and discharging your weapon with calm and calculation is another thing entirely. Not everyone is equipped for such a deed."

"*I* am, that's for damn sure." Baker's tone

179

didn't match the boldness of his words.

"Then that should serve you well," said McNulty. "If it's true. As for me, I know from experience I am indeed equipped for such cool violence. Not long ago, you mentioned that marshal in Buford. You weren't there at the moment I killed him, Baker, but that lawman accosted me in the street with his pistol drawn. By all rights, he should have slain me there and then. But, you see, he was a younger man than I — perhaps your own age — and lacked my experience with mortality. When our eyes met, I saw death in his pupils. Not my death, mind you, but his own. And I believe he saw his death in *my* eyes. And so, transfixed, he froze, and in that split second of hesitation, I drew my revolver and fired."

"True enough," T.C. put in. "That's just how it was."

McNulty nodded. "Yes, T.C. was there and can bear witness. The point of my tale, Baker, is that when I face down a man, I can see his fate. Perhaps the ability comes from my Celtic blood . . ."

"Yeah, the Irish are a spooky lot," T.C. said.

"To be honest, Baker," McNulty continued, "staring now into your eyes, I don't see a favorable outcome for you. That is, should you go for your gun. However, if you stay your hand, then —"

"Then the world's your oyster!" T.C. smiled. "Seems like a clear choice to me, Baker. But then I'm not the gun hawk you are."

Baker's resolve had wavered. Seeming to shrink in place, he removed his hand from the pistol.

"You're showing great wisdom," McNulty said to him.

Rather than accepting the compliment, Baker let out a string of vile curses, ending with, "I'm done with you bastards! I'm riding out. You won't see me no more."

Baker stalked off in the direction of the livery.

McNulty exhaled deeply. "That could have been ugly. I won't regret his absence."

"I always figured Baker for a bully," T.C. said. "All wind and no sails. You called his bluff nicely."

"Thank you for backing my play."

"Glad to. The only thing is, to the best of my recollection, your account just now wasn't entirely accurate. If memory serves, the marshal's pistol misfired. That's how you got the drop on him. There wasn't time for you and him to stare into each other's eyes to behold Death or George Washington or anybody else. It all came down to a misfire."

McNulty gave a little shrug. "Sometimes it helps to rearrange the truth."

T.C. grinned. "Well, you've got a knack for doing so, I'll give you that. I do admire a man who fashions his own reality."

CHAPTER TWENTY-TWO

The cougar hunched on a narrow ledge, muscles tensed, in keen observation of the riders passing below. Its tan hide contrasted clearly with the dark, gray stone, and had any of those below looked up, they would have noted the creature's presence. No one looked up.

The cougar had been moving along the ridgeline for several minutes, its yellow eyes locked on the horses and riders, carefully gauging their movements. Its vigilance now paid off as the rider in the rear halted, allowing the other two to continue forward. Seemingly unaware of this pause, the others put some distance between themselves and their companion. Seeing this, the beast made its move. It swiftly loped from rock to rock till it was less than a dozen feet above its quarry. Then, with a great thrust of its hind legs, it sprang outward. A hundred and eighty pounds of flesh and muscle descended on the separated rider. Whether it had been the cougar's intention to strike the human or the horse mattered little at this point. Perhaps the cougar saw the two beings as one intertwined entity. In any case, here was prey.

The weight of the descending body dislodged young Tom Sawbridge from his saddle. He hit the ground hard. His horse, still on its feet and realizing the danger, abandoned its rider and raced forward. The big cat, having landed on its side, quickly righted itself and rushed toward Tom.

Though he'd had the wind knocked out of him, the boy reacted automatically and kicked outward, landing a boot heel on the cougar's snout. The cat snarled and advanced again but was met by another kick. The cougar now adjusted its attack, half circling the boy, then darting forward to clamp its jaws down upon his right arm.

Tom had no time to give in to fear. He could only fight, though he knew he was no match for the beast. Fortunately, his coat was made of thick wool, which momentarily kept the sharp fangs from tearing into his arm. But one heavy forepaw now raked across his stomach, causing him to scream out. He thrust his free hand through the dirt, seeking a stone or anything else to use as a weapon. He found the canteen that he had just paused to drink from. Gripping it tightly, he began striking the cougar's head. This only served to enrage the animal, which gripped Tom's arm tighter and pressed both forelegs across the youth's body to pin him down.

A shot rang out. The cougar immediately released Tom and backed up a few paces. A second shot found its mark: the cat yelped as a bullet tore into its right shoulder. The cougar staggered, hissed fiercely, then spun about and fled. Tom Sawbridge, still sprawled on the ground, turned to look up at his sister Elizabeth and Saturn Hayes, both still mounted. Elizabeth stared down at him, horrified. Saturn was lowering his Winchester rifle, gun smoke drifting about him.

"Dear God, Tom!" Elizabeth dismounted and ran to her brother. "Are you hurt badly?"

It took the boy a moment to evaluate his condition. "Just my belly, I think," he said tentatively. He lifted his shirt to reveal a trio of parallel red lines across his stomach.

Elizabeth drew in her breath and studied the marks for a moment. "Not too deep, thank heaven. Just scratches really." She handed Tom his hat and helped him to his feet.

Saturn was now standing beside them, his rifle still in hand. "Could have been a lot worse, that's for sure. I've seen cougars do more damage in less time."

"You saved me, Saturn." There was real gratitude in the boy's tone. "You and your eagle eye."

"First shot was just to scare the cougar away from you," said Saturn. "To get it to move a touch back so I could strike it without hitting you."

"You surely did a fine job." Elizabeth was making an effort to steady her voice. "I don't want to think what would have . . ." She let the words trail off and drew Tom to her side.

Saturn looked grim. "It ain't too common for a cat to pounce on a human being like that. Especially a human up on a horse."

"Then why'd that one attack?" A note of distress had found its way into Tom's voice. The full realization of what had just happened seemed to be creeping over him.

"Couldn't say what compelled him," Saturn said. "It's unnatural. All I know is that everything tied in with this journey, coming and going, has been full of devilry."

"I told you that you didn't need to make

the ride with us, Saturn," Elizabeth said. "We were prepared to find my cousin on our own."

Saturn tugged at his mustache. "No, no, that wouldn't set right with me. You got spunk all right, Miss Elizabeth, but you don't have my experience out on the rough. Or, for that matter, my experience with devilry. We put in a day's worth of riding yesterday, and there's still a good ride ahead today before we hit Black Powder. I wouldn't want to think of you and the boy making this trek alone."

"We're in your debt." Elizabeth said.

"Don't think nothing of it." Saturn slid the Winchester back into its saddle pouch. He winced and touched his left shoulder; his wound was still aching.

Elizabeth noticed. "Are you all right?"

"Just feeling my years," Saturn lied. He hadn't mentioned that he'd been shot yesterday. If Elizabeth knew, she'd have no doubt refused his assistance. Better to keep the misfortune to himself.

"I fought a cougar!" Tom announced to the world at large. Distress had shifted to youthful pride. "A cougar jumped me, and I gave it some good licks!"

Elizabeth looked hard at her brother. "Is this really an occasion for bragging? If it wasn't for Saturn, you might well be sitting in that beast's belly right now waiting to be digested."

This stark image silenced the boy. He now looked somewhat queasy.

Saturn approached Tom and rested a hand on his shoulder. "Well, no use in fretting over what coulda been. You're hale and hearty, and that cat's on the run. It's all satisfactory. Now let's go round up your horse and head on out."

Saturn took his sorrel by the reins and, with Tom by his side, headed up the trail.

Elizabeth started toward her own horse, then paused to look back at the spot where the cougar had downed Tom. She shuddered. She found herself reflecting on Saturn's words: was everything about this journey truly full of devilry?

CHAPTER TWENTY-THREE

Three hours into the morning's ride, George Gault's wound was again getting the better of him. The renewed energy he'd felt upon rising, heightened by his fiery anger at Alworth's desertion, had by now largely drained away. Once more, grimacing and ghostly pale, he struggled to stay in the saddle.

They'd just passed through a rocky gully when they came upon an odd sight: a Chinese woman, unaccompanied, diligently digging a hole. She was some distance away, laboring beneath a cottonwood tree with two horses tied nearby. On the ground beside her, next to the mound of dirt, lay something sizable, covered over with a blanket. The woman paused, shovel in hand, to take in the riders, then immediately looked away and resumed digging.

The thud of the shovel in earth made Billy Fowler wince. "Should we stop and help her?"

"Why the hell would we do *that*?" Gault spurred his horse forward, and the others followed.

Soon the woman was well behind them, beyond sight and sound. Only then did Gault slacken his pace. The sprint seemed to have further weakened him, and after another mile's ride he pulled up and called for a break. His men dismounted, and Lampo went to help Gault down. Gault cursed and waved him off, easing himself out of the saddle. On unsteady legs, he made his way over to a fallen pine and sat down on it. He stared off into the distance, breathing hard and pulling on his mustache. After a while, he took out a cheroot and rolled it between his fingers for a full minute, never lighting it, before shoving it back into his duster pocket.

Something wasn't right. Gault knew it was still morning, but the sun seemed to be flickering on and off, a lantern caught in a strong wind. The sky had turned an un-natural color, not really a color at all, more like a high, quavering field of emptiness. Were those birds flying overhead or were they shifting cracks in the clouds? No, not right at all.

Suddenly, Ida stood before him. She must

have climbed down from the mesa. Somehow she had become very young, as young as she'd been that day, that vile evening when he'd finally had enough and left. He'd been sixteen then, too old to let tears burn his eyes. But they did burn. Then and now, Ida appeared like some earthbound angel, her gentle smile touching his burning eyes, easing the pain and shame.

His father wasn't nearby now, but still not far enough away. A hundred miles away would be best. Two hundred. Five hundred. He would steal a horse and put those miles between that man and himself. *I'll miss you, George,* young Ida had said, then and now, *but do what you must do.* Wait, wasn't Ida dead? Wasn't his father dead, as well? Was Gault himself dead? Hadn't he been shot yesterday?

The other three men, standing a distance away, studied Gault and talked quietly among themselves.

"Our general there still don't look too sound, does he?" Nash said. "I figure we've got a couple more hours' ride to Black Powder. I'm wondering if he can make it."

"Gault's tough," said Lampo.

"No one's claiming otherwise," Nash conceded. "But, like I say, we've got a ways to go. And what if Pompay's already pushed

191

on from Black Powder? What then?"

"Then we follow." The Finn removed his derby and ran a hand through his tangled red hair. "Leave if you want."

"I take it Gault doesn't favor men leaving on him," Nash said. "Besides, I think I'd like to stick just to see how this all plays out."

Billy still stared over at Gault. "I'm starting to have my own concerns, I gotta say. Mr. Gault ain't looking his best, that's a fact."

"He's tough." This seemed to be Lampo's default statement. He replaced his hat, smoothed his long beard, and grunted. "Damn tough."

Billy sighed. "Sure, but even a tough man can crumble. Even a man like Gault."

Gault heard his name spoken, and Ida faded away. He turned abruptly to look straight at Billy. With some effort, he pushed himself off the log and stumbled over to the men.

"I heard that, Billy," he growled into the young man's face. "Who do you think is crumbling? Me?"

"I didn't mean it that way."

"Whatever goddamn way you meant it, it's wrong!" Gault's eyes were wild. "Dead wrong! What do you know about being a man? You ain't even close, are you? Not even eighteen, yeah?"

"All I was saying —"

"You were feeling your oats yesterday, weren't you, boy? Standing up to me like that?"

"Hey, Mr. Gault, I wasn't —"

"I don't crumble!" Gault was shouting now. "You hear me? You all hear me? I'm going to see this thing through."

"Sure, Mr. Gault," Lampo said calmly.

In his rage, Gault didn't hear him. "I'm going to bring a hard reckoning to Pompay and his people! Do you think I'd see Ida go unavenged?"

No one answered him. Gault let go an animal cry, then staggered back a few steps and yanked out his Colt. Three men's hands flew down to the grips of their own pistols. Gault spun away, putting his back to the others, and rapidly fired three times into the air. He cried out again and dropped to the ground face first. He spasmed once, then lay still.

Nash snickered. "Guess he crumbled after all. Crumbled and crumpled."

"Shut up." Lampo knelt down and turned Gault over.

"Has he gone crazy?" Billy asked.

"Fever." Lampo's hand rested on the

193

fallen man's brow. "He's got fever."

Nash snickered again. "Fever or not, he almost got himself plugged skinning his gun like that. Maybe we should take his weapons off him."

Billy nodded. "Might not be a bad idea,"

"He wouldn't like that," Lampo said.

"Well, *I* wouldn't like getting shot by a man who's out of his head," Nash said. "What's say we just snag that Colt for safekeeping?" He leaned over and reached for the revolver on the ground.

The Finn's hand shot forward, scooped up the weapon, and slid it back into Gault's holster. "You don't take a man's gun."

Nash smiled darkly. "Oh? Is that the code over in Sweden?"

"Finland," said Lampo.

"What's that?"

"Lampo's from Finland," Billy said. "Not Sweden."

Nash threw up his hands. "Fine. Split hairs if you want. The point is, your man here is passed out. What's our move now?"

"We keep going," Lampo said.

"What? To Black Powder?" Nash gestured toward Gault, still sprawled on the ground. "What about *him*? He's not likely to stay in his saddle, is he?"

They were all silent for several moments.

194

Then Lampo stood, walked over to his horse, and removed a loop of rope from around the saddle horn. He draped it over his shoulder and walked back to Gault.

Nash cocked his head. "What are you fixing to do? Hang the poor bastard?"

Sometime later, back on the trail, they crossed paths with a stagecoach. As the coach rolled by, the driver and well-garbed passengers all strained their necks to stare at the sight of the upright but dazed-looking Gault, firmly tied to his saddle, with the rope crisscrossing his chest.

Billy, who was riding alongside him, smiled at the passing observers and called out, "We're getting him to his wedding!"

Had his employer been more lucid, Billy would never have chanced the joke, but Gault was barely conscious. Such was his condition since he'd been hoisted into his saddle and bound there.

Nash rode up beside Billy. "His wedding! That's a good one!" He laughed. "You Nubians got a sense of humor. I've always said as much."

If Billy had disliked Nash before, this last remark confirmed the feeling. "Go to hell," he snapped.

Nash looked offended. "What's with you?

The bunch of you for that matter. I try to be amicable, and all I get is sassing."

"I ain't sassing you. I'm telling you to go to hell."

"Oh, well beg my damned pardon. Sorry I got that wrong. Jesus Christ! What a lousy mob I've fixed myself with. An uppity boy, a surly Swede, and a leader who's gone off his nut."

"Like Lampo told you, you can leave anytime. Gault's beyond caring."

"I've been promised some pay for my troubles, and I aim to collect."

"Then keep your trap shut and just ride."

"I goddamn will!"

Nash dug his spurs into his horse's ribs and shot forward. He stopped short of Lampo, who was riding foremost. Billy was alone again beside Gault.

After several minutes, Gault spoke, the first time since they'd resumed their ride. His voice was raspy and detached. "They threw it away."

Billy turned in his saddle. "What's that, Mr. Gault?"

"They threw it away, damn 'em."

"Who threw what away?"

"My uncle and aunt. Ida's parents. They threw it away."

"What was it they threw away, Mr. Gault?"

196

"The kaleidoscope, damn it! The one I bought for Ida."

"I see."

Gault went silent again. After a minute he continued, speaking quickly now, breathlessly. "First time I came back home after I left, I brought Ida that kaleidoscope. Got it in Denver. Her parents threw it away. They'd heard of things I'd done, said I'd gone bad. They didn't want her to keep any gifts of mine." With unfocused eyes, he looked over at Billy. "Ain't that sad, Saturn?"

Billy started to correct Gault, to tell him that Saturn wasn't with them, but thought better of it. "Yes, very sad, Mr. Gault."

Gault again lapsed into silence. When he spoke again, it appeared his thoughts had shifted elsewhere.

"It was a hoe . . ." The words seemed to distress him. He shook his head back and forth as if in pained disbelief. "A rusty old hoe. Rusty but sharp. How could someone . . ." His voice cracked.

"Don't distress yourself, Mr. Gault," Billy said. "You just ride easy."

Gault now looked down at his chest, bound with rope, and his wrists, tied to the saddle horn. "Did the law get to me, Saturn?"

"The law?"

"Is that why I'm trussed up? Was it for killing that teamster in Laramie?"

Billy answered softly. "No, nothing like that."

"Or that fella in Crook County?"

"No, Mr. Gault."

" 'Cause those were all self-defense." Gault sighed and stared off. "More or less . . ."

CHAPTER TWENTY-FOUR

Stepping into a saloon called the Bronze Spur, T.C. immediately forgot about McNulty's orders. Instead of inquiring as to the whereabouts of a theater troupe, he invited himself into an early morning poker game now in full swing. As he had the day before, he was feeling the tingle of his ghost caul and figured luck was with him. This belief seemed borne out by his first few hands, which he won handsomely.

His fellow players were a fairly agreeable lot. There appeared to be no equivalent to yesterday's hostile blacksmith. In addition to T.C., the table was composed of another white man, three Mexicans, and a well-dressed black man in spectacles. Many saloons refused admittance to non-Caucasians, but the Bronze Spur apparently was of a more egalitarian bent. Which fine with T.C. — he was happy to win any man's money, regardless of his complexion.

The other white man was the only one who'd been souring the mood a touch, not with hostility but with a level of anxiety T.C. found annoying. It was clear the fellow had been losing handily all morning, and his bad streak hadn't stopped with T.C.'s arrival. He was a skinny, twitchy man who accompanied each of his losses with a pitiful moan.

"Don't carry on so," T.C. advised. "Your luck's bound to turn around . . . one of these years."

T.C.'s accompanying laugh only served to draw out another wretched moan.

The next dealer was the bespectacled man, who distributed the cards with a bouncy patter. "No one knows what fortune will allow. Will the tides turn for some? Will they stay their course for others? Let's see, why don't we?"

"Just deal," Skinny groaned.

"Glad to," said Spectacles, passing out the final cards.

T.C. swept up his hand and fanned the cards. Three sevens and a couple throwaways. Not bad at all. When the bet came around to him, he raised confidently, but not enough to chase away his companions. Only one of the players folded, and, after the draw and another solid bet, T.C. won his fourth hand in a row. Yes, the phantom caul hadn't steered him wrong.

Spectacles, whose pair of kings had not held up, accepted the latest loss placidly. "You're living under a lucky star, aren't you? Well, forgive me, but I hope it moves my way soon."

T.C. grinned. "Sorry, friend, but I think me and my star are gonna be yoked together for a spell. I just have that feeling."

Skinny, coming off his latest moan, fixed T.C. with a hard stare. "Maybe that star of yourn ain't exactly right. Maybe you nudge it some. Maybe not in a proper way."

T.C. returned the stare. "Are you insinuating something, mister? 'Cause it sure sounds like you are."

Skinny sniffed and twitched, but kept his eyes on T.C. "I'm just having my thoughts, is all."

One of the Mexicans, a hard-looking man, studied Skinny. "Those are dangerous thoughts. To accuse this man of cheating . . ."

"That's right," Spectacles put in. "This is a friendly game we're having."

"I can always tell when a man cheats," continued the Mexican, nodding toward T.C., "and this one was not cheating."

"Was I saying he was?" Skinny now looked

on unsteady ground. "I wasn't doing no such thing. Let's keep playing."

"Yes, let's," said T.C. gathering in the cards. "My deal." He offered his accuser a toothy smile. "And, just so you know, I never cheat at poker. I'm not that clever. Tried it but once and wound up swindling myself out of a stack of quarter eagles. Been an honest man ever since."

He neglected to add that he'd shifted his dishonesty to bank robbing. No sense bringing up unrelated facts. Spectacles won the next hand, but T.C. hadn't invested deeply in it. The hand after that went to T.C.'s defender, the hard Mexican. Just when T.C. was beginning to think his luck had gone fallow, he pulled up a bold full house on the draw — aces over jacks.

After favorably reviewing his cards, he looked over at Skinny, peering at his own hand, and noticed his widened eyes. Clearly, the fellow had drawn something strong and didn't possess a poker face. After some jousting bets, only T.C. and Skinny remained in the hand. Having faith in his full house — though wary of what Skinny held — T.C. ventured a large bet. Larger, he guessed, than Skinny would want to chase. The twitchy man stared intently at his closely held cards as if scrutinizing his last will and testament.

Skinny finally tore his eyes away from his hand and set them on T.C. "I want to meet your bet, but I ain't got enough cash on me."

"Ah! You've got yourself some nice cards I'm guessing."

"Maybe I do." Skinny tried to sound sly. "But like I say —"

"You're short on funds. I understand. Got anything you could toss in the pot to even things up? A pocket watch maybe? Something like that?"

Skinny seemed to probe the recesses of his mind, which didn't take long, before calling out, "A hat! How about a hat?"

T.C. shifted his gaze to the man's bare head. "Unless my eyesight's failing, you're not wearing one."

"It's right here on the floor." Skinny stooped down and, indeed, lifted up a hat T.C. hadn't before noticed. Skinny held it high as if proudly displaying it to the room.

"I'll admit, it's a real beauty you got there," T.C. said.

The hat was a large green sombrero, well-constructed and elaborately embroidered. Silver threaded flowers and intertwined vines decorated much of the surface, and the wide brim was edged with gold trim.

"Sure, throw it in the pot," said T.C.

The bet was covered and the hands laid out. T.C. hooted at the sight of Skinny's club flush.

Skinny looked confounded. "What are you crowing about? My straight flush beats your full house."

"It would if you *had* a straight flush," T.C. said. "But you don't."

"Whatta you mean? It's right there!"

"It's surely not. Can someone back me up here?"

Spectacles leaned over the cards and adjusted his eyeglasses. "Sorry, sir," he said to Skinny. "It's true. You're one card shy."

The three Mexicans chimed in their agreement.

"You're all wrong!" Skinny began frantically naming his cards. "Four of clubs! Five of clubs! Six! Seven! Eight!"

"That's not an eight," Spectacles gently corrected. "Look again. It's a nine. There's a gap there. All you have is a flush."

"Which comes short of a full house." T.C. tossed his battered old hat on the table and reached for the sombrero. "Sorry to part you from your chapeau, pardner, but I'll give it a good home."

He set the green sombrero firmly on his head and beamed.

Skinny's twitchiness had reached new heights. Looking as if he might lose his breakfast, he managed to get to his feet.

"I'm leaving this godforsaken town," he said and shoved himself out the saloon doors.

T.C. began pocketing his winnings. "Hate to conquer and run, but I'm expected elsewhere. You can throw my old hat into the next pot. I won't be needing it. What do you reckon, fellas? Does my new sombrero suit me?"

Spectacles smiled. "It makes you look dapper as a duke."

T.C., unsurprisingly, was late meeting up with McNulty.

"I didn't find out anything about your performers," T.C. said truthfully, "but I ran into some gents who insisted on giving me their money."

"I see." McNulty eyed the sombrero. "And where did you acquire *that* monstrosity?"

"Hey, watch your tongue! I've taken quite a fancy to this hat. I earned it with an ace-heavy full house. With this on my head, I'll be the talk of the town."

"That's what concerns me. It will certainly make you stand out for the next round of wanted posters."

"Aw, you're just jealous 'cause you can't boast anything as fine on your own noggin."

McNulty smiled thinly. "Yes, that's it. I'm consumed with jealousy. Come, let's fetch the horses. I've discovered that the performance troupe left town earlier today. It's the one I'm looking for. We'll gather up Quinny, then continue north."

McNulty led the way down the street toward the livery. At one point, two young women, twirling lace parasols, passed them and exchanged smiles with T.C.

"Lookee there, McNulty!" T.C. laughed. "My sombrero's already paying dividends. All the young gals will be flocking around to see who this Flashy Dan is."

McNulty paused and looked over at the mercantile to his left. "Wait a moment. I want to pick up a provision or two. I won't be but a minute." He entered the store.

T.C. remained outside, amusing himself with his reflection in the store window. He fiddled with the sombrero, giving it a tilt he deemed stylish. After a moment, his gaze shifted to an arrangement of objects on the other side of the glass, lingering on one in particular: a cloth doll in a floral calico dress and little white bonnet. The painted eyes were a vivid blue.

Should he go in and buy the doll for

Quinny? Not that Quinny was a child, of course, but neither was she a full-grown woman. If he presented the doll to her, she was unlikely to offer much gratitude, but that didn't matter really. Maybe she'd take some quiet comfort in the toy, even if she'd never acknowledge it.

T.C. was just about to enter the mercantile when a male voice called out behind him. He couldn't understand the words, but the tone was confrontational. His hand dropped to his pistol, and he turned. The rifle blast caught him full in the chest. It happened so quickly, he never saw his attacker. T.C. gasped and stumbled out into the street. The sombrero tumbled from his head and landed at his feet. He fumbled desperately for his pistol, but a second blast caught him in the right shoulder and jolted him backward. He fell heavily to the ground, feeling as if he'd fallen from a great height.

McNulty tore out of the store, his revolver in hand. He glanced down at T.C., then at the man standing across the street holding a smoking rifle — a tall Indian in a coonskin hat. McNulty thrust out his arm and fired. The shot just missed. The other man stared ahead coolly, then took aim at McNulty. Before the Indian could fire, McNulty got off another shot, this one tearing into the

Indian's ribs. The man bent over, discharging his rifle into the dirt, then promptly straightened and again took aim. Once more the Irishman fired, this time striking his foe's chest dead center. The tall Indian wavered on his feet for a few seconds, then fell backward, hitting the earth with a thud.

McNulty strode over and kicked the rifle away. The man still lived, though barely. His eyes were wide and unfocused, and his breaths came in rasping sputters. McNulty left him and hurried over to where T.C. lay staring up at the sky. After glancing about to make sure no other assassins waited in the wings — bounty hunters perhaps? — McNulty holstered his pistol and knelt beside his friend. He clasped T.C.'s hand.

"It hurts . . ." T.C. managed to say, his voice hardly a whisper.

"It won't hurt for long," said McNulty, knowing this was true. "Rest easy, lad."

He squeezed T.C.'s hand and felt the other's response. After a minute, T.C.'s grip slackened, and his eyes glazed over. McNulty sighed deeply. Releasing T.C.'s hand, he drew his fingers over the young man's eyelids, closing the eyes forever. He offered a brief silent prayer and rose.

By now, seeing the danger had passed, a fair number of people had spilled out into the street. Gunfights were enough of a rarity as to be of great interest when they occurred. Those now standing around the fallen men included several respectable-looking townspeople, the parasol girls among them. A short man, his face sprayed with old smallpox scars, bent to check T.C.'s pulse, then shook his head and walked away. Also in attendance was a pair of unkempt men who appeared to be twins. By their buckskin garments, stained with grease and tobacco juice, and the bullwhips looped through their belts, the pair looked to be bullwhackers by trade.

One of the twins grinned and nudged the other. "Looks like we pulled into town just in time for the festivities."

"Appears so," his brother agreed. "Guess this place was worth the visit."

McNulty cast a cold eye on the two men. "That's my friend lying dead at your feet. I'll thank you to show some respect."

"We didn't mean no harm," said the first bullwhacker. "We just don't happen on excitement like this too much."

"That's right," said the other twin. "It's like that O.K. Corral a couple years back in Tombstone, ain't it?"

"No it's not," McNulty said firmly. "That gun battle was the result of a longstanding feud. What happened here was completely unprovoked. I've no idea why the assailant killed my friend."

"I've got a notion." A man stepped out from the crowd and addressed McNulty. "More than a notion."

He was tall and solidly built and looked to possess Indian blood. McNulty immediately noticed the badge on his shirtfront. The outlaw never liked being this close to the law and wondered if his wanted poster had made its way to Black Powder. He dearly hoped not.

"That one over there . . ." The lawman nodded toward T.C.'s killer, still sprawled in the street. "He just pulled into town about an hour ago. Name's Low Moon. Arapaho. I spoke to him when he rolled in."

"Sheriff Little is half Arapaho his own self," someone in the crowd felt compelled to state. "So he talks the lingo."

"I spoke to him," the sheriff repeated. "And it seems Low Moon was hunting down a man who killed his brother two weeks ago. Shot him in the back."

"My friend had nothing to do with any killing," McNulty insisted.

Sheriff Little eyed him steadily. "Well, mister, Low Moon said the one he was look-ing for was a white man who wore a fancy green sombrero. A sombrero that was pretty special looking."

"Dear God." McNulty looked down at the sombrero lying inches from T.C.'s body. "That wasn't my friend's hat. I mean it was, but he'd just won it at a poker game. Only about a half hour ago."

"He's right, Sheriff."

McNulty took note of a black man in spectacles who'd just stepped forward.

"I was at the same game," this man said. "That other fellow, the one who bet his sombrero, was another stranger. I believe he rode out of town after he left the table."

"Bad damn luck for your friend," Little said to McNulty. "Looks like Low Moon saw the sombrero and thought he'd found his man. It's real tragic."

"Indeed it is," McNulty said quietly. "Tragic and bizarre."

"This one's still alive." The short man who'd examined T.C. was now kneeling over Low Moon.

"Will he make it, Doc?" The sheriff walked over there, followed by McNulty.

"Not a chance," said the doctor. "He's just about gone."

McNulty knelt down next to the dying Arapaho and spoke gently to him. "I can't fault you for this. You made a mistake, a

211

terrible one, but, Lord knows, I've made more than my share myself in this life. I hope your passage to the next world is a good one. Maybe you'll meet your brother there."

McNulty waited till Low Moon had taken his final rasping breath, then stood and walked back over to where T.C. lay. The sheriff followed him.

"I want to make sure my friend gets a proper burial," McNulty said.

Little nodded down the street. "Here comes our undertaker now."

A small woman, bespectacled and dressed in black, was approaching.

McNulty's eyebrows rose. "You have a female undertaker here?"

"Miss Peppers' father was the old one," Little explained. "When he died some years back, she took on the job. Seemed kinda natural."

"Lady undertakers and Indian lawmen!" one of the bullwhackers exclaimed. "What a caution."

"Yessir," said his twin. "Black Powder sure is an uncommon place."

The crowd parted to allow Miss Peppers to come through.

"Two deceased," the sheriff told her. "Both strangers to town."

Miss Peppers studied the dead men. " 'I have been a stranger in a strange land,' says the Good Book. Most assuredly, all strangers deserve a peaceful repose."

McNulty took out his billfold, withdrew several bills, and passed them to the petite undertaker. "This is to see to my friend's interment. And to Low Moon over there. As you said, he was a stranger, too." He turned to the sheriff. "Being of the same tribe, maybe you can see that things are done for him in the proper manner."

Little nodded.

"You don't plan to attend the burials?" Miss Peppers asked.

"My responsibilities call me elsewhere," said McNulty.

"Very well. What was your friend's name?"

McNulty hesitated. He didn't intend to provide the name T. C. Heckett, which appeared on numerous wanted posters. Especially not with an officer of the law standing inches away.

"Brennan," McNulty said after a moment. "Matthew Brennan." It was the name of a priest he'd known back in County Kerry. A perpetually inebriated one. McNulty thought T.C. would have appreciated the jest.

He bent down, removed a money pouch

from T.C.s coat, and pocketed it. He then undid his friend's gun belt and draped it over his own shoulder.

A scruffy young boy now appeared and grabbed up the fallen sombrero. "Hey there, mister, can I keep this?"

"No, youngster. No one shall." McNulty seized the hat from the boy and handed in to Miss Peppers. "I'd appreciate, ma'am, if you'd see that this gets destroyed. By raging flames, if possible."

He turned and walked off, intent on leaving the streets of Black Powder without delay.

CHAPTER TWENTY-FIVE: JOURNAL OF ALWORTH B. NEVINS

Torn from my sleep by the sound of gunfire, I threw off the bedclothes and scrambled to my feet. For a moment, I forgot where I was. Perhaps I even forgot *who* I was, other than a human being in proximity to danger. The gunshots had occurred in rapid succession, four or five in total, before yielding to silence. I stood there for a minute or so, now remembering that I was in a hotel room in the town of Black Powder.

The image of George Gault intruded on my foggy brain. Was he the one responsible for the gunfire I'd just heard? At present, he was for me the symbol of all things dangerous and violent. I crossed the room to the one window, opened it, and leaned out to see if anything was happening in the street.

I was on the second floor, so my view of it all was from above. The street was steadily filling with people, and in their midst lay two unmoving forms — two men, both with shirtfronts blotched by bright-red patches. One of the two had long braids splayed out in the dirt; I believe he was an Indian. Despite my fears, I saw no sign of George Gault. A gray-bearded man seemed central to the activity. Although I couldn't make out all his words, he seemed to have an accent, either Scottish or Irish.

Then I saw none other than Miss Peppers, my acquaintance from earlier, standing central to the activity. She seemed to be intently surveying the two lifeless men, and I heard someone utter the word *undertaker*. The gray-bearded man walked off, and Miss Peppers appeared to take charge of the situation, issuing firm commands as to the handling of the bodies. I understood now her reference to clients who reposed in the churchyard. Her job, it appeared, was to act as conductor for the final journeys of the departed — in this case, from the dirt of the street to the dirt of the grave.

Seeing that the present unpleasantness had no real bearing on me, I withdrew from the window and returned to bed, hoping to gain another hour or two of slumber. As it turned out, I did little more than toss and turn, battered by fractured visions of blood and bullets.

CHAPTER TWENTY-SIX

At first, McNulty couldn't find Quinny. She wasn't there on the rock outcropping where he'd last seen her and seemed to be nowhere in the immediate vicinity. He called her name several times but received no response. He rode a short way ahead, coming up on the other side of the outcropping, and there saw a pair of sprawled legs stretched out from behind a cluster of boulders. He thought he recognized the boots but rode around the boulders to make certain.

Baker lay there slumped against the rocks, his limbs splayed out in all directions. A dark red hole was positioned centrally in the forehead, with thin red rivulets reaching down over the bridge of the nose. The eyes gazed off at nothing at all. The mouth was twisted half open, revealing the gap in the front teeth. McNulty dismounted, drew his pistol, and looked around carefully should whoever had done this still be nearby. After a moment, Quinny appeared from behind the rocks. The look on her face was even more unreadable than usual.

"My God, child." McNulty stepped forward and drew her to his side. "Who shot Baker? I didn't even know he'd returned here."

"I did it," Quinny said flatly.

"You?"

"I did it," she repeated. "I shot him with the little derringer T.C. gave me. Shot him in the head."

McNulty stared incredulously at the girl for several moments before finding his voice. "Why? Why did you do that, Quinny?"

"He showed up and said he was angry at you. He said he wanted to get back at you and was going to do it through me." Quinny looked down at the ground. "He said I wasn't too ugly to spend an hour on."

"Dear Jesus," McNulty muttered.

"He came at me, tried to grab me and push me down." Quinny was speaking dreamily now as if reciting some tale of yore, some legend from a distant land. "He was scarier even than he usually was. I remembered I had that little gun in my pocket. It was loaded, so I pulled it out and pointed at his head. I pulled the trigger."

218

"I see," said McNulty softly.

"I pulled the trigger. And he was dead then. I'm sorry I killed your pardner."

"He wasn't my goddamned pardner." McNulty pulled the girl into an embrace and rested a hand on her head. "I'm so sorry you had to go through that, child. So very sorry. He was a wicked man and deserved his fate."

Tentatively, Quinny returned the embrace. But only for a moment. Then she stepped back and sighed. "I threw the derringer away after. As far as I could. But maybe I should go find it so I can give it back to T.C."

McNulty took a few seconds to respond. "T.C. won't be needing it, lass. He won't be needing anything anymore."

Quinny stared at him, and understanding slowly came to her eyes. "Oh. Then I won't bother to look for it."

"Right. There's no need."

The girl turned away and stood with her back to McNulty for a minute. When she turned back around, he saw that her eyes were not quite dry.

"He saved me," Quinny said quietly. "T.C. did. He gave me that little gun the night before last. If I hadn't had it with me today . . ." She trailed off, then nodded to herself. "Yes, he saved me."

McNulty gestured toward the dead man. "I'd best bury Baker now. I won't bother to plant him too deep, but I'll at least cover him up. Then we can head out."

"I didn't like Baker," Quinny said firmly. "Didn't like him at all. But I didn't like shooting him either."

"Yes, I understand."

"I've decided I don't like being around guns."

"I understand."

McNulty retrieved his shovel from his saddle and began to dig. The girl walked away.

When he was done, McNulty mounted up and went to find Quinny. After searching for several minutes, he caught sight of her, some forty yards away, sitting on the bank of a stream, her pony tied nearby. She had taken out a fishing line and was meditatively moving it through the churning waters. He called her name, and she looked up. She held his gaze for several seconds, then gave a little wave. Seeing how things were, McNulty took a moment to respond, offering his own small wave. Quinny nodded and turned her attention back to the stream.

That was how he left her, there by the

edge of the tumbling waters, alone, calmly fishing.

CHAPTER TWENTY-SEVEN

That morning Viola had rousted her companions with grumbles and blasphemies, insisting they pack up and hit the trail at once. She declared that her sleep had been choppy and filled with nightmares — just as she'd predicted — all on account of their proximity to the graveyard. She'd no wish to spend one more minute sharing ground with the moldering dead.

Major Pompay berated Viola's superstitious soul but complied with her request. As the sun crested the sky, they rode out of Black Powder, headed due north. The plan was to reach the town of Bordeaux well before nightfall and set up for another show.

Their exodus did not go smoothly. A few miles out, the wagon wheel that had given them past problems finally failed them. Pompay hadn't noticed that a crack had expanded drastically — to the point where the wheel actually broke apart.

Just as despair and recriminations were reaching a peak, a pair of bullwhackers had come riding up. They were twin brothers, equally unkempt, who'd just finished escorting a freight wagon and, having been paid off, were bound for Black Powder to pursue base activities. The major, employing his best oration, talked them into continuing into town, purchasing a new wheel, and immediately delivering it back to him. In exchange, he'd add to the men's coffers. The bullwhackers accepted the deal. With enough of Pompay's cash to buy the wheel and his promise of their reward upon returning, the men headed out.

Two hours later, just as Pompay and his companions were thinking they'd been abandoned, the bullwhackers returned, dragging the wheel between their horses. The men said they'd have been back earlier, but they'd arrived in town just in the wake of a bloody gunfight and, of course, such lively entertainment had distracted them. Pompay paid the twins off, offering them extra if they'd do the work of putting the wheel back on, but they declined. They wanted to waste no time in returning to Black Powder to sample more of its wonders.

Now, as the day was sliding past the noon

hour, the major and Viola crouched in the dirt replacing the shattered wheel. Viola seemed to be doing the lion's share of the labor, with Pompay taking on most of the moaning.

"This is not what I was born for," the major complained. "I'm a man of the gentle arts, not a beast of burden."

"Ain't no one would ever accuse you of overstraining yourself," said Viola, positioning the new wheel. "But I guess keeping hard work at bay is how you stay in such tip-top condition."

Pompay cursed and plopped his wide posterior in the dirt. "My knees are giving out."

"So's my patience. C'mon, Major, the sooner you quit grousing, the sooner we'll get this done and be on our way. Or would you prefer to stay here in the middle of nowhere and wait for the buzzards to come feed on you? I figure you'd make a plentiful meal for 'em, a real feast."

Weary of her companions' bickering, Two Robes kept her distance. Tilting her head back, she looked up into the blue, cloud-streaked sky. Despite Viola's warning, no buzzards were in sight. And no eagles. In fact, nothing with wings. Certainly no angels, though her teachers at the white man's school had told her those celestial beings were always up there watching over the affairs of men.

When she asked one of the teachers why angels couldn't be seen, the woman berated her. It was a heathen thing to ask, Two Robes was told. She should simply believe. She remembered thinking at the time, *How can I believe in something if I'm not allowed to ask anything about it?* Fearing a hard smack on the cheek — or worse — Two Robes had held her tongue. Now that she was free of that place, she could choose to believe or not believe in whatever she wished. Maybe someday she would decide to believe in angels, but, for the present, she felt no need to do so.

She looked back at the others who were just finishing up replacing the wheel. What did she feel about them, these odd chattering ramblers? They always seemed to be talking — debating, commenting, prattling on about everything and nothing. What compelled them to do this? Did they find no solace in quiet things? In the patter of creatures moving through high grasses? In the low, lonesome hush of the wind? *The wind.*

In the Lakota tales, the wind spirit was called Tate. He blew across the world connecting the past and the future. If Two Robes was to believe in something in the sky that couldn't be seen, she thought she would prefer Tate over any white angel. The wind was blowing now, though not very strongly. She could feel it on her skin, easy and untroubling. It felt like a prayer.

Viola was laughing at something or other. Probably at her own joke. When she laughed, it sounded like the breaking of crockery dropped on a hard floor. Did Two Robes have affection for this loud, boisterous woman? Well, yes, yes certainly. In the few weeks that Two Robes had been with the troupe, Viola had been nothing but kind to her. But they were clearly opposites in temperament. The Lakota girl was content to go long intervals without expressing her opinion on the world. For Viola Hall, such abstinence would be downright impossible. Painful even.

Regarding the major, Two Robes felt no strong affection. Not that she disdained him, no, nothing as extreme as that. He just struck her as rather absurd . . . and not particularly trustworthy. The man's smiles and florid words lacked sincerity, and much of what he presented as truth seemed suspect. His claim to being an officer in the war was probably a lie. As were the benefits of his elixir. Even his name was not really his own. But, on that point, she couldn't fault him. Though she herself had two other names — the one her people bestowed upon her and the one the whites gave her — she had created a new one for herself, the name Pompay and Viola knew her by. That name alone felt real.

For better or worse, Pompay and Viola were as close to family as Two Robes had in this region, and, up until the last few days, she'd been fairly at ease in their company. But something had changed. She couldn't put her finger on it, but a new feeling of disquiet had been growing in her. It wasn't that she feared some betrayal from either of her companions. Rather it was the fact of them being together, the sum of their parts, that in an indefinable way suggested something dark and impending.

It was a strange, vague notion, and, when it intruded on her, as it did now, she focused on driving it away. At the present moment, she concentrated on the gentle wind caressing her face. It was comforting to think of it blowing across the world, uniting her past and her future. Or, perhaps, erasing the first and ensuring the second.

CHAPTER TWENTY-EIGHT

Like a tot on a seesaw, Gault's state of mind had been teetering back and forth all morning. At present, just past noon, if his mind hadn't exactly found a place of balance, it had at least succumbed to exhaustion.

"Black Powder . . ." Gault muttered as they rode into town. He seemed barely interested in the fact that they'd reached their destination. His companions made inquiries, and Gault was soon delivered to a pox-scarred doctor who berated them for dragging a wounded man around roped up like a stray steer. The doctor told Gault's men to leave him in his care and return in an hour.

Lampo and the others now wandered down the main thoroughfare, discussing their next move.

"We should ask around about Pompay," said the Finn.

"We should ask around about a decent

place to eat," Nash countered. "We never had breakfast, and all the riding and agitation has left my belly churning."

"We're not here for your belly," Lampo said.

The debate continued until Billy Fowler stopped in his tracks and pointed to the ground. "Hell, is that blood?"

The other two paused as well and studied the spot Billy indicated.

"Blood it is," Nash said. "And looks pretty fresh. There's some over there, too. Guess we missed somebody's showdown."

"Was a gunfight!" A scruffy boy of about ten who'd been sitting on the nearby steps of a mercantile jumped up and approached the men, eager to impart his news. "Happened a couple hours ago. Injun killed a white man, and another white man killed the injun."

"You saw it happen?" asked Nash.

"Aw, nope." The boy's disappointment was acute. "Sure wished I had though."

Nash laughed. " 'Course you do. Any boy would. I'll tell you, kid, couple years back I was down in El Paso and got to see Marshal Dallas Stoudenmire kill three men in five seconds. Now *that* was a gunfight. Not to take anything away from your one here, but mine beat all."

"Sounds like it!" The boy's eyes went moon-wide.

Lampo waved a dismissive hand. "Never mind all that, boy. You see folks doing a show here in town?"

"There was one last night, but I didn't get to see it." The boy sounded forlorn. "I miss all the good stuff."

"Know where those show folks are now?" Lampo asked.

"Heard they left town," the boy answered.

Lampo waved his hand again, letting the boy know his presence was no longer required. The Finn had a dangerous look to him, so the child felt it best to make a hasty retreat.

As the boy ran off, Nash called after him, "Hope you get to see a good killing someday, little bit!"

"Leave him be, Nash," said Billy. "He's just a kid."

"Sure, one with a taste for bloodshed. All right, we know now that Pompay's left town. Might as well eat, right?"

"Might as well," Lampo now agreed. Noting a restaurant sign down the street, he started toward it, with Nash trailing.

Billy was turning to follow when, out of the corner of his eye, he glimpsed a horse coming up behind him at a trot. He looked up at the man in the saddle and froze in place. The rider saw him at the same moment and came to a halt.

"Alworth . . ." Billy said under his breath. He looked back and saw that Lampo and Nash had entered the restaurant without waiting for him. Or noticing Alworth Nevins.

Billy hurried to join the Easterner.

Alworth looked down at him. "Didn't know if I'd get to see you again, Billy."

"Jesus, Alworth! If Gault finds out you're here —"

"I thought I'd be gone before you arrived. I didn't think Gault was capable of riding with any speed today."

"We had to tie him to his saddle, but he made it here all right. And he ain't feeling too charitable toward you right about now."

"I suspect not. Where is he?"

"Getting mended up by the local doctor. Look, I don't know what's pushing you on like this, but you're playing a risky game."

"A girl." Alworth said, though he hadn't really meant to.

"A *girl*? What do you mean a girl?"

Alworth looked away. "An Indian girl who's traveling with Pompay. I don't want to see harm come to her."

Billy stared intently. "Bull's balls, greenhorn! It's 'cause you read all them books with romance and adventure in them. It's left you in a foolish state."

Alworth looked back and smiled. "I'm sure you're right, Billy."

Billy shook his head "Don't that beat the devil. Did you see your girl before Pompay's people left town?"

"No, they were gone by the time I arrived."

"If you favor your health, you'd better get going, too. When Gault has it in for someone . . . well, you should just go."

Alworth nodded and touched the brim of his hat. Billy returned the gesture and watched as Alworth rode briskly down the street and out of Black Powder.

The doctor's office was a cramped, cluttered room, all mahogany shelves and glass cabinets, that reeked of various astringents and alkaloids. The first thing Gault asked upon being left there was if the doctor knew anything of Major Pompay. On being told that Pompay had come and gone and was said to be heading north, Gault lapsed into a ruminative silence. While cleaning the gash in Gault's side and applying new bandages, the little doctor chastised him vigorously for having ridden so many miles with a bullet wound gnawing at him.

"By all rights, Miss Peppers should be fitting you for a coffin right now!"

"Who's Miss Peppers?" Under the doctor's ministrations, Gault's mind and body were experiencing a renewed strength. "I don't know any damned Miss Peppers."

"She's our feminine undertaker," said the doctor, tightening the bandage across Gault's ribs. "Lucky thing you haven't keeled over, seeing as she's got two other corpses to attend to this morning. Both killed in a gunfight. A wandering Arapaho and a young stranger, that one white."

"Young stranger?" Gault found himself suddenly thinking of Alworth Nevins. Was there any chance the little fool would have made his way to Black Powder? Why would he do that? Probably no good reason, but, then again, who could predict what an addle-pated tenderfoot like him might do?

"What's that stranger look like?" Gault asked.

The doctor sneered. "Like a young dolt who got himself killed."

"Where are those bodies right now?"

"Over at Miss Peppers' place. Four buildings down on the right. Gray door."

The doctor tossed Gault's shirt back to him. "Interesting old scars you have there

233

on your upper back and neck. Like they were made by a shovel or maybe —"

"A hoe," Gault said quietly.

The doctor *hmmed,* but didn't push the issue.

The dark memory, which Gault always strove to suppress, now pressed in on him with fierce clarity. On that day — long ago but never far away — the beatings from his father, while always brutal and frequent, reached a vicious extreme. For some minor infraction, now lost to memory, his father had cornered him in the barn, picked up an old hoe lying there, and begun striking him without restraint.

Of course, the man had been drinking — that was to be expected — but even the moonshine and his chronic anger couldn't account for the unprecedented violence he now rained down upon his son. When George, barely sixteen, turned to escape, his father struck his fiercest blows, the edge of the tool digging deep into the boy's back and neck. The attack might well have reached a fatal peak had the hoe's handle not snapped. Sated or exhausted by his efforts, old Gault staggered out into the coming twilight, leaving his son bloodied and sobbing in the hay-strewn dirt.

It was Ida who found him there. It was

always she who'd find him after a beating, but she looked particularly distraught when she saw the damage this one had done. Though little more than a child herself, at thirteen she took on the role of consoler, holding him there in the shadows and whispering that everything would be all right, yes, yes, all right.

But he knew at that moment that this could never be so, not as long as he remained there in the sphere of his brutal father and indifferent mother. If not for Ida's comforting heart, he would have right then considered drowning himself in a river or dashing his brains out against a stone. But her words and embrace gave him strength.

He told her then what he needed to do, and she said she understood. After Ida had bandaged him up as best she could, George told her good-bye, stole the family horse, and rode off into the darkness. He would not return till nearly three years later, after he'd learned the cholera had taken both his parents.

"That'll be one dollar for my work." The doctor's voice broke into his memories.

Gault shook himself out of the past "A whole dollar?" He pulled on his shirt. "I had a bullet taken out of my thigh a few years back in Rawlins and only got charged fifty cents. You didn't even have to dig out any lead."

"No, but I just hauled you out of the fangs of death. You were in spitting distance of blood poisoning. Isn't that worth a buck?"

Gault handed over the money. "I'd say it smacks of banditry."

The doctor sat on a stool and began to roll himself a cigarette. "Should've charged you *two* dollars. Total lack of respect for the medical profession."

The door opened, and Lampo entered the cramped space. "You okay, boss?"

"As much as can be expected."

"We found out Pompay left town already."

"Yeah, I heard." Gault pulled on his duster. "The others outside?"

Lampo nodded.

"What've you all been up to?"

"Breakfast. We saved you some bacon."

Gault led the way out. They found Billy and Nash waiting in the street.

"You're looking more fit, Mr. Gault." Billy handed Gault a folded napkin. "Brought you some food."

Gault shoved the bacon into his mouth, wiped his lips, and grunted. "We're riding north."

"You sure you're up for that?" Billy asked.

"I mean, you just got fixed up by the doc. Maybe you should —"

"We're heading north," Gault said again. "But first I want to check on something."

He led the way down the street, stopping at a small gray-doored house. Not bothering to knock, he entered, his men in tow. They were met in the hallway by a tiny woman dressed in black.

"You Miss Peppers?" Gault asked.

The woman straightened her eyeglasses and stared up at him. "Can I help you?"

"I understand you got a couple bodies here. Two men gunshot."

"Yes, I had them brought in an hour ago. You have an interest in them?"

"Maybe."

"Are you perhaps acquainted with one of the deceased?"

"Maybe. I want to set eyes on the white man."

"Well, if you see the one, you'll see the other," said Miss Peppers. "I have them laid out side by side out back. The white and the red. I've never been one for separating the races in death. I figure the Lord sees all souls in the same light. Come along."

She led them to a back room where two bodies lay together, pressed shoulder to shoulder, on a low wooden platform.

"It's to be an exceedingly simple burial," explained the undertaker. "No embalming, no paid mourners, the coffins of the most basic cut . . . That is, unless, sir, you wish to pay for something more respectful."

Gault studied the face of the dead white man, looking displeased. "No, I would not."

"Why are we here, Mr. Gault?" Billy asked.

"I heard some young buck got himself killed. Just wanted to check if it might be Nevins."

Billy looked quickly away; he could easily have told Gault that Alworth wasn't dead.

"Hey, wait now." Nash was leaning over the other corpse. "Blamed if I don't know this one! Sure, ran into him two days back down south, him and a couple of his Arapaho pals. Ornery cuss name of Low Moon. Him and I nearly traded bullets."

"Apparently, he did indeed trade bullets this morning," Miss Peppers said. "That's why he's now in my care. He who lives by the sword, dies by the sword."

Nash grinned. "Beg to differ, ma'am, but I believe it was an Enfield rifle he was pointing at me when we met. If it'd just been a sword, I wouldn't have minded so."

Miss Peppers eyed him coolly. "I'd thank you not to make jokes in my parlor. I keep a somber mien within these walls."

Billy nodded. "That's right, it's never good to be cocky around the dead."

Gault turned away from the bodies. "Thank you, Miss Peppers. We're done here."

The little undertaker made a final plea. "A bit of extra coin can go a long way, you know. Are you certain you don't wish to upgrade the services?"

"Damned certain." Gault led the others back outside.

"We ride now, boss?" Lampo asked.

"We ride. We'll fetch our horses and head out. And this time nobody ties me to my damned saddle."

Gault started up the street. The others followed him, Billy bringing up the rear. As he trailed his companions, the young man's thoughts went to Alworth, sincerely hoping the dang fool had gotten a decent start on them. Gault had looked disappointed when the white corpse turned out not to be Alworth Nevins. Billy guessed Gault wouldn't mind at all seeing Alworth laid out with several bullet holes puncturing his hide. What's more, Gault would no doubt be pleased to make those holes himself, something Billy wouldn't want to see come to pass.

You'd best be galloping right brisk, green-horn. Hell is on your heels.

CHAPTER TWENTY-NINE

Pompay and Viola had just finished replacing the wheel when a rumbling sound made them all look up the trail. Coming toward them, from the direction they'd been heading, was another horse-drawn wagon, a man at the reins and a woman beside him. As it drew closer, the two people became clearly visible. The man, slender with a long nose and curling black mustache, wore a stovepipe hat and blood-red coat. The woman, heavyset with long, tangled black hair, was draped in a voluminous shawl.

"Is that who I think it is?" Viola asked.

"Alas, yes," Pompay said. "The unavoidable Count LeSage. I had hoped not to cross paths ever again."

Two Robes came over to stand beside Viola. "Who's Count LeSage?"

"A charlatan!" Pompay huffed. "A finagler and a slyboots!"

Two Robes whispered to Viola, "Is he sure

he isn't describing himself?"

Viola laughed and whispered back. "You've got a bit of bite to you after all, girlie! You should show it more often."

Pompay was still steaming. "I'd wager he's not even a true count. And if that's an actual French accent, then I'm Napoleon Bonaparte."

Viola again whispered to Two Robes, "One's as much a count as the other's a major."

Pompay twisted around to face the women. "What are you two murmuring about? Sharing secret information or just engaging in hen-ish gossip?"

"We're only discussing the weather," Viola said with a look of innocence. "It's a lovely day, ain't it?"

Pompay snorted and turned back to watch the new wagon, as audaciously painted as his own, pull up alongside him. Two Robes took note of the words on the side: *Count LeSage's Celebrated Traveling Emporium.*

"Major!" The driver grinned and tipped his stovepipe.

"Count!" Pompay grinned and tipped his Panama.

"Delighted to see you again." LeSage's accent was indeed suspect. "It's been too long, *mon ami.* Your absence has been a

242

burden to me."

"Not as burdensome as yours to me, I assure you."

LeSage climbed down from his seat, and the two men shook hands, their disingenuous smiles lingering a few seconds more.

Pompay now addressed the woman in the shawl. "And how is sweet Angie, the Pearl of the Prairie?"

"I'm alive," the woman acknowledged.

"And for that I'm thankful," said LeSage. "My wife keeps me honest."

Viola's guffaw drew the count's attention. "Of course the virtuous Miss Hall is still at your side." LeSage now eyed Two Robes. "And I see your little team has expanded along aboriginal lines. And a comely female she is! An admirable acquisition indeed."

"Best save your admiration for your own wife," Viola suggested. "Wouldn't you agree, Angie?"

Angie grunted.

"Where have your journeys taken you, Count?" Pompay asked.

"Most recently Bordeaux. We made quite an impression up there, I must say."

"What? Bordeaux?" Displeasure was obvious in Pompay's tone. "That's *our* next stop on our tour."

"Then I do hope I've warmed its citizens

up for you. They certainly turned out enthusiastically for my own appearance. My lecture entitled 'The Avoidance of Turpitude' was marvelously well attended. And my newest exhibition drew a teeming mob . . . and earned me rather a nice profit."

"What exhibition?"

"Ah! My dear major, I'd have thought word of my good fortune would have made its way to you. Why, sir, I've come into possession of an artifact of tremendous value and interest."

"You don't say."

"*Mais oui!* Would you like to see it?"

"Are you going to charge me for the privilege?"

"Of course not, Major! Consider it a professional courtesy. Here, I'll get the object."

LeSage went to the back of his enclosed wagon and quickly returned carrying a lacquered box a foot in length. He unhinged it and opened the lid. Inside, on a bed of plush burgundy velvet, rested a polished blue-black revolver. Affixed to the inner lid, a small bronze plaque bore the legend: *The Pistol with which the famed Outlaw Jesse James of Missouri was slain by Robert Ford, April the Third 1882.*

"Jesse's only been in his grave 'bout a year

and a half," Viola noted. "And already you're cashing in on his memory? That irks me, LeSage. I once shared a couple nights with a nomadic cousin of his."

"You must be very proud of that fact," said LeSage with a smirk.

Viola smiled sweetly. "I'm always glad for a brush with fame."

Pompay was still studying the revolver. "This gun here is a Colt Paterson, is it not?"

"You know your firearms, Major," said the count. "Undoubtedly from your illustrious time in uniform."

Pompay ignored the jibe. "From what I heard, the pistol that killed Jesse James was a Smith & Wesson. Not a Colt at all."

"You've been misled, sir."

"I've heard it from several sources."

"Unfortunately, your sources must be misinformed."

"Must they? I suppose so. Because surely you wouldn't stoop to chicanery by trying to palm off a counterfeit article as the genuine one."

"As you say, Major, indeed I would not. Just as you yourself would never so stoop. By the way, do you still have that missing link you used to display? The one that looked oddly like a modified monkey?"

"No, Count, I parted with that some time ago."

"Probably for the best. As I recall, it was beginning to look rather mangy."

The two men stood staring eye to eye, neither blinking, for several long seconds.

Finally, Pompay nodded down at the pistol. "You say you've made some good coin exhibiting that weapon?"

"Can't complain."

The major stroked his double chin. "Would you consider selling it? That is, if someone were interested in it purely for its historical import."

"I would not." LeSage slammed closed the box. "*Mes pardons.* At this point, it has too much sentimental value."

Viola let out a laugh. "Sure, Count. Outlaw-killing six-shooters are just *dripping* with sentimentality."

"Still the inveterate wag, aren't you, Miss Hall?" LeSage returned the box to the back of his wagon.

"Can we go now?" Angie, still seated, barked at her husband. "Or do you have more shit to spill?"

Viola laughed again and gave the other woman a little salute. "I've always liked you, Angie!"

"We'll journey on soon enough, *ma ché-*

rie," LeSage told his wife before turning to Pompay. "What say you, Major? A little game of skunk throw before we part ways?"

"I wouldn't balk at the suggestion."

"Then let's fetch our pieces."

The major and the count left the women to go rummaging through their respective wagons.

Two Robes looked perplexed. "I don't understand. Are those two friends or enemies?"

"They sure ain't friends," said Viola. "And they don't do too good a job at being enemies neither."

"What's skunk throw?"

"A game those two came up with," Viola answered.

"A damned stupid game," Angie put in.

"How's it played?" Two Robes asked.

"No one knows," said Viola. "Not even those two, I think."

Almost simultaneously, the two men returned, each holding a cloth sack. They then seated themselves on the ground — Pompay with some effort — facing each other. After exchanging a brief nod, each dumped the contents of his sack into the space between them.

"Bones," Two Robes identified the objects. "Lots of little bones."

"Skunk bones to be specific," Viola explained.

Pompay's were dyed green; LeSage's, red. Each of the sets contained a small dyed skull. In anticipation of spirited play, Pompay removed his Panama hat and set it beside him. LeSage did likewise with his stovepipe. Without further ceremony, the two men began an elaborate and incomprehensible series of moves, sometimes resembling checkers, sometimes backgammon.

Most often, though, to the women observing, the moves seemed totally arbitrary. Every once in a while, one player or the other would swear and pass a greenback to the other. Clearly, betting was an aspect of the game. The contest had gone on for over half an hour (accompanied by Viola and Angie's demands to finish up) when the count made a move that the major felt compelled to challenge.

"Hold on now!" Pompay cried out. "You just flipped a hip bone."

"Yes, what of it?" LeSage responded.

"You can't do that, damn it!"

"Oh, can't I?" The count gave his mustache a twirl. "I'm pretty damn sure I just did."

The facade of civility had apparently been dispensed with by both parties. What's more, LeSage's accent now suggested less of Parisian boulevards and more of Kansas cornfields.

"Two moves ago, you hopped a hip bone with a thigh bone," Pompay insisted. "You know you can't flip a hip after you've just hopped over one. Not when your skull's already been spun."

"Your eyesight must be failing," LeSage countered. "That was *not* a hip I hopped with my thigh. That was a shoulder bone."

Pompay's face grew red. "*My* eyesight! *My* eyesight, you say! It's your own eyesight that needs examining. Or, more likely, your conscience. You know damned well you hopped a hip."

"Attack my conscience, will you? Where was yours five minutes ago when you tried to go triple-up with your tail-tip?"

"That was an honest mistake."

"*Honest?* Ha! The only thing honest about you, Pompay, is your honest need for a thrashing. Maybe then you wouldn't be such a raging lout."

"You go to hell, LeSage!"

"Meet me there, you unsavory hog!"

That did it. The game promptly gave way to a fervent but unskilled wrestling match. The two combatants, clumsily interlocked, rolled madly through the dirt, disarranging the skunk bones and themselves in the process. Two notable casualties were the men's hats. The count's stovepipe was thoroughly bashed in, and the major's new Panama, like its predecessor, was crushed beyond salvage. In the heat of battle, Le-Sage fully abandoned his French accent, and both men traded their mock eloquence for the ugliest curses they could summon.

Before the engagement could end in blood, Viola began kicking, not much minding which of the men she contacted with. "Break it up, you imbeciles! You're gonna slaughter each other!"

At some point, Angie had left her seat and hurried to the back of her wagon. Returning with a long, sturdy broom, she wasted no time in swinging it with great gusto. Like Viola, she made no distinction between one gladiator and the other in dispensing her blows. Between Viola's kicks and Angie's beating, the men seemed to become aware of the ladies' displeasure. They at last separated, transferring their curses from each other to the women.

For her part, Two Robes had watched it all — from the unfathomable game through the absurd fight — in silent awe. Done with this foolishness, she now climbed into the back of her wagon and sighed deeply. She didn't know to what to attribute the lunacy she had just witnessed: the inclinations of white men, the unsavoriness of these two particular men's professions, or the overall nature of the male species. She shook her head and smoothed out her calico dress, noticing once more the tear there. It still needed mending.

Their battle ended, Pompay and LeSage stumbled to their feet and brushed themselves off with unconvincing dignity. After glancing at the ruins of their headwear, they groaned, and climbed into the seats of their respective wagons. Neither had bothered to round up his skunk bones.

Viola extended her hand to Angie. "Nice separating numbskulls with you."

Angie tossed her broom back in the wagon and accepted the handshake. "Likewise."

The two amazons took their places beside the men. Without exchanging another look, Pompay and LeSage each shouted at his team of horses and set his wagon in motion. The two parties rolled off in opposite directions.

Viola laid the shotgun across her lap. Ever since Nash had deserted, she'd taken to keeping the gun at hand. Now she gave the barrel a little pat.

"If Angie's broom hadn't worked, my next

251

move was to grab the ol' man-tamer here."

"I'm in no mood for your tomfoolery."

"Who's fooling, Major? You don't know how close you came to getting your britches full of buckshot. You wouldn't have sat down for a month."

"You think you're quite the wit, don't you?" Pompay scowled and gave the reins a shake. "Oh, so quick with the repartee."

Viola burst out laughing. "Hell! I don't know what *repartee* is, but it sounds mighty racy. Most likely I've had a go at it in my time. Quick or otherwise!"

CHAPTER THIRTY

As he rode on, McNulty fixed his memory on the face of Viola Hall, framed by its cascade of blond curls. Had he been asked a week ago whether or not Viola's face possessed beauty, he'd have been hard pressed to answer. But, since the dreams had come, it was as if the visage of Helen of Troy floated before him. Though fully aware of the absurdity of the notion, he couldn't manage to shake it. Nor did he really wish to.

He had found himself on a quest, such as described in the knightly tales of Mallory he'd read as a boy. If he remembered the accounts correctly, some of those journeyers found what they sought while others never did. Galahad had achieved the grail, while proud Lancelot, due to his transgressions, ultimately failed. What was to be his own lot?

If the men he'd often mixed with had been

party to these musings, they'd have ridiculed him without mercy. Perhaps not to his face, but certainly behind his back. Frank Baker, though, would have had no hesitation about expressing his disdain. But Baker's disdain and malice were no longer part of the world.

Not for the first time, McNulty reflected on the hard fact that while this morning he'd led a band of four, now he alone pursued the trail north. He'd lost many comrades in his time — to violent death or capture or other circumstances — but few he truly missed. T.C. and Quinny he would miss.

He pushed those thoughts away and returned to Viola. How many times had he shared her bed? Well, not *her* bed, but one of those in the Lowfield sporting house where she worked. Perhaps four times? Or five? Certainly no more than that. Not enough to explain the mighty impulse now propelling him forward. Having lived six decades, he couldn't justify his actions like some romantic schoolboy might. No, he was weathered and worn and, as such, should be beyond the folly of romance. And yet here he was.

So, was it four or five? He counted off the times and in doing so discovered that he could chart their relationship through the ways she had addressed him. The first time Viola hadn't called him anything; he was one of a thousand rovers whose names weren't worth knowing. The second time, upon learning his surname, she had called him McNulty. The third time it was John. After that, it was Johnny, but interspersed with *lambkin.*

Of course, it wasn't rare for hired women to toss off terms of affection as tools of their trade. Casual *dear*s or *honey*s were easy investments that could ensure repeat customers. But this seemed to be something else. He remembered his discomfort the first time Viola called him *lambkin.* The word, with its suggestion of childlike purity and innocence, struck him as foolish and unsuitable. At best it was inaccurate; at worst, a blasphemy. He was a fornicator, an inveterate thief, and a killer of his fellow man. His soul, demonstrably impure, was surely beyond the grace of God. And yet . . .

When she bestowed the name upon him — not the first time, but after that — he received it as a sort of blessing. Lying there in their nakedness, after passion, with their arms around each other (in a way uncommon to the customary exchange), they spoke of many things, meaningful and meaningless, and she called him lambkin, and he, indeed, felt as if he might be clean and innocent. The dark truth that he was an outlaw and she a whore was momentarily kept at bay. He was allowed the illusion that they were simply man and woman, their flesh intertwined and their stories shared. Perhaps Viola bought into the illusion, as well. He thought maybe she did, for he suspected she was capable of such a belief. She was younger than he, by fifteen years or more, and, though the coarseness of her life had no doubt marred her, something bright and buoyant still shone in her eyes.

And she was capable of song. Not their first time together, but possibly the second, she had sung to him. For all her rascality and coarseness, her voice was surprisingly sweet. She offered him a ballad or two, then a song of her own creation. As he recalled, it had something to do with lonesome lilacs floating in the wind. The lyrics were rather pretty, and the melody, though a bit warbly, had a haunting quality. He'd been surprised to hear such a delicate tune issue from lips so given to vulgarity and cutting jests. Perhaps there was more to this woman-for-pay than met the eye.

Up until now, McNulty had dwelt little on all this. The visits to Lowfield and the cathouse there had all occurred in somewhat of a cluster, over perhaps an eighteen-month period, and none in nearly three years. If pressed, he would have acknowledged that he'd been particularly drawn to Viola's company, but it wasn't unusual for customers to have preferred girls. He hadn't given more weight to his preference than that or, rather, hadn't given himself permission to consider anything deeper.

As it turned out, the rounds of his illicit work had kept him from Lowfield, and so he'd banished thoughts of Viola. In his hazardous profession, it was best to keep one's mind on the task at hand and not get distracted by things of the past. But now the dreams had come. The dreams and the lunacy and the quest. Galahad or Lancelot, he would ride on, ride north, and see what awaited him.

He hadn't been too long on the trail when he saw a rider coming up on his left at a steady pace. About ten yards out, the man drew up his horse, and McNulty did the same. They sat facing each other.

The man studied McNulty for a moment or two, then said, "I know you."

McNulty appraised the rider. Young, not far into his twenties. Dressed in the garb of a ranch hand but somehow not fitting the mold. The tan Boss of the Plains hat seemed too clean, too crisp. There was nothing in the youth's appearance to suggest hardness or experience. And yet, the revolver on his hip, a serious-looking Remington '75, had to be considered. Though the young man hadn't the cut of a seasoned bounty hunter, that didn't mean he wasn't trying his hand at the enterprise. McNulty had known several yearlings who thought they'd toughen themselves and show their sand by drawing on better men. Was this one of that type?

"I know you." The youth said it again, this time adding, "I recognize you from back in Black Powder."

Although McNulty hadn't noticed any of his wanted posters back in town, that didn't mean they weren't there. He slid his hand smoothly to the ivory grip of his Starr revolver. *All right, boyo, if you do intend to show your mettle, then proceed.*

The youth caught the motion, as subtle as it was, and his hand moved to his own pistol, not smoothly but with haste. His eyes grew wide, and his mouth tightened.

McNulty gauged the situation. "It seems we've found ourselves at a somber moment. Two strangers meeting in a place of solitude, both wondering what will happen next."

He saw the youth's fingers twitch, the ones

wrapped around the Remington.

McNulty continued, speaking evenly, almost melodically. "Tell me, young sir, have you ever actually shot a man face to face? That is, have you locked eyes with an opponent, as you and I do now, and discharged your weapon with calm and calculation? I ask because not everyone is equipped for such a deed. As for myself, I know from experience that I am indeed equipped for such cool violence."

The youth stiffened in the saddle and tightened his grip on his pistol. "I'm not seeking trouble."

"Sometimes trouble seeks out the man," said McNulty. "Not the other way round. The point of my words, young man, is to tell you that when I face down an adversary, I can see his fate in his eyes. Perhaps that ability comes from my Celtic blood . . ."

"If you're intending to shoot me, mister, you should know this . . ." The youth's voice had a tremor to it. "I won't go down without a fight. Chances are you'll win the day, but you never know. I might get off a lucky shot."

"You might. But, then again, you might never get the chance to raise your weapon."

The youth, a look in his eyes of panic more than resolve, yanked free his pistol.

McNulty had not expected such rashness — or quickness. His own gun cleared the holster just as the youth squeezed the trigger.

A metallic click signaled a misfire.

Shock and dismay showed on the youth's face, and he stared at his pistol with a look of betrayal. Shifting his gaze back to McNulty, he saw the barrel of the older man's gun pointed at his chest.

"That was foolish," said the Irishman. "Foolish and nearly fatal for you. Now toss aside your weapon."

McNulty kept his pistol trained on the youth, even after he complied.

"Very good. Now who are you?"

The young man gulped. "My name's Alworth Nevins."

"And a fine name it is," said McNulty calmly. "It'd be a shame to see it on a tombstone, you being of so tender an age. Thought you'd get the drop on me, aye?"

"No . . . I mean I . . ."

"You damned near did, lad. The thing is, I seem to have grand luck with misfiring guns. I've escaped tragedy more than once in such situations. Guess you won't be collecting any reward on these old bones."

"Reward? I don't know what you mean."

"Oh, come now. You said you knew me.

You no doubt figured you'd reel me in and earn a sizable bounty."

"I swear to you, mister, I've no idea who you are. I just noticed you back in town after that gunfight. You were talking to Miss Peppers. I recognized you from there, that's all. I was just riding up now to ask if you'd come across the people I'm looking for."

"Do you have any more firearms hidden on your person?"

"No, sir."

"I imagine you don't." McNulty holstered his revolver. "You don't seem like the kind who would. So who are you looking for?"

Alworth exhaled. "A group of traveling players."

"Players?" McNulty narrowed his eyes. "Performers you mean?"

"That's right. They're led by a man called Pompay. And there's a Lakota girl . . ."

"What about a blond woman in her forties? She sings songs. Name of Viola."

"Why, yes, there was someone like that. And I do believe Viola was her name."

"I'm seeking them as well. I need you to tell me why you're on their trail."

Alworth was suddenly bold. "Only if you tell me first. If you mean any harm to those people . . ."

"Quite the opposite, lad. Let's share

261

information, shall we? It may be to our mutual benefit."

They spent the next few minutes exchanging what they knew about Pompay's group. In McNulty's case, he had little to offer other than the fact that Viola seemed to be one of their number. While he touched on his desire to reunite with her, he didn't give voice to his full ardor, which seemed too much to share with this stranger.

He did ask Alworth what he remembered of Viola's performance. The youth recalled that she sang several songs including one rather bawdy one admonishing "naughty, naughty men," accompanied by winks and wiggles. McNulty smiled to hear this. Alworth, for his part, told of his experiences over the last couple of days, including joining his employer's blood hunt and his subsequent desertion. Like McNulty, he held back on sharing the full depth of his feelings toward the woman he sought, only saying he wished to spare Two Robes from harm.

McNulty took in Alworth's account. "So this man of yours, George Gault, believes Pompay's band is responsible for his kinswoman's death. And he aims to hold them accountable."

"Yes. And Gault is a violent man."

McNulty nodded. "So it seems. I've known violent men. I know what they're capable of."

"Perhaps because you're one of them?" Alworth surprised himself with his nerve. "I'm recalling now that I saw a poster two days ago about an Irish outlaw who wears a Van Dyke beard."

McNulty smiled faintly and gave his beard a little stroke. "Is that so?"

"I believe the man is wanted for murder, among other crimes. I don't remember the man's name."

"McNulty. John McNulty." The outlaw rested his hands on his saddle horn. "It's somewhat well known in these environs. Hear me out, Alworth. We could easily part ways now. If so inclined, you could always gather up a posse and hunt me down later to earn the bounty. Or we could throw our lots in together for the time being. Yes, I'm a man of many sins, but, at present, we seem to have a shared goal in finding Pompay's troupe before this Gault does."

"True."

"It may well be the will of Providence that we've encountered each other. And that your pistol misfired."

McNulty dismounted and picked up Alworth's revolver from the ground. He felt its weight, eyed the barrel, swung open the cylinder, and checked the weapon over before handing it back up to its owner.

"Seems to be in good working order, Alworth. Misfires just happen sometimes. I must say, I didn't expect you to be as swift on the draw as you were."

Alworth reholstered the pistol. "I've practiced some."

"I can't recall ever being outdrawn before. Which concerns me. Perhaps the onslaught of time is gaining on me." McNulty remounted and considered his companion. "So, what do you say? Shall we blend our paths?"

Alworth took a moment to answer. "For the time being."

McNulty nodded. "Understood. You needn't pledge yourself to the devil indefinitely, only for the present. Your soul is still your own."

CHAPTER THIRTY-ONE

Realizing he'd left his hat back at the doctor's office, Gault told his men to wait at the livery while he went to retrieve it. He declined Lampo's offer to fetch it for him. Although he didn't say so, Gault wanted to be alone with his pain.

As he made his way back down the street, he gave himself over to the throbbing in his right side. It washed over him, coating his flesh and radiating outward from his ribs. Still, the doctor seemed to have known his business, and, for the first time since he'd been shot, Gault felt reasonably assured his wound would not kill him. He understood that earlier this morning his mind had fled, and he felt angry and shamed by the fact. It was bad enough that his strength had given out without having to worry about what mad garblings had fallen from his lips.

He thought he remembered babbling to someone about Ida's kaleidoscope, and he hated himself for doing so. The searing hurt of a bullet wound he could accept, could comprehend, but not the disarray of his mind and the corruption of his thoughts. George Gault was not built for crazed whimsy. No, he was a man of calculation and iron-willed intent. The pain in his side was comforting because it *was* pain, and pain was something he could understand and hold close. A disloyal brain was something else entirely. A thing to be desperately feared.

When he reached the doctor's office, Gault found his hat there but not the doctor, satisfying him all around. He had no desire to encounter the pockmarked little sawbones again. A goddamned dollar for his time. For that amount, the bastard should have added in a haircut and shave. Gault had barely left the office and started back up the street when he heard his name being called from behind.

Specifically, he heard the summons, "Wait, Cousin George!" Turning, he saw Elizabeth coming toward him, flanked by her brother, Tom, and Saturn. It took Gault several seconds to absorb the reality of the sight.

"What the hell?" he said in a near whisper as the three newcomers formed a half circle around him.

"Saturn told us you'd been shot," Elizabeth said. "How are you?"

Gault ignored the question. "What the hell are you doing here, Elizabeth? And Saturn . . ." He eyed the cowhand. "Didn't I send you back to the ranch?"

"I was heading there," Saturn said. "But then I ran into Miss Elizabeth and Tom. They were seeking you out, and it didn't feel right to let them go it alone."

Gault returned his gaze to Elizabeth. "What were you thinking, coming all this way? What'd you have to say to me that was so damned important it couldn't wait till I got back?"

"It's not what *I* have to say to you, it's what Tom does." Elizabeth nodded at her brother, standing to her left. "Go on, Tom. Say your piece like we discussed."

The boy cast down his eyes and ran a boot tip through the dust of the street. He blinked and gulped.

"Tom!" His sister squeezed his shoulder. "This is what we came for, isn't it? Why we rode all the way here?"

"Yeah, Lizbeth." Tom's voice was barely audible.

"Then tell him."

"Tell me what, boy?" Gault's tone was harsh. "Don't stand there wasting my time."

267

"The kid's nervous," Saturn said. "He just needs to —"

"Goddamn it, Tom!" Gault took a step forward and lifted the boy's chin, meeting his eyes. "Spill it!"

Tom's words came out in a rush. "I drank it, Cousin George! It was me! Not Mama, it was me! I'm sorry — real, real sorry! I swear to God!"

Gault's face twisted in confusion. "Drank it? What do you —"

"The stuff in the blue bottle."

"The elixir? You drank some of the elixir?"

"Not just some," Elizabeth added. "He drank half the bottle. The portion that was missing. My mother never touched a drop. Tell him, Tom. Tell him it all."

Gault released the boy and took a step back. "Tell it."

Tom drew in a deep, trembling breath. "At the show that night, I heard some cowboy say the stuff was probably just trumped-up liquor. So, after we got home and Mama and Lizbeth had gone to sleep, I snuck over and took the bottle off Mama's bed table. Then I went outside and took to tasting it. More than tasting it really. I meant to have just a sip or two, but I guess I got carried away. Drank a bunch of it and got all dizzy. I went back inside, put the bottle on the table again, and pretty much passed out. I wasn't thinking straight, or I would've known that everyone would see half the bottle was gone."

"Understand, Cousin George?" Elizabeth said. "Mama never drank any."

"How do you know for certain?" Gault asked. "She might've had some beside what the boy downed. Either before or after he had his share."

Tom shook his head. "No, I know for a fact she didn't. The bottle was full to start. And the cork was in real deep when I snuck the bottle away. Took me awhile to pull it free. Then after I was done drinking, I made sure the cork was in real deep again, so no one would guess I'd been tampering. Even banged it some with a stone. In the morning it was just like I left it."

Gault scowled. "You took the trouble to do all that but didn't bother with the fact you left the bottle half empty?"

Tom cast his eyes down again and resumed kicking at the dirt. "Like I say, I wasn't thinking straight."

Elizabeth took on the narrative. "In the morning I was so shocked and preoccupied, finding Mama the way she was, I didn't take notice of how peaked Tom looked. Or, if I did, I just assumed it was due to Mama's death. The point is, no one drank from the elixir but Tom. I brought him all this way because I felt he should be the one to tell you the truth. Now that you know, there's no need for you to keep chasing after those actors."

Gault stood there for several moments staring off without focus. Finally, he cleared his throat and spoke. "Nothing's changed."

Elizabeth's gave a little start. "What do you mean nothing's changed? You just heard it was all a horrible misunderstanding. The elixir didn't poison anybody. Tom's a testimony to that. And we just told you, Mama never even had a taste of it."

"Then why did she die?" Gault demanded. "She wasn't but forty-six and sound. You said she just woke up hacking and right off upped and died. Makes no damned sense."

"Sometimes things like that happen," Elizabeth said softly. "They happen, and they're terrible, and we don't know why they occurred. It's just part of being human."

"Are you lecturing me, girl?" Gault snapped. "I don't need your view on life and death! You should have tossed all that foolishness into the grave with Ida. Let it rot with her bones."

"Boss!" Saturn looked pained. "You don't want to be saying things you'll be sorry for."

"I ain't never been sorry in my life. I didn't get to be where I am now by harboring doubts. A man does what he does and pushes on."

"Maybe, but this clearly isn't the time to push on." Elizabeth locked eyes with her cousin. "There's no longer a reason for you to hunt down those people — if there ever was. It's time for you to gather your men and head home."

Gault's face darkened. "You do *not* tell me what it's time to do! I'm going to follow through with what I began. By God, this is my chance to do right by Ida."

Elizabeth let out an incredulous laugh. "Do you even hear what you're saying? It makes no sense. No sense at all. Do you mean that, after what we just told you, you still —"

"I'm done talking with you, girl." Gault turned to the other man. "Saturn, if you were fit enough to ride all the way here, you're fit enough to join back up with me. Go get your horse. We're heading north where Pompay's bound for."

"Now look here, boss," Saturn said. "Like Miss Elizabeth laid out, there ain't no reason for you to keep on with all this. Let's go round up the other fellas, and we can all ride on home together."

"I told you I'm heading north." Gault paused and smoothed his mustache. "All right, all right. If you want to accompany Elizabeth back home so no harm befalls her and the boy, I'll let you do it. But I'm keeping on."

Saturn clicked his tongue. "Mr. Gault, I gotta say, you don't look right. Or for that matter, sound right. I'm thinking getting shot has taken a toll on you. Lord knows, getting shot my own self has been vexing. We all know now those actor folks didn't do harm to Miss Ida, so why don't we all just head on home?"

"I told you that you can take Elizabeth back," Gault said. "Me, I'm not done with things."

Gault turned and started to walk away.

Elizabeth threw up her hands. "Saturn! Has he lost his mind?"

Saturn stepped forward and caught Gault by the arm. "Boss, I don't believe you're thinking straight. Now, why don't we just —"

Gault spun about and drove his right fist into Saturn's jaw, dropping him to the ground. Elizabeth gasped, and Tom looked away. Gault stood there wincing and gripping his side, his wound asserting itself. A strange mix of defiance and regret came over his face, as he looked down at the sprawled man.

"I took no pleasure in that, Saturn," Gault said quietly, then turned and continued up the street.

A few townspeople standing off to the side had witnessed this exchange. Elizabeth heard one say to his companions, "It's barely afternoon, and already we got two shootings and one punching. It's looking to be a lively day!"

Elizabeth helped Saturn to his feet. He gingerly touched his injured shoulder and grimaced.

Elizabeth handed Saturn his fallen hat. "He shouldn't have struck you."

"There's a lot of things your cousin shouldn't have done, Miss Elizabeth. And probably a lot of such things ahead of him."

"I don't understand him at all. Why would he keep on like this?"

"A man of his cut can't be easily understood." Saturn tugged his hat down over his forehead. "I guess there's a fire in him, a wretched blaze, that just goads him on. Even when there's no sense to it, it goads him on."

CHAPTER THIRTY-TWO: JOURNAL OF ALWORTH B. NEVINS

If I have indeed made a deal with the devil, I pray it's a worthwhile one. Partnering with a man of John McNulty's experience — unlawful and immoral as his experience might be — would seem to better my chances should I need to face down George Gault.

Though being shot at by the vengeful Deputy Oakes two days back was distressing, it wasn't at close range, so nowhere as chilling as my meeting with McNulty. Staring into the barrel of the Irish outlaw's gun made me acutely aware of my limitations, of my failings. I've never felt so close to death, and my dread was overwhelming. Though, to be fair to myself, I wasn't fully overwhelmed, was I? For didn't I rise to the occasion and draw my Remington in defense of my life? Of course, my pistol failed, and only McNulty's restraint saved me from the grave, but still, I made an effort.

It seems to have become my lot to align myself with men of dark design. Gault, Lampo, Nash, and now McNulty . . . All men for whom violence is as natural as breathing. By the end of this interlude, will I become like them? A spiller of blood? A killer? Marcus Aurelius, that ancient ponderer, wrote: *Accept the things to which fate binds you, and love the people with whom fate connects you.* Should I take his advice and embrace these rough companions and fierce outcomes, all in the service of some metaphysical balance? Damned if I know. Having taken one class in Stoicism doesn't make me a philosopher. Best not to dwell on such things. Best just to ride on and see where the trail takes me.

As we rode side by side, McNulty attempted to draw me out, asking about my background and experiences. Though I felt I should ignore the entreaties of this wrongdoer, my resistance soon weakened, and I fell into conversation.

On hearing that I'd attended Yale, McNulty brightened. "Ah! An educated man. I admire you, Alworth. My own education has been piecemeal at best. A few years in the hedge schools — illegal under English law — and whatever books I could lay my hands on for my own edification."

"You sound learned enough," I offered.

"That's a bit of trickery on my part. To be sure, I've acquired a fair number of fine words and phrases and know how to wield them. But, overturn the rock, so to speak, and you'll find nothing but the crude son of a peasant farmer and a dairymaid."

"Well, you fooled me."

"As was my intent. But tell me more of this Two Robes. Obviously she's made an impression on you."

After a moment's hesitation, I began to speak of the Lakota girl. At first, I only touched on her appearance and her knowledge of Shakespeare, but before long I'm afraid I started to wax poetic, fully divulging my feelings toward her. I went on and on about my belief that she and I were kindred spirits and that we might understand each other if given the chance to commune. McNulty listened patiently until I sputtered out, suddenly self-conscious of my ramblings.

He looked over at me, a smile on his lips. "You trumpet your affection quite loudly, my young friend."

My face reddened. "I may have overstated things."

"I think not. Tell me, Alworth, do you believe in destiny?"

"I don't know."

"An honest answer. I don't know myself, but, when something resembling destiny beckons, I try to follow. Such as I'm doing now."

He then spoke at some length about Miss Viola Hall, apparently a woman of ill repute, but also the object of his infatuation. And he shared with me the dreams that led him in pursuit of her. He explained that, despite the gray of his beard, he was feeling a surge of youthful exhilaration such as he hadn't felt in a long time.

Returning to the topic of destiny, McNulty said, "It strikes me as no coincidence that you and I, seekers of our respective Guineveres, should find our paths crossing like this. If men are indeed destined in their lives, this would appear to be sound evidence of that. Do you agree?"

"It *is* curious," I admitted. "But, as for it being destiny, I can't really say. It's fortunate maybe. Yes, I can agree to that."

"Fortune, destiny, the whim of the universe . . . Whatever the scheme may be, we can merely gird our loins and press on."

And so we did, the Western outlaw and the Eastern tenderfoot. Before long, we received confirmation that we were on the right path. At first we thought that our objective was coming to meet us directly for, from a distance, we spied a colorfully painted wagon rolling our way. Only when it got closer did we see that the name on the side wasn't Major Pompay, but Count LeSage. A skinny man was at the reins, a bulky woman beside him, neither looking particularly amicable. When we inquired as to whether or not they'd encountered Pompay's wagon, the woman snickered, and the man huffed. Further pressed, the man tersely conceded that, if we continued on as we were, we should come upon Pompay within a few miles.

Quickening our pace, McNulty and I rode onward. It was somewhat past one in the afternoon when we found whom we were seeking.

CHAPTER THIRTY-THREE

It was Two Robes who saw them first. Sitting in the back of the wagon with her legs dangling, she noticed the pair of riders coming up behind her at a gallop.

She leaned out and called to Pompay and Viola up front. "There are two riders moving up on us."

Pompay called back. "Is it those bullwhackers returning?"

"No. Someone different. I don't recognize them. They're coming fast."

Pompay leaned out himself and looked behind. "I don't recognize them either."

"At the pace we're going, we won't outrun them," Viola reasoned. "We'd better halt up, Major, and see what they want."

Pompay pulled up the horses, and all three of the wagon's occupants climbed down, Viola still gripping her shotgun.

"They're making haste," Pompay noted. "I hope their intents are honorable."

Viola tightened her grip on the gun. "Well, if they ain't, then — Wait! My God, I know one of them, the bearded one."

"Is he a peaceable man?" the major asked.

"I wouldn't go so far as that," Viola answered. "That's John McNulty."

"*Bloodless* John McNulty?" Pompay's eyes widened. "The outlaw chieftain?"

"That's a gaudy way to put it but, yeah, that's the one."

The two riders soon drew up beside the wagon and dismounted.

"Johnny . . ." Viola lowered the shotgun, and her voice took on an uncharacteristic softness. "Criminy, I didn't think we'd ever cross paths again, it's been so long. What are you doing here?"

McNulty smiled gently. "Ah, Viola, there are no simple answers to your question. But there *is* an urgent one. I think my friend Alworth here is the man to explain."

Alworth had been staring intently at Two Robes, overcome by the fact that he now stood in close proximity to her. The infatuation was one sided: Two Robes didn't seem to take notice of him in the least.

"Alworth?" McNulty rested a hand on the younger man's shoulder. "Tell them of your man Gault."

Alworth shook himself out of his stupor

280

and offered a concise account of George Gault's motivations and dark intent. He did his best to describe Gault's character and to caution why such a man should not be taken lightly, even when hampered by a bad wound. Omitted were his own reasons for coming to warn the performers, other than to say he feared what Gault might do upon finding them.

Pompay immediately began protesting. "You say I'm being accused of poisoning the man's relative? That my fortifying elixir is responsible for her death? Preposterous! Why, I've often sampled the potion myself."

"Sampled?" Viola snorted. "Hell, Major, I've seen you obliterate a whole bottle if there was no whiskey at hand."

Pompay puffed up his chest. "An exaggeration, but the point is that I've often drunk the elixir — as have countless of my customers — to no ill effect. This Gault fellow is woefully mistaken in his claims."

"Be that as it may," replied Alworth, "he thinks he's in the right. And, that's all George Gault needs to make him dangerous. He and his companions arrived in Black Powder just as I was leaving. He would have found out you all left there this morning. Likely, he decided to keep following you, just as McNulty and I did, which means he may not be far behind us."

"We shouldn't tarry here," said McNulty. "Alworth and I will accompany you. To ensure your safety, you understand."

Pompay looked unsettled. "I don't like the sound of this. We're just trying to follow our performance circuit. Bordeaux is our next stop."

"We can continue in that direction," McNulty said. "But perhaps we'll veer off a bit in hopes of throwing Gault off."

"But what if he catches up with us?" Pompay asked. "What if we're not able to avoid him?"

"The truth is, from what Alworth has shared, I don't think Gault is a man who can ultimately *be* avoided. No, in the end, it's quite possible he must be confronted."

The major gulped. "This is all very troubling. My horses are little more than old nags. They can't be depended on to travel at any great speed."

"Then we'd best be on our way," said McNulty

Pompay returned to the wagon seat, and Two Robes took her place again in the back. Alworth started toward his horse, but McNulty caught him by the elbow and drew him aside.

"Do me a favor, will you, lad?" said the

Irishman. "Let Viola here ride your mare for a spell so she and I can have a personal chat. You can squeeze yourself into the back of the wagon with Miss Two Robes. I'd wager you wouldn't mind such an arrangement, aye?"

Alworth responded with a gape. "I don't know . . . uh, that is, I . . ."

"You *what,* son? Are you saying you're delighted by the prospect of spending time with your young lady? Yes, I thought that might be the case. Oh, Viola! Come join me, won't you?"

Arrangements were made. Alworth, somewhat apologetically, took his place in the back of the wagon as Two Robes eyed him suspiciously. Viola climbed astride Steadfast and was soon riding beside McNulty, trailing the wagon at such a distance that their conversation was theirs alone.

"I don't mind riding your friend's horse," Viola said. "But you didn't think to just toss me behind you on your own steed?"

McNulty noted the touch of coyness in her tone. "I didn't wish to be too bold, Viola, seeing as we haven't seen each other for such a while. Besides, I knew you were at ease on horseback. I recall you once telling me how, as a young lass, you locked a foul-hearted farmer in his barn and took his workhorse for an afternoon's jaunt."

Viola laughed. "You remember that, do you?"

"I remember many of your tales."

"Yeah? Then I hope some of them were true."

"In one way or another, I'm sure they were."

Viola studied him for a moment. "Fess up, Johnny, why have you tracked me down like this?"

After some hesitation, McNulty told her about his dreams.

"You came looking for me just because of dreams?" There was awe in Viola's voice. "Because my face popped up when you were sleeping?"

"Dreams have power," said the Irishman. "Your face appeared to me right at the time when you might be in danger. Is that just by chance? I think not. Somewhere in the Bible it says our dreams come to us as visions in the night, bearing heavenly instructions. It's the Book of Job, I believe."

"You know your Bible."

"I know fragments of it. Just as I know fragments of countless other books and things I've encountered. That's what my life amounts to, I'm afraid. Fragments of the world, but nothing whole and complete."

"Were you thinking that maybe . . ." Viola's words trailed off and she looked away.

"Yes?"

"Were you thinking that maybe meeting up with me again would . . . oh, I don't know, help make things whole?"

"I think maybe I was," McNulty said softly.

"Aw, you're crazy, lambkin."

On hearing the old term of affection, the aging outlaw grinned widely — and he was not a man given to such expression. "If you label me lambkin, I may have to retaliate by calling you *acushla.*"

"What's that?"

"It's Gaelic. It means *darling.* Or, more accurately, pulse of my heart."

"Pulse of my heart!" Viola pulled tightly on the reins, bringing the mare to a halt. Seeing this, McNulty drew up his own horse. The man and woman sat for a long moment appraising each other.

When McNulty finally spoke, it was with a shyness more suited to a younger man, perhaps a boy. "I'm glad I found you, Viola Hall."

"I'm glad you did, too," said the woman with equal shyness.

"We should keep moving."

Viola nodded, and they resumed riding. They kept close together, heads bowed toward each other, and continued talking.

In the back of the wagon, Alworth and Two Robes sat facing each other, though largely silent and avoiding eye contact. Once, the wagon hit something bumpy, throwing the two of them into each other. After awkwardly disengaging, Alworth had made an attempt at conversation, but as intimidated as he was by Two Robes' company, he barely made it beyond a few words.

The Lakota girl was preoccupied with mending the edge of her skirt, which she held in a tight bunch as she worked, revealing a bit of the petticoat beneath. At one point, Alworth started to comment on what a pleasing garment the blue calico was but caught himself. Was that too intimate an observation, taking note of what a woman wore next to her body? Certainly, he wouldn't mention the petticoat, but was even the dress too much to discuss? He wished he'd logged more time with the females of the world. As it was, he understood as much of their ways and inclinations as he did, say, those of a giraffe. True, he had encountered more women than giraffes, but that didn't ease his discomfort at the moment.

Finally, Two Robes looked at him directly and spoke. "Are you and the other one — Johnny — good friends?"

Alworth started. "What? McNulty? Lord, no! I just met him perhaps an hour ago. I'm not at all of his kind. The man is a known out—" He stopped himself. There was no good to be had by making Two Robes and her companions aware of the unsavory background of one of their protectors.

But Two Robes couldn't be fooled. "You were going to say outlaw."

"No, no, I was going to . . . Ah . . ."

"No? Then were you going to say outhouse? The man is a known outhouse?"

Noting the slight smile on the girl's lips, Alworth tried to summon his own, awkward one. "Oh, a joke! You're making a joke."

Two Robes looked at him with something like pity. "Yes, a joke. Major Pompay says your friend is a leader of outlaws."

"He's not my friend," Alworth repeated. "He's just someone I fell in with. Sometimes you find yourself throwing in with people you'd never imagine keeping company with."

Two Robes paused in her mending. "Yes, I know what that's like."

"Then you know one shouldn't be judged by one's companions." Alworth sighed. "At least I hope not. To be honest, I don't know much these days. Back home, back in Connecticut, I used to fancy myself somewhat clever. Since I've been out West here, I don't really feel clever at all anymore."

"Your name is Alworth, yes? Is that your Christian name?"

"Yes."

"I've never heard it before."

Alworth smiled, starting to feel a bit more at ease. "No, you wouldn't have. I'm named after an English town clerk who wrote a history of municipal corporations. Not very inspiring, is it? Somehow a copy of the man's book ended up in my family's home, and my father thought Alworth was a noble-sounding name for a son. Though he's just a hatmaker, Father's always aspired to a higher station. That's why he was rather disappointed in me when I squandered my chances at a university education. But, what about your own name? How is it you're called Two Robes?"

The young Lakota inclined her head. "How do you know my name? I haven't said it."

"Oh! But didn't — Didn't I mention I saw your show back in Willerton? You were quoting Shakespeare. I thought you had great, well, poise. Yes, poise."

Two Robes accepted the compliment with a small shrug.

"But, back to your name," Alworth went on. "I know Indian people bestow names having something to do with a person's character or deeds."

"It's not the name I was given at birth. Nor the one I was saddled with at the white man's school I attended. I began calling myself Two Robes not long ago when I left the school and traveled west."

"Why Two Robes?"

"Because I wear the ways of two people, the red and the white."

"I see. That must not be an easy thing to do."

"No. No, it isn't."

"I think I understand somewhat how you feel. Like you, I've never felt at home, really, in the world."

"But you *did* have a home. And a family. You just said so yourself."

"Yes, but —"

"Then you can't compare yourself to me." Something flared in Two Robes' eyes. "To an Indian girl who was torn from her people and made to dress in white clothes and learn white manners and speak white words.

289

Now can you?"

"I suppose not," said Alworth quietly, no longer at ease. "I didn't mean to offend you. I just meant — Oh, never mind. I don't know what I meant."

Two Robes studied the young man for a moment before resuming her mending. "I didn't mean to make you feel bad, Alworth. I don't know what's in your heart."

Hearing the girl make reference to his heart stirred something in Alworth. Immediately, he wanted to pour out his thoughts and dreams to her. He caught himself, fearing that laying his feelings bare in such a way would earn him rebuke or ridicule.

As for Two Robes, she surprised herself by exposing something of her own heart. "It's not that I don't appreciate Shakespeare, you understand. I do. It's just that I wish his words hadn't been forced on me like they were. Actually, I've always loved Juliet, high up on her balcony, so full of hope and affection."

Alworth kept silent but nodded.

There was a sincerity in him that made Two Robes want to keep sharing her experiences, her observations. Soon, she set her needle aside and plunged into an oration touching on childhood remembrances, the days at Carlisle, Eagle Singing, her Quaker benefactor, the train ride west . . . So many things she hadn't given voice to in a very long time. Perhaps never. When she finally stopped, she was struck by the realization that she hadn't shared this much with anyone since arriving in Wyoming Territory. Not even with Viola, and certainly not with the major. But, for some reason not easily explained, she felt drawn to reveal herself to this young man.

CHAPTER THIRTY-FOUR

The barrel of a fierce-looking Navy Revolver was pointed directly at Count LeSage's head, and he didn't seem pleased. In fact, he looked like he might swoon and tumble off his wagon seat to the earth below. Beside him, his wife's demeanor was markedly different than his. Angie stared at the mounted gunman with a glare of disdain.

"If you're gonna rob us, then rob us," she said. "If you're gonna shoot us, shoot us. Don't waste our time."

"Shut up, Angie!" LeSage made no effort at a French accent now. "Just let this gentleman . . ."

He went silent, unsure of what he wanted the gentleman to do. They were only a couple of miles short of their destination, Black Powder. So close, yet far enough away that their bodies might not be discovered for days.

George Gault cocked his revolver. "Okay,

Pompay. Your reckoning has come."

"Pompay!" Lesage's voice rose an octave. "Dear God! You think I'm Pompay?"

At that moment, Gault's three men, who'd been trailing behind, rode up and took their place beside him.

"Hell, that's not Pompay," Nash declared. "Pompay's a fat fellow. This one's mostly bones."

Gault kept the gun leveled at LeSage. "I saw the wagon. It's painted like the one there that night."

"Sure, he's got a fancy, spiffed-up wagon like Pompay's," said Nash, "but this fellow's not him. I thought you said you attended one of the shows, yeah? Then you know this fellow looks nothing like Pompay."

"And the name on it ain't even Major Pompay," Billy put in. "It says Count *Lesage*. Whole different thing."

Gault kept his gun hand still extended. "All these traveling hucksters probably know each other. How about it, 'Count'? Have you come across Pompay today?"

LeSage stared back at the man threatening him. After a few seconds, he pushed out the words, "No, no I have not. I've run into him once or twice, but not for at least a year."

Gault shifted the pistol toward Angie.

293

"How about you?"

"Not for a year," she answered curtly. "Maybe more."

Slowly, Gault lowered his gun. "Be on your way."

LeSage needed no more encouragement. He screamed at his team, and the wagon rolled forward and away.

"I saw the wagon all painted up." Gault spoke hesitantly. "I just assumed . . . All right, let's keep on."

He dug his spurs into the mustang's flanks, drawing blood, and shot forward. Lampo followed directly. Nash and Billy held behind for a moment.

"No way anyone could mistake that skinny fellow for Pompay," Nash said. "I'm thinking Gault is still tilting at windmills."

"What's that mean?" Billy asked.

"Not sure exactly. Just an expression I've heard. It means when someone's acting crazy and not seeing things right. You disagree, Billy? You think Gault's acting normal? Me, I can't rightly say, not having known him but a couple days. You're a better judge than me."

Billy offered no response. Instead, he nudged his dun forward, leaving his companion behind.

Nash hesitated. He glanced behind to

where they'd come from, then forward to where they were headed. He pursed his lips and shook his head. Reaching into his trouser pocket, he extracted the three-cent nickel he kept for such occasions. It was the same one he'd consulted yesterday when he abandoned Pompay. He flipped the coin in the air, caught it in his right hand, and slapped it down on the back of his left.

"Tails." He cursed and again shook his head.

Nash pocketed the coin and rode after the other men.

CHAPTER THIRTY-FIVE

Following McNulty's instructions, the wagon party soon left the common trail north and veered off to the left. Within the hour, while passing through a low, pine-bordered valley, the travelers caught sight of a cleared-out area directly ahead. On reaching the area, they were met with the evidence of a past fire: scores of blackened, partially consumed boards, edged by the long grasses. McNulty pulled up, Viola beside him, and the major followed suit, stopping the wagon on the edge of the debris field. A solitary stone building was visible a ways beyond.

Pompay looked about, taking in the charred wood. "Seems like there was a conflagration here recently."

"Not recently," McNulty said. "Close to twenty years ago from what I've heard. Burnt wood keeps its look for years. Major, I noticed one of your lead horses appears to be flagging."

"Vesuvius? I'm afraid I agree. Alas, he's well beyond his youth, and our present pace is a bit much for him."

"In fact, none of those nags of yours looks particularly spry. We'd best rest them for a few minutes. Losing a little time now is better than running the beasts into the ground later."

McNulty and Viola dismounted, and the others climbed down from the wagon.

The Irishman looked around him. "I've been by this place a few times over the years. The story goes that a pair of young brothers moved here with their wives, intending to carve out a new town. Called it Tiny Eden. They spent months putting up houses in anticipation of all the new citizens who would one day join them. But then the war came. One brother joined the Union, the other the Confederacy, and both fell in battle within weeks of each other. Afterwards, their widows upped and left. But before they did, out of grief, they put the town to the torch. At least that's the tale I've been told." He gestured at the stone building across the clearing, which appeared to consist of only walls, the wooden roof no doubt having been burned away. "That was meant to be the chapel. Now, it's all that remains of the brothers' dream. The last remnant of Tiny Eden."

"Seems like there should be some quote about flames and dreams," Alworth mused. "One found in some ancient book or other."

McNulty smiled. "If there isn't, perhaps you can summon up one yourself. An educated lad like yourself must be stuffed with clever quotations. Anyway, this place is supposed to be haunted. Those two brothers are said to wander the ruins, calling out for their missing brides."

"Stop it, Johnny!" Viola gave a little shudder. "I hate that sort of morbid patter. Talk of ghosts and such."

"It's not ghosts I find worrisome," said McNulty. "It's men of flesh and blood with desperate aims. Like the men who are on our trail. Let's have the horses catch their breath for a few minutes, then move on. Now, might there be anything handy to eat? I wouldn't mind a bite of something."

Viola brought some jerky and biscuits from the wagon and distributed them. While most of the group remained behind, Alworth and Two Robes made their way to the chapel. There they stood before the stone arch where, prior to the fire, a door had once existed.

"This was once someone's great aspiration," said Alworth. "Their hope for the future." He removed his hat. "I'd like to go in."

Two Robes gestured toward the arch. "Let's go."

"You're not afraid?" Alworth asked.

"Of what? Ghosts? No, the road behind me is filled with so many of them I'm beyond fear, really. When someone goes through enough bad times, it hardens their skin."

"But not their hearts, I hope."

The two exchanged a look, then entered the chapel. It was a large enough space that, had it seen its potential, it would have allowed for several dozen worshippers. Apparently, no pews had ever been placed inside, or their charred remains would have been evident. Likewise, the lack of burnt lumber on the ground suggested the floor had never been anything other than dirt. As it was, only the four stone walls stood witness to what might have been.

Alworth peered slowly around. "I wonder what prayers were said here."

He raised his eyes to the open gap where the roof should have been. Two Robes followed his gaze. The sky, pure blue only moments ago, had become a somber, murky gray. Perhaps a storm was moving in.

■ ■ ■ ■

If McNulty's party believed altering their path would offer them any protection, their belief was soon to be dispelled. On a ridge overlooking Tiny Eden, George Gault stood staring through a spyglass. Some distance below he could make out the presence of several people moving about. Though they were too far away to identify, the brightly painted show wagon beside them stood out clearly. This time, the large letters on the side heralding *Major Pompay* were unmistakable. Gault gave a grunt of satisfaction and lowered the glass.

"Tie up the horses here," he said, turning to his men. "We'll go down on foot and move through the trees there till we get into the clearing. That way we won't announce ourselves till we're pretty much on top of them."

"We're going to talk to those people first, right, Mr. Gault?" Billy forced a smile. "Never hurts to palaver a bit to see if things can be worked out."

Gault stared at the youth as if looking through him. "I'm going straight down. Lampo, you and Nash flank me on either side at a distance. Keep hidden till I call for you. Billy, you're with me."

Billy started to speak, but Gault brushed firmly past him and made his way over to his horse. Gault exchanged the spyglass for the Trapdoor Springfield, but left the Peacemaker, figuring the rifle and his Colt would suffice. He tied off the mustang to a nearby ponderosa as the other men tied off their own horses. Shouldering the Springfield, Gault started down the ridge. After a moment's hesitation, Billy fell in behind him.

"Guess we're in for it," said Nash to Lampo. "I'm hoping Pompay didn't recruit some new nursemaid to replace me. Probably not likely though, you figure? I mean, it's only been a day since I lit out on them."

The Finn didn't answer. Instead, he pulled on his long red beard and grunted.

"Guess there's no sense dallying here." With a deep sigh, Nash turned and began making his way downhill, to the left of where Gault and Billy had descended.

Lampo drew his revolver and began his own descent, heading to the right. A bank of dark clouds moved slowly across the ridge and over the valley below.

"Company's coming," Viola called out as she watched the two men emerging from the pines about a hundred yards away.

301

Pompay, along with McNulty, came to stand beside her. "Why are they on foot I wonder?"

"Maybe they wanted to get close before we noticed them," McNulty said. "So we wouldn't hear their horses approach. Viola, go find Alworth and bring him here. He can tell us if this is his man Gault."

Viola hurried off. The team of horses, facing the direction the newcomers were approaching from, stirred restlessly, as if aware of impending peril. Pompay fumbled nervously with his shirt collar.

"Shouldn't we hide?" he asked. "If these men are dangerous, we should hide, yes?"

McNulty cast him a sidelong glance. "And then what, Major? Wait till they drag us out of our holes and hope for their good graces? No, best to face things dead on."

"I don't like the 'dead' part of your notion. I'm not equipped for this type of situation, Mr. McNulty. Not at all. I'll leave you to sort things out."

Pompay spun around and headed in the direction of the stone building, soon passing Alworth and Viola, who were hastening forward. He found Two Robes standing at the entrance of the chapel.

"Ah, my little Sioux friend." Pompay patted the girl's shoulder. "There's wisdom indeed in remaining in the rear here. We'll let the more violent element have their day."

"What's happening, Major?" Two Robes asked.

"Nothing that either you or I need be involved in, I assure you."

Two Robes studied Pompay's face for a moment, noting his tense smile and twitching eye. "But we *are* involved," she said. "Every one of us here is involved."

It had come. As Viola watched from beside the wagon, McNulty and Alworth walked forward to meet the approaching men. Both parties stopped simultaneously, with no more than fifteen yards separating them.

"That's him, cradling the rifle," Alworth whispered to McNulty. "George Gault. The one with him is my friend Billy."

"Well, let's hope your friendship maintains," McNulty whispered back. Then he called out, "Good day, Mr. Gault! I suppose a conversation is in order."

Gault ignored him, fixing his eyes on Alworth. "Nevins! What the hell are you doing here?"

Alworth cleared his throat. "Just trying to help everyone find some common ground, Mr. Gault. So any unpleasantness can be avoided."

Gault sneered. "Ain't that thoughtful. As for you, mister" — he addressed McNulty now — "whoever you are, far as I know we have no quarrel with each other. It's the fat bastard who just ran off I'm concerned with. Him and his band. And Nevins here, too, now that I've set eyes on him again."

"You seem to have a fair number of enemies, sir," said McNulty.

"Some men do. I take it as a show of character."

"You may be right. I'd like to suggest, though, that seeing these people here as enemies may not be in your best interest."

Gault's eyes narrowed. "Yeah? How so?"

"Because if you choose to make enemies of them, you'll also need to count me in among their number."

"Should that bother me? You haven't said yet who you are."

"The name's John McNulty, and, in my time, I've put several men beneath the sod. I take no pleasure in saying so, mind you, but I believe it's something you should know."

"I've heard of you all right. But I've laid out several men myself. So if your claim is meant to set my nerves on end, it doesn't."

Thus far, none of the men's hands had drifted toward a holster, and Gault, for his part, had kept his rifle pointed downward. Still, tension filled the air, as heavy and dark as the storm clouds that had rolled over the valley. For the first time since McNulty and Gault had begun their exchange, the two younger men beside them met each other's eyes. The look exchanged between Alworth and Billy was one of deep concern, perhaps fear. Billy bit his lip and blinked. Alworth, reacting to a gust of wind, instinctively pressed down on his Stetson. It wasn't necessary — the wind was not very strong — but the act provided distraction, as if his worst concern at the moment was a blown-off hat.

Next to the wagon, Viola now inched closer to the shotgun that she'd left leaning against one of the wheels. As her fingers closed around the stock, she heard footfalls behind her. Turning, she found Two Robes standing there.

"Is that Gault?" the Lakota girl asked.

"Seems to be." Viola drew the shotgun to her side. "You might want to get behind the wagon, girlie."

As the canopy of gray clouds spread out overhead, the sunlight grew weak and brittle. It occurred to Alworth that the moment was almost too fitting, too theatrical, as if some master impresario had designed it to match the accompanying drama. A soft sprinkle of rain now began to fall, adding to the bleakness. All remnants of the bright-blue afternoon had, in a matter of minutes, given way to this premature twilight.

"No need for you to risk your health, McNulty," Gault called out. "I'm guessing you have no real stake in this."

"You'd be wrong there," McNulty answered.

"Have it your way then."

Gault leveled his rifle and fired from the hip. The gunshot echoed through the valley.

CHAPTER THIRTY-SIX

Whether or not he'd been the intended target, Alworth was the one who felt the bullet's hot sting. He cried out, clutched his right leg, and dropped to the ground. Without sparing a look at his fallen comrade, McNulty yanked free his revolver and fired. Gault's grunt testified to the shot finding its mark.

The bullet glanced off Gault's left hip, not embedding itself but causing him to stumble backward. Regaining his footing, he swiftly brought the Springfield to eye level and again squeezed the trigger. The bullet whistled past McNulty's left ear, a missed shot.

By now, Billy Fowler's pistol had also cleared the holster. The youth's eyes were wide as he raised his gun hand, but McNulty had already retorted and did not miss. Billy cursed and fell to his knees, his left arm bloodied and dangling. The trigger finger of his right hand convulsed, resulting in a shot that went wildly astray. Now the only one of the four not wounded, McNulty again fired. Once more, it was Gault whom the bullet touched, though only barely, leaving a red gash in his right cheek. Undaunted, Gault again aimed at McNulty, this time directly at his chest.

Another resounding shot rang out. From her place back near the wagon, Viola had added the double barrels of her shotgun to the volley. Buckshot skinned Gault's left leg, ruining his aim at McNulty. In the course of seconds, George Gault had been struck three times, though none of the shots had brought him down. He fired his rifle again. While this shot again missed piercing flesh, it clipped the brim of McNulty's hat, thus serving to distract the Irishman enough so Gault could grab Billy by the collar and pull him to his feet.

Not bothering to reengage in the firefight, Billy staggered back toward the tree line, his torn arm trailing blood. Lampo now appeared and ran into the clearing, firing as he came. Billy stumbled into his arms, and the Finn pulled the wounded youth back toward the trees. George Gault, limping slightly from the wounds to his left leg, had also fallen back, and all three vanished into the pines.

The rain was falling more notably now, dispersing the drifting waves of gun smoke. Viola broke open her shotgun, quickly reloaded, and went to stand by McNulty's side. They both fired again, despite the fact that their adversaries were no longer visible. Two Robes, who'd also come forward, helped Alworth to his feet and began half dragging him through the field of black, rain-moistened boards toward the wagon. The horses — the four of the team and the two saddled ones — while agitated by the gunfire, had not bolted. Viola fell back to join Two Robes, and together the two women brought Alworth behind the wagon and laid him on the earth there. McNulty got off one more shot, then joined them.

The speed with which everything had happened left them stunned. Viola exhaled deeply and clutched the shotgun to her chest. Two Robes gave a slight shudder as she knelt beside Alworth and took his hand in hers. Only McNulty appeared calm, methodically reloading his Starr revolver while glancing around the side of the wagon in the direction Gault had vanished.

Taking some comfort in the warmth of the girl's hand, Alworth panted through his pain. So this is what it felt like to take a bullet. Not long back, he'd heard a bunk-mate tell a jocund tale of being shot in the thigh over a rivalry for a saloon girl. The cowhand had laughed and claimed the pain was minimal compared to the real hurt of losing the affections of a pretty wench. When Gault and Saturn were shot yester-day, they spoke little of their wounds, neither man being given to complaining. But lying here now with a bullet in his leg, Alworth was struck with the stark revelation that being shot was a hellish thing indeed.

Two Robes squeezed his hand. "Don't worry. We'll take care of you. We need to undo your trousers and see to your wound."

Despite the pain, the young man nearly blushed. "No, no, that won't be necessary."

"Would you rather bleed to death than expose your knees?" Two Robes asked sternly.

McNulty looked down at them, then returned his gaze to the tree line beyond. "No time for undressing and doctoring right now. Just bind up his leg tightly with some-thing. Such a measure will serve for the present."

Without hesitation, Two Robes gathered up the edge of her dress, still not fully mended, and ripped a lengthy strip from it. Deftly, she bound it around the wound over

310

the pant leg and pulled tightly, to which Alworth responded with a groan.

"Sorry if I hurt you." Two Robes tied off the wound. "But we need to stop the bleeding."

Standing next to McNulty, Viola was reloading the shotgun. "Not the best situation, is it?" she said quietly so only he could hear. "One man down and a pack of jackals waiting to move in on us."

"I've lived through worse," said McNulty. "I've led a tumultuous life, you know, Viola. Danger often seems to be nipping at my heels."

Viola managed a smile. "You've always had a way with words, Johnny. It's like every damned thing you utter is a little chunk of poem."

McNulty smiled back. "If so, a god-awful poem it is. Anyway, I'll agree our odds aren't the most desirable. From what Alworth said, there are four of those fellows out there. We've seen three so far. Not sure where the fourth is keeping himself, but no doubt he'll show up with as much unpleasantness as his *compadres.*"

"Looks like we wounded two of the lot."

"Yes, though our friend Gault seems damn near invulnerable. Alworth says he'd already been shot once yesterday, plus what he received just now. The man has iron, I'll give him that."

"I'd rather you just give him lead."

"That's what I've been attempting to do," McNulty said. "Now I think you and the girl had better get Alworth over to the chapel. We're too exposed where we are. I'll cover your retreat and join you shortly."

When Viola and the others had gone, McNulty fired once, then launched himself into a zigzagging run, not in the direction of the chapel nor toward where Gault lay, but for the stretch of pines to his right. The awareness that he was crossing open ground propelled him on, giving fleetness to his less-than-youthful limbs. Though three gunshots rang out in rapid succession, he made it to the trees untouched. Once there, he knelt among the closely packed pines and began to scan the immediate area. Before he'd made his run, McNulty had noticed someone moving among the trees here. What's more, he was certain one of the three shots he'd just eluded had come not from Gault's position, but from this stretch of woods.

Yes, there the man was, crouching perhaps forty feet away. Despite the intervening tangle of pine branches, McNulty could make out his shoulders and head and the hat, from which a black feather sprouted. The fourth man. He seemed not to know where McNulty was hidden, for he looked about furtively, his revolver raised and ready.

McNulty aimed his own pistol, but just then the man turned and spotted him. Both men fired, almost overlapping. McNulty felt the shot rip across his right shoulder blade. It knocked him over, leaving him sprawled on his back. Having heard the thud of a bullet against wood, he knew his own shot had missed its mark, instead burying itself in a tree trunk. McNulty quickly righted himself and fired again, as did his enemy. This time, two thuds indicated that both bullets had struck trees.

McNulty took a moment to assess his wound. He drew his coat back from his right shoulder and saw blood had begun to seep through his shirt. He pulled the shirt back, tearing several buttons as he did so. The bullet looked to have creased the shoulder blade but not embedded. Luck was with him.

He eased himself belly down on the damp forest floor and began crawling forward, not directly toward the man, but around him. McNulty moved slowly and carefully, taking care to make as little noise as possible. The pelting of the rain on the earth and tree branches helped muffle his progress. The man seemed to have lost track of him, for McNulty could see him popping in and out from the shelter of the pines, looking desperately in all directions.

McNulty's stealth paid off. After snaking his way around his quarry for a minute or two, he was able to flank him. When he'd come within twenty feet of the crouching man, McNulty rose to his knees and took aim.

"Don't move an inch," he called out. "If I see you twitch, I'll put a bullet in the nape of your neck. I don't like to shoot a man from behind, but I will if need be. Throw down your weapon."

After a moment's hesitation, the man complied.

"Stand and turn around," said McNulty. "Good. Now move away from the gun."

When the man followed through, McNulty stepped forward and picked up the pistol, tucking it into his belt. "Who am I addressing?"

"I'm Nash." He tried to force a smile. "Look, friend, this is all Gault's game. I just sort of got roped in."

"Really? My colleague Alworth spoke of you and offered a different take."

"I just got caught up in the excitement

of things."

"Yes, it has been exciting, hasn't it? I can feel that excitement in my shoulder at the moment."

"Like I say, I just got caught up in all this," Nash insisted. "I'm actually pals of sorts with Major Pompay. Ask him yourself. Until just yesterday, I rode with him and his folks, protecting them against hostiles and such."

"So was that your intention at present? To protect him? Enough talking. Walk ahead of me."

McNulty gestured with his pistol, and the two men made their way through the pines and back into the open space that had once been Tiny Eden. Entering the clearing there, McNulty pressed the Starr's barrel against the base of his prisoner's neck and, with his free hand, grabbed the back of Nash's coat collar, pushing his forward. When they reached the spot where McNulty had first encountered Gault, the Irishman halted, still maintaining his grip on Nash. By now, the rain had ceased, though the sky remained gray and dark clouded.

Keeping Nash well in front of him, McNulty called out toward the tree line. "Can you hear me, Gault? As you see, I've seized one of your men. I'm thinking we might work out some sort of understanding."

McNulty waited for a reply. When none came, he continued, "We've traded blows, your lot and mine, and have both drawn blood. I know two of you are wounded, and I have Nash here disarmed and under the gun. It might be wise now to call an end to hostilities. What do you say, Gault?"

This time a reply did come from the tree line, but not a verbal one. Instead, a rifle burst reverberated loudly, and Nash, taking the impact of the blast, was flung back against McNulty. As Nash fell, the Irishman stumbled backward, managing to keep on his feet, and fired twice. He then pivoted and ran back toward the wagon, leaving Nash bloodied and broken on the ground.

Chapter Thirty-Seven

"What the hell'd you do *that* for?" Through gritted teeth, Billy Fowler managed to push out the words. His pistol now holstered, he leant against a tree, clutching his wounded arm. "You just shot down one of your own men."

"Wasn't really one of my men." Gault, kneeling close by, his cheek dripping blood, again sighted his Springfield and fired once more at the retreating McNulty. A miss. Not having brought down more ammunition for the rifle, he tossed it aside. He stood and withdrew his Colt. "Nash just fell in with us yesterday. And he got himself captured like a goddamned fool. Hell if I was going to let him be used against me."

"Christ," Billy muttered.

"What now?" Lampo stood nearby. "We circle them?"

"That's right," said Gault. "We'll move along those trees on the edge of the field.

The same ones Nash was in, only we won't be goddamned fools. Let's go."

Billy shook his head. "Not me. I'm done."

Gault stared hard at him. "Far as I can tell, you ain't dead. That means you ain't done."

"I tell you I'm hurt bad. My arm . . ."

"It's not your shooting arm that got hit, is it? All right, stay put for now, but let off a couple shots every minute or so. That way they'll think we're all still here. When you hear things getting hot up ahead, it means the Finn and I got the drop on them. You can come up then and help mop up."

Billy watched Gault and Lampo disappear into the thick of the woods, then slid down the base of his tree to a sitting position. He felt a strong urge to close his eyes and give over to sleep, but the pain in his arm was an angry, burning thing that wouldn't let him go. Alone now, torn and undone, he tried to breathe through the hurt, one labored breath at a time.

He wished desperately he was back at the ranch where a runaway steer was the worst of troubles, and no one was inclined to shoot him. Oddly, the realization now struck him that in just over a week he'd be turning eighteen. He wondered if he'd be allowed to see his birthday.

■ ■ ■ ■

Having rejoined Viola and the others, McNulty caught his breath and again reloaded. They were now all inside the roofless walls of the stone chapel. Two Robes knelt beside Alworth, holding his hand and offering words of comfort. Pompay and Viola crowded around McNulty as he finished his report of what had just occurred.

"So Nash admitted he'd been with us?" the major asked.

"He did," said McNulty. "And he boasted he was a bosom friend to you all."

Viola let out a gruff laugh. "Friend? Hardly! Not in *this* world."

"In point of fact, I believe he's not in this world any longer," McNulty said. "Not after Gault saw fit to gun him down during a peace parley."

"Why would Gault do such a thing?" Pompay asked. "After Nash had thrown in with him?"

"I really don't know, Major. From my brief acquaintance with Gault, I'd venture he's not a man who can be measured by common standards."

"The horses!" Pompay went pale. "What if he decides to shoot our horses? We'd be

319

stranded and at his mercy."

"Hell, ain't we already at his mercy?" said Viola.

"True, Gault may decide to shoot them," McNulty acknowledged. "But, then again, he may not. Some men are fine with sinking a bullet into an unarmed human but are averse to harming a healthy horse."

Pompay was growing more agitated. "Why is this happening? *Why?* All I've tried to do in my life is provide the people with a little entertainment, a little distraction. And help heal their bodies and spirits."

Viola's eyes flared. "You mean with the elixir? Healing bodies and spirits, are you? Goddamn it, Major, it's your stinking potion that's landed us in this trouble."

Pompay turned on her. "I've told you, my elixir never hurt anyone! On the contrary, it —"

"It damn well hurt *him,* didn't it?" Viola pointed to the sprawled Alworth. "And before the day is done, we may all be laid out gushing blood. Thanks to you and your fabled fortified *swill!*"

"Listen, woman, you can't accuse me of —"

"Enough!" McNulty held up a hand. "We don't have time for this. We still have our foes to contend with. Two, maybe three of them."

"You shot Billy," Alworth said from the ground. "He's probably out of this."

"Yes, I shot him, but I didn't kill him, so we can't factor him out. What about the other man Gault has with him? Is he much of a threat?"

"Lampo's cold blooded. A violent man."

"All right, good to know what we're up against," McNulty said. "Here's what I'm thinking. I imagine Gault won't be content to just wait for us to appear again. In gunning down his own man, he's shown he's remorseless and relentless. He'll no doubt try to move upon us. The woods to our left now are too far away for him to reach us without being seen well in advance. So I'm guessing he'll come up through the same stretch Nash did, to our right. Those woods curve in alongside our present spot, and behind as well, at a distance of no more than a few dozen yards."

"Too close for comfort," Viola said.

McNulty continued. "I suggest we plant ourselves among the pines over there and lie in wait for Gault's attack. It's a sounder play than waiting for him to ambush us."

"But we're safer just staying inside here, aren't we?" Pompay was noticeably sweating now. "Better than any of us exposing himself. We're in a solid stone structure after all."

McNulty smiled grimly. "The Alamo was a solid structure, wasn't it? And an intended place of worship, as well. Just like this building."

Viola nodded. "And none of that helped 'ol Davy Crockett and his pals, did it?"

Pompay gulped. "Then maybe you're right, McNulty. You should go out there in the woods and wait for Gault's attack."

"I wasn't planning on going alone. Are you armed, Major?"

"Me? Why no, I never carry a gun."

McNulty pulled the pistol out of his belt and thrust it at Pompay. "Take it, Major. It belonged to your old chum Nash. I checked, and it's still got three rounds. Don't waste them."

Pompay began to back away from the weapon. "No, no, I'm not the man for that sort of work."

Viola snickered. "What's wrong, Major? Don't want to relive your glorious days in Gettysburg and Shiloh?"

McNulty forced the gun into Pompay's hand. "I wasn't asking your opinion on the matter, Major. Our friend Alworth is incapacitated, so that leaves you and me as the only able-bodied men still standing."

"Hold on now." Viola stepped forward, still brandishing her shotgun. "You're not leaving me out of this. I can shoot a lot more steady than Pompay; you can bet on that. I'm coming."

"Is there any sense in arguing with you?" McNulty asked her.

"No sense at all."

"Very well. But you're not off the hook, Major. The three of us will head out together." McNulty looked down at their wounded companion. "Alworth, you're armed and have proven yourself a quick hand. If any of Gault's band make it in here, can you fight?"

"I'll do what I have to," said Alworth.

"Good. Two Robes can stay with you."

"If I had a gun, I'd fight, too," the Lakota girl declared. "Viola taught me how to shoot."

"Barely," Viola muttered.

"We can use every hand." McNulty reached into his coat pocket, drew out the pistol that had belonged to T. C. Heckett, and held it out. "This served a young friend of mine. It's a reliable firearm."

Two Robes accepted the revolver.

"Still, it's best you stay with Alworth," McNulty said. "In case anyone gets past us."

"Johnny!" For the first time, Viola noticed the stain on McNulty's right shoulder where blood had seeped through his jacket. "They shot you!"

"It's a mild injury," McNulty said. "The bullet just slid by. I'm not hindered at all. Let's go, Viola. You, too, Pompay."

"I'm just an entertainer," Pompay muttered, but he followed the other two out the doorway.

Alworth and Two Robes were alone now in the chapel. Alworth withdrew his right hand from hers and slid out his revolver. He set the gun on his chest, his finger resting on the trigger guard.

Two Robes studied the gun in her own hand. "I wonder what became of the man who owned this before."

"Maybe better not to know," Alworth said.

"The Sioux are a warrior people. I don't know if that's been bred out of me at the white man's school."

"I hope you don't need to find out." Alworth paused to let a wave of pain pass through him. "Two Robes, I need to tell you . . . *Want* to tell you . . . I didn't just follow you all out of some general sense of decency. I came all this way because I didn't want any harm to befall you. You particularly, Two Robes. From the moment a few days back when I saw you on that stage, I told myself that I . . . that I . . ." Another wave of pain surged in, silencing him.

With her free hand, Two Robes stroked his forehead. "Yes, you've said this already, Alworth. I understand."

Though Alworth had closed his eyes, he felt he could still see the girl leaning over him, her own eyes holding no judgment regarding his foolish head and heart.

CHAPTER THIRTY-EIGHT

McNulty distributed his small force among the pines, separated at intervals of roughly fifty yards. Major Pompay, set farthest back, had found a low boulder to crouch behind. He rested his arm across the flat of the stone, his pistol (Nash's pistol) aimed outward, and made an effort to not tremble. McNulty had placed Viola next, not too deep in from the clearing. This way she'd have the chance to cross back to the chapel if necessary. He positioned himself foremost, fairly deep into the woods.

Though the rain hadn't returned, the sky remained overcast, the clouds now the color of tarnished steel. A profound silence filled the forest, broken only by the sporadic drip of raindrops from high tree branches. McNulty stood behind a thick ponderosa, his left hand pressed against the rough bark and his right tight around the grip of his revolver. The pain in his shoulder was troublesome but not severe. He welcomed it in a way because it gave him focus.

This was the first gunshot wound he'd ever experienced, and the thought filled him with mild awe. He'd lived nigh on six decades, fought in rebellions, robbed numerous banks and trains, killed several men and wounded others, and had never once felt the bite of a bullet. Not until now. McNulty smiled. He'd beaten the odds, hadn't he? It had been a grand stretch of untorn flesh, and he had no cause to complain. But Bloodless John was a thing of the past.

He scanned the woods in all directions. His enemies might try to sneak up at a crawl, just as he had done with Nash, and catch him unawares. Their leader wasn't a man to take lightly; that was clear enough. From what Alworth had said, Gault, even when unperturbed, was of a severe and unyielding character. Now, with vengeance in his heart, he was a thing of pure ferocity.

Though McNulty knew nothing of Gault's history, he could guess at the road that had led him to this hour. A bitter boyhood, reckless early manhood, brutal encounters, and vicious choices . . . Yes, such would likely have been the blueprint of George Gault's life.

McNulty had known such men in his time. Baker had been one — though, compared to Gault, a trifling version. And was he himself not of that general cut? True, McNulty liked to think himself a fair and even-handed man, slow to anger and quick to forgive, but wasn't that just a veil to protect himself from the black truth of who he really was? Habitual thief, flaunter of the law, slayer of men. Perhaps not all ten commandments lay shattered in his wake, but surely most. As for any left intact, no doubt given time he would topple those as well.

McNulty drove those thoughts away. This wasn't the time to gauge the weight of his soul. This was the time to dispense death. *To everything there is a season . . .*

Viola held the shotgun waist high and stared into the gray expanse of pines. The forest floor directly ahead was uneven, dipping in places, rising in others. Every once in a while, a squirrel would burst out of nowhere and scurry along, causing Viola to flinch. Her back pressed firmly against a tree, she waited in tense anticipation for whatever was to come.

She prided herself on being someone accustomed to facing the tides of life dead on, but waiting in this manner, with danger lurking unseen like a ghost, was another specialty. Having the major positioned somewhere behind her gave no comfort, but the fact that John McNulty stood up ahead — beyond sight, but as sure as the risen sun — helped calm her.

He had come to her. Urged on by nothing more than whirling dreams, he had come to her. Nearly three years had passed since they'd last seen each other, but he hadn't forgotten. And she hadn't forgotten. Though Johnny's face never appeared to her in a dream, it had still hovered in her conscious mind, never fully abandoning her. Just as Johnny himself, in the flesh, had not abandoned her. If they got out of this — this dire situation — who knows what might lie ahead?

It wasn't until the man was nearly upon her that Viola heard from behind the crack of a dead branch underfoot. She turned quickly. He was just rising from a crouch, bared teeth showing above a long red beard and a large Bowie knife in his raised hand. Viola discharged the shotgun, but, at the same moment, the man shoved the barrel aside with his free hand, and the shot went astray. As gun smoke enveloped them both, the man swept downward with his knife. Viola twisted away in time to avoid the full

329

thrust, but the blade slashed across her right arm, causing her to drop the shotgun. Clutching her arm, she staggered backward but was able to stay on her feet. Her attacker switched the knife to his left hand and, with his right, pulled out a long-barreled pistol. He paused for a second as if deciding which weapon to do his work with, then advanced on the unarmed woman.

"You ugly son of a bitch!" Viola screamed in his face.

If the bearded man intended a reply, he was denied uttering it by the bullet that tore into his stomach. He gasped and doubled over, his pistol falling from his hand. Seconds later, he righted himself and began swinging the knife desperately through the air. There was no one to make contact with now, for Viola had quickly stepped away. A second pistol shot rang out, and the man was flung backward. He landed on his back, lifeless but with the knife still in his grasp, as blood oozed from his chest to blend with his red beard.

McNulty appeared, smoking pistol in hand, and looked down at the dead man. "I'm guessing this is the one Alworth called Lampo. His death betters our odds."

Still holding her arm, Viola slumped against a tree trunk and cursed softly.

McNulty now noticed her wound and hurried over, kneeling beside her.

"Let me have a look." He set his revolver on the ground, near at hand, and pulled back Viola's coat and shirt to examine the cut. "It doesn't appear to be too deep at all."

McNulty removed his neckerchief and used it to bind the arm.

Viola tried to smile. "You've got a tender touch for sure, Johnny. But don't linger on me. Gault's still somewhere out there."

McNulty nodded, took up his revolver, and stood.

A gunshot sounded from deeper in the woods. Then another. Without pausing, the Irishman grabbed up Viola's shotgun, put it in her hands, and hurried off in the direction of the gunfire.

Back in the stone chapel, Two Robes, along with Alworth, had heard Viola's outcry, followed by the first two shots.

The young Lakota woman rose, balancing T.C.'s pistol in her hand. "I have to go to her."

"It's not safe," Alworth said from the ground. "Stay here. McNulty can help her."

"Viola's my friend. I'll be back. Stay alert, Alworth."

Then she disappeared out the doorway.

Alworth pulled himself to a sitting position, his back against the wall facing the doorless threshold. He pointed his revolver at the empty space there, keeping his finger near but not on the trigger. If Two Robes or one of his other companions should suddenly appear in the doorway, he didn't want to react rashly and fire. If it should be Gault or Lampo, though, that would be another thing entirely.

But what if it was Billy Fowler who appeared? What if McNulty's bullet had not taken the young ranch hand out of the fight after all? If Billy stood there, framed by the stone archway, gun in hand, was Alworth prepared to end his friend's life?

His concern for Billy now merged with his fear for Two Robes' safety and the sharp pain of his wound. It all made for a stressful blend. The Remington felt heavy in his hand, heavier than he remembered it feeling before. The man he'd purchased it from last year had lavished the weapon with praise: *Oh, this one's a beaut, yessir! A real coffin-filler. It won't never let you down.* Standing there in the general store, Alworth had swung the gun back and forth, delighted with how comfortable it felt in his hand.

Not so now.

■ ■ ■ ■

The major staggered out from behind the boulder where he'd been hiding, his shirt-front a bloody chaos. Having realized too late that someone had crept up behind him, he'd stood and turned just in time to receive the two bullets, one in his side and one in his chest. The shots spun him about so swiftly, he never saw his assassin. The pistol he'd been given slipped away and was forgotten. He used the boulder to steady himself before stumbling in the direction he knew his comrades waited. They would receive him, save him. *They must.* But then he fell, fell through infinite space, never arriving.

When McNulty saw Pompay crumpled on the ground, face half pressed into the damp earth, he knew at once the man was dead. Stopping twenty feet from the body, the Irishman began scanning the area for signs of Gault. Yes, possibly Alworth's friend Billy might still be in the mix, but McNulty believed it had come down to the two of them: John McNulty and George Gault. Hearing a movement directly ahead, a ways past the boulder, he stepped behind a tree, aimed, and fired. Seconds later, the shot was returned. McNulty heard the bullet whistle by, several inches from where he stood.

"Your shot missed, Brother Gault," he called out. "Did mine find its mark?"

After a moment, Gault called back, "You missed, too."

"Then we're even on that score." Though he couldn't see him, McNulty realized his adversary was less than thirty yards ahead, hidden behind a tree-lined rise in the land. "Here's the thing, Gault. A minute ago, I dispatched your man Lampo. Yes, he's gone to Satan. And you yourself saw fit to lay down poor Mister Nash. As for your last cohort, Billy, he's presently lying somewhere bleeding his young life out. So that leaves just you, doesn't it?"

"I'm enough," the unseen Gault answered. "Always have been."

"To continue our tally, I see the major here has died by your hand. That was your purpose in tracking us down, wasn't it? To kill Pompay for perceived wrongs he committed against your loved one? Well, you've accomplished your goal. Why not accept your victory and move on?"

"That ain't my plan."

"Listen now. Some of my own party have

suffered wounds today, but I'm willing to overlook that. In the interest of peace, you understand. I strongly suggest you vanish into the woods, gather up your wounded man, and ride out. Simply ride out. No one else needs to suffer today."

"You're wrong. There's two more still left in Pompay's traveling show."

"Two women, Gault! Are you really intending to kill two women?"

"They were all part of that goddamned show. And one of them's an Indian."

"What in hell motivates you, Gault? It can't just be —"

The conversation abruptly ended with a gunshot. This time the bullet struck McNulty's tree, right at the level of his head.

McNulty didn't return fire then, instead taking a moment to reload his half-empty gun. This complete, he made a decision. The thought of further injury to Viola being unacceptable, he must be brazen in his actions. He was through with reasoning and subterfuge, and the time had come for less subtle measures. A recollection came to him, an incident back in Tipperary during his young rebel career. That day, unarmed and without assistance, he'd found himself cornered in a dead-end alley by a trio of constables.

Rather than give in to fatalism, he had decided mad abandon might win the day. With a wild whoop, he'd seized a trash bin sitting there and rushed at the coppers, screaming as if his mind had fled him. The audacity of his charge completely unnerved the public servants. When he flung the bin at them, they all fell back in confoundment, and he made good his escape. Such boldness could serve him now. Though McNulty no longer had youth on his side — nor the inclination to wail like a banshee — he had the wits of age to rely upon. And, in place of a trash bin, his fully loaded Starr revolver would make a suitable substitute.

McNulty drew in a deep breath and darted out from behind the tree. In several long strides, he passed Pompay's corpse and reached the shelter of the low boulder. He dropped into a crouch as a shot pinged loudly off the top of the rock. Again, his mature legs had not failed him, sparing him from harm. He nodded to himself. Good, now for the next part of the effort.

He'd noted that, just to his left, the land slanted gradually upward. If he could make his way quickly up the slope, moving within the protection of the pines, he could reach a point where he was looking down on Gault's position. Then McNulty would have the advantage. Hopefully a lethal one.

Yes, that would be his play. He reached over the top of the boulder, fired once, then rose and ran for the slope. Two shots rang out, both close but not finding him. He made the bottom of the slope and, without pause, began an upward scramble from tree to tree. Another two or three bullets tore into tree trunks as McNulty's luck held out. When no more shots came immediately, he guessed Gault was reloading. McNulty moved upward and to the right until he reached his desired position: there stood Gault below, not sixty feet away, staring up at him. Their eyes met. Both men fired, almost simultaneously.

Gault was flung backward, struck just below his left collarbone, and landed heavily on his spine. The impact jarred loose the Colt from his hand. McNulty, from his upper vantage point, gazed down at Gault for several seconds before toppling forward. He tumbled headfirst down the slope, losing his own weapon in the process. His descent was checked when he slammed into the base of a thick pine, ten feet from Gault. McNulty rolled over on his back, groaned once, then lay unmoving.

With much effort, Gault forced himself to his feet. He looked about for his revolver, but it had landed among some underbrush and was hidden from view. It occurred to him that maybe he should have also brought along the Peacemaker, but he'd always favored the Colt. And hadn't it done well just now? For there lay that Irish bastard who'd been too much a fool to stay clear of this business.

Gault walked over and looked down at his victim. Dead or dying, shot through the heart. All right then. Gault now took note of his own wound. Bad but not graveyard bad. How many times had he been shot today? Four, wasn't it? Add in the one from Oakes yesterday, and it made for five. All in little more than twenty-four hours. He couldn't be slain was the plain truth of it. He was of some unique mythical breed of men, composed of iron and bone and scorn, who flat out refused to die. Yes, he, George Gault of Wyoming Territory, was unkillable.

As Two Robes entered the woods, she heard two more gunshots, close together as the first pair had been. At brief intervals, several more shots rang out. Though she hadn't found Viola, she soon came upon the body of the major. She had no time to weigh how she felt about his death, for more shots echoed from somewhere close by, and she hurried toward the sound. If Viola was there, in the midst of violence, she must try to help her. Though the older woman was inclined to profanity and endless babbling, she was truly the only one in all this time who'd shown real kindness to the Lakota girl. Viola mustn't end up like the major — a wasted husk from which the spirit had been torn out.

Almost immediately, Two Robes came upon them: John McNulty sprawled out, seemingly dead, and, standing above him, a tall, mustached man, hard looking and covered with blood. This, she knew, must be Gault.

He turned to look at her, and a thin, terrible smile came to his lips. "Well now, it's the poem injun."

Two Robes started to raise her pistol, but, with a speed that shocked her, Gault crossed the space between them and slapped fiercely at her hand. Her gun went flying. Instead of trying to retrieve it, Gault threw his hands around Two Robes' throat and pressed her against a tree. Her own hands enwrapped his thick wrists as she struggled to free herself, but, despite his multiple wounds, Gault was too strong, too enraged, and he squeezed tighter and tighter.

"Good-bye," he snarled in her face. "You

339

can go to hell now."

"Gault!"

At the sound of his name, he released the girl, stepped back, and turned to see who'd summoned him.

"Damn you, Gault!"

It was the greenhorn Nevins, leaning against a pine to steady his wounded leg, but pointing his revolver straight at Gault with surprising control.

"What do you know," Gault said. "Look who's found his manhood."

Released now, Two Robes let out a low moan, and slid down the tree to a sitting position. When Alworth's eyes shifted toward her, Gault saw his chance. He bent quickly and scooped up the girl's pistol at his feet. Straightening, he took aim at Nevins. His finger barely touched the trigger when the world exploded.

In the wildness of the moment, Alworth couldn't have said what part of Gault's body he was aiming for, but his shot struck the forehead, almost squarely. Gault never had the chance to fire. Instead his body dropped backward, falling straight and unbent, like a toppling tree. The gun never left his hand.

Alworth grasped a moment to take in the enormity of what he'd been forced to do, then limped over to Two Robes and sprawled out beside her.

"Are you all right?" he asked.

Touching her neck gingerly, she nodded. "You came out here . . ."

"I heard all the shooting, and I knew you'd entered the woods. So I just had to . . ." He trailed off. Words seemed hard to summon right now.

"My God!" Viola had appeared. After glancing around to take in Two Robes, Alworth, and the dead Gault, she hurried over to where McNulty lay, his shirt stained crimson, and knelt beside him. Placing her shotgun aside, she took up his hand and spoke his name.

McNulty opened his eyes, but she saw at once that the light was leaving them. "Viola," he said weakly.

"Right, Johnny. It's me."

"Turns out . . ." He was struggling to speak. "Turns out he was the one."

"What's that, Johnny?" She leaned close to better hear him.

"The one to send me from this world. I always wondered who it would be. Turns out it was Gault."

"Stop talking now. You need to rest."

"I will, Viola. I will rest." His voice was barely above a whisper now. "I'm sorry we didn't have more time together."

"Oh, Johnny."

"Acushla . . ."

At the sound of the word, Viola broke, and her body trembled with sobs.

McNulty's labored breaths continued for perhaps half a minute, then ceased. When he was gone, Viola released his hand and brusquely wiped away her tears.

"Good-bye, lambkin," she said softly, then rose.

"You've been hurt too, Viola." Two Robes was on her feet now. "Your arm."

"Nothing much. Looks like it's all over now. Gault and his men are dead. Pompay's dead and . . . and Johnny's dead. We need to get Alworth here to a doctor. Let's haul him out to the wagon."

The women helped Alworth up, and, with one supporting him on either side, started out of the woods.

Just as they entered the clearing, Two Robes looked up and saw, at a distance, a large bird making wide, graceful circles in the sky. It was too high up and far away for her to identify, but she found herself thinking it might be some manner of creature that no one had ever seen before. It was a very strange thought, but somehow she found the notion comforting. Above the sanguine plains of earth, perhaps there was a place where such beings dwelt. Maybe not eagles or angels, but something of another kind altogether. Something that looked down on the mad thrashings of humanity with great pity and understanding.

Chapter Thirty-Nine:
Journal of
Alworth B. Nevins

They delivered me into the back of their wagon. There Two Robes remained with me while Viola took the reins up front. We were headed back for Black Powder. Deciding that getting my wound treated was the first priority, Viola planned to send later for the bodies of McNulty, Pompay, and, I supposed, our enemies. As we were leaving the barren field of Tiny Eden, I heard Viola curse loudly and felt the wagon slowing down. As we came to a stop, I looked out the back and saw that we had just passed a man who stood there swaying on his feet. His coat and shirt were smeared with blood from a wound to the shoulder.

It took a moment for the reality to hit me. It was Nash. Not dead after all.

Suddenly Viola was standing before him, pointing her shotgun at his chest. "You lousy rat, Nash! You threw in with Gault to bury us all, didn't you? What was the pay?

Thirty silver coins, I'm guessing. Well, you bastard, you got some of us, but not all of us."

"I never meant any real harm, Viola." Even as Nash uttered the words, you could tell there was no truth behind them. "Just let me get to my horse, and I'll ride out. You won't see any more of me."

"Damned right I won't," said Viola. "Because there won't be nothing more of you to see."

She sighted the gun and cocked it. Nash grimaced and took a step back.

"Viola, no!" Two Robes had climbed down from the wagon. "We've had enough killing here, haven't we?"

Viola kept the shotgun raised. "Do you really want my answer?"

"Yes," Two Robes said.

After a moment, Viola lowered the gun and spat in the dirt. "All right, Nash, you just got a chance you don't deserve. If you can make it to your horse, you can ride away from all this. Go and be damned."

Viola climbed back up front, and Two Robes rejoined me in the back. As we rolled on, I watched behind as Nash slowly, painfully made his way across the dead field.

Not long after, we found Billy. He had left the woods and was sitting at the edge of what had been Tiny Eden, clutching his shot arm and looking dazed and unwell. At my insistence, the women got him into the back of the wagon, where we lay beside each other, two young men who had passed through fire and survived.

Once we'd returned to Black Powder, things got somewhat hazy for me. I was seen to by a grumbly little doctor, who gave me some vile liquid to drink while he went to work. He dug the bullet out of my thigh and sewed me up proper, though, thanks to the tonic, I remember none of it. At one point, just after the operation, I heard the doctor speaking to someone in the room. My eyes flickered open briefly, and I saw a man with a star on his vest standing next to the doctor.

"I wonder, Little," the doctor was saying, "if this shootout will wind up as famous as the O.K. Corral one."

"I doubt it," the man with the star said. "When the Earps did their business, there were several dozen witnesses to it. Here, there's just the participants."

"Too bad," said the doctor. "I hear they're making plays and ballads about the O.K. Corral. It'd be something if Black Powder got its own bit of fanfare."

Then I passed out. Apparently, I slept deeply from early that evening until nearly noon the next day. During the interval, I later learned, Viola contracted with Miss Peppers to take some men to Tiny Eden to gather up the bodies of McNulty and Pompay, plus the several horses and firearms that were to be found scattered about. Viola told her not to bother with Gault and Lampo. She said vultures could conduct the funeral for those two. The small undertaker's professional dignity would not abide this suggestion. She said even the worst of men deserved an adequate interment, and she would see to it at no cost. Viola struck a bargain with Miss Peppers: whatever money was discovered on the four bodies would be split evenly between both parties. Both ladies made out well by this arrangement.

When I finally awoke, I found Two Robes seated by my side. She informed me I was in a back room of Miss Peppers' establishment. For a brief addled moment, I wondered if I'd succumbed to my wound, but Two Robes explained that several rooms of the building doubled as a sort of boardinghouse.

I thought this an odd business design but was glad I'd wound up in the wing where the living were housed. I asked to see Billy.

After determining I could walk with Two Robes' assistance, she led me to a sort of parlor, where I found not only Billy and Viola but, to my great surprise, Saturn Hayes, as well as a young woman and a boy whom I recognized as Ida Sawbridge's daughter, Elizabeth, and son, Tom. The latter two were seated, as was Viola, but Billy and Saturn stood together along one wall. Billy's left arm was in a sling, and, in the course of things, I'd notice Saturn glance over at him from time to time with a look of almost parental concern.

There was one free chair, which, in a gentlemanly fashion, I tried to yield to Two Robes. She would have none of it, pretty much shoving me into the seat. Elizabeth had just commenced to explain how she, Saturn, and Tom happened to be in Black Powder. The trio had ridden all this way here to track down Gault and convey some crucial information to him. They'd arrived in town yesterday, not long after I'd ridden out, and had encountered Gault almost immediately.

What Elizabeth told us next was fairly unbelievable. Ida Sawbridge had never even tasted Pompay's elixir. Instead, it was Tom who drank it, to no ill effect beyond what would befall a boy unaccustomed to alcohol.

(At these revelations, I noticed Tom looked considerably uneasy.) When presented with this fact, Gault had bizarrely ignored it and continued on his quest for vengeance — a quest he now knew was based on a lie.

"Why would he do such a thing?" Two Robes asked. "Knowing there was no longer any reason to come after us?"

Elizabeth sighed and shook her head slowly. "I've no answer for you. I can't say what was in the man's head. Did my mother's death undo him so much that he couldn't think straight? Did his wound cloud his brain with some wild fever? Was it none of those things? I truly don't know. Even if Mama hadn't died, maybe he'd have found something else to give his rage to. Saturn here thinks my cousin had a kind of blaze in him that just wouldn't let him be."

"That's the way of it." Saturn stared off, looking thoughtful. "Things that make fine sense to most folks just never sat right for George Gault. No telling why. For one reason or the other, he never could let the world just keep to its proper order. He had to shift it about to make his own way. I don't think even *he* knew why he did the things he did. He just did 'em."

"And four coffins will be filled because of it," Elizabeth said. "But what's important to

349

know" — she turned to look up at Two Robes, then over at Viola — "is that nothing you people did caused any harm to our family. I'm so sorry for the trouble that came to you."

"Ain't your fault, ma'am," Viola said. "We don't pick our kin. If we could, I'd've picked one of those rich Vanderbilts."

Viola's joke lightened the mood and drew a few chuckles. I glanced over at Two Robes. I could tell she felt relieved that she'd had no part in Ida's death. Miss Peppers entered the room and informed us the burials of McNulty and Pompay would take place later in the afternoon, in tandem. Those of their killers would be held the next day so as not to sour our mourning. She added that, of course, none of us would be expected to attend tomorrow's interments.

We separated then for a few hours, with myself getting more bed rest, and reconvened for the funeral. A preacher had been rounded up to say some good words, and the proceedings were conducted with dignity. Miss Peppers had arranged for John McNulty to be interred beside a young man who she said had been a friend of his. For some reason, Viola set a bugle atop the major's coffin and instructed that it should be buried with him. When it came time to put McNulty to rest, I looked over at Viola and saw she'd somehow combined tears and a smile as she watched his coffin being lowered.

Afterward, when we'd all left the graveyard, Elizabeth informed us that she and Tom would be staying for their cousin's burial tomorrow. Despite what he was, what he had done, he was still their relation. What's more, she knew that upon Gault's death, his sizable ranch and all his holdings passed to her and her siblings. Since her sisters lived far off, she planned to take over the responsibilities of running the ranch. She had invited Saturn to stay on and assist in this, and he had readily agreed. Billy, as well, would be joining in those efforts. And young Tom Sawbridge would grow up learning the ways of a rancher and, it was to be hoped, become a far better man than his cousin had ever been.

After Elizabeth had said all this, she turned to me. "Alworth, you're also most welcome to return with us and take part in what's to come. I'd be glad to have you."

Before I could reply, Viola cleared her throat loudly and theatrically. "Just a minute. Two Robes and I have our own offer to make to Alworth here. Not to start a tussle over the little fella, but we were hoping he might join in with *us*. We're continuing on with our show-making and could use a new player. Seeing as he's such an educated dandy, we figured he might take nicely to the stage life."

"Well, Alworth," Elizabeth said, "you seem to have an array of offers. What's your choice?"

I looked from Elizabeth to Viola, back to Elizabeth, then back to Viola. Finally, I shifted my eyes to Two Robes. I could be wrong, but I'm fairly sure I saw a look of expectation on her face. After a moment, I gave her a little smile, and she returned one of her own.

I turned back to Elizabeth. "Thank you for your kind proposal, ma'am, but I guess I'll be trying my hand on the stage."

Elizabeth smiled. "Then good luck to you, Alworth. Feel free to keep the gray mare for your travels. Good luck to all of you."

"Then it's settled," Viola said. "Let's pack up. We can hit the road before dark sets in. Oh, one more thing. Hey, kid!" She addressed Tom Sawbridge.

Tom looked a bit startled. "Me, ma'am?"

"Yeah, you. There's a fine horse over in the town livery, a blood bay. If Alworth is keeping the mare, you oughta have the bay. It belonged to a real good man, and I'm sure he'd be happy for you to ride it."

I knew Viola was talking about McNulty's horse. She turned, and with Two Robes by her side, headed down the street to where the wagon was waiting. Elizabeth and Tom headed off in their own direction, leaving me, Saturn, and Billy standing in a little circle.

Billy grinned at me. "Well, greenhorn, I guess this is it. Don't let the actor's life go to your head now."

I smiled back. "I don't think that will be a problem."

"Hell, I might've joined you if I didn't need to stick with this old saddle tramp here." He indicated Saturn. "Lord knows if I wasn't around to mind him, he'd likely get into all sorts of nonsense. Probably end up roping a pile of jackrabbits, mistaking 'em for prize steer."

Saturn snorted. "Look who's talking nonsense. Why, boy, you don't have the smarts to keep from getting yourself all shot up. You're lucky the doctor didn't lop off your arm and toss it to the rooting hogs."

Billy laughed. "Hell, Saturn, remind me now. Didn't you get your own damned self shot a couple days back? Or was that my eyes playing tricks on me?"

Saturn snorted again. "Cocky pup." He

offered me his hand. "You take care of yourself."

I shook his hand, then Billy's. "I'm glad to have known you both."

Billy gently elbowed Saturn. "Alworth is just including you in that, 'cause he don't want you getting all pouty."

Ignoring him, Saturn gave me a parting wave, turned, and headed down the street. "Come on, young blood," he called over his shoulder. " 'Less you plan to keep standing there waiting for some golden coach to come carry you off."

"Wouldn't mind that at all." Billy gave me a wink, then turned to follow Saturn. "Hold up, old man!"

Then they were gone.

I made my way to the wagon and found Viola and Two Robes standing beside it. I saw they'd already fetched Steadfast from the livery and had tied her to the back.

"It'll be good to have the extra horse," Viola said. "We can use it for scouting or as a replacement if one these nags finally collapses. Glad to have you in the fold, Alworth. I've got big plans for our troupe. And none of them involve elixir! 'Course, we'll need to have a new motto painted on the side. How's 'Duchess Viola's Raucous Review of Fun and Fanciness' strike you?

Anyway, let's take to the road. You two can ride in back together for a spell till I need a break."

Viola took her seat in front and grabbed the reins. Since my leg was still hampering me, Two Robes needed to help me into the back. Once she'd joined me, we rolled on, intending to catch the last hours of light. For several minutes, we stared out the back in silence, watching the town of Black Powder shrink away in the distance.

Finally, Two Robes turned to me and spoke. "Do you think you'll like this life?"

"I honestly don't know."

Two Robes nodded. We went quiet. As we traveled on, we could hear Viola up front singing to the world at large, perhaps something raucous, perhaps something sweet. It was hard to tell.

ABOUT THE AUTHOR

Michael Nethercott is the author of two suspense novels, *The Séance Society* and *The Haunting Ballad* (St. Martin's Press). His writings have appeared in numerous periodicals and anthologies including *Alfred Hitchcock Mystery Magazine, Abyss & Apex, The Magazine of Fantasy and Science Fiction, Flame Tree Press: Terrifying Ghosts,* and *Best Crime and Mystery Stories of the Year.* He is a winner of The Black Orchid Novella Award, the Vermont Writers' Award, the Vermont Playwrights Award, the Clauder Competition (Finalist and Best State Play), and the Nor'easter Play Writing Competition.

Printed in the USA
CPSIA information can be obtained
at www.ICGtesting.com
JSHW020722171123
52215JS00001B/15